On The Other Side

On The Other Side

Marianne Smith

NEW HANOVER COUNTY
PUBLIC LIBRARY
201 CHESTNUT STREET
WILMINGTON, NC 28401

AuthorHouse™
1663 Liberty Drive
Bloomington, IN 47403
www.authorhouse.com
Phone: 1-800-839-8640

© 2013 Marianne Smith. All rights reserved.

No part of this book may be reproduced, stored in a retrieval system, or transmitted by any means without the written permission of the author.

Published by AuthorHouse 3/8/2013

ISBN: 978-1-4490-5699-5 (sc)
ISBN: 978-1-4490-5698-8 (hc)
ISBN: 978-1-4490-5700-8 (e)

Library of Congress Control Number: 2009912965

This book is printed on acid-free paper.

Because of the dynamic nature of the Internet, any web addresses or links contained in this book may have changed since publication and may no longer be valid.

The views expressed in this work are solely those of the author and do not necessarily reflect the views of the publisher, and the publisher hereby disclaims any responsibility for them.

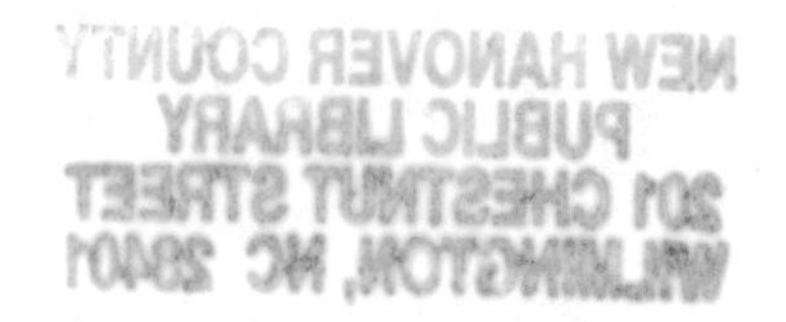

^ Thoughts from the writer's heart ^

To three special people in my life, without whom I would not have begun to write this book much less made the journey to completion, I wish to acknowledge the following:

Firstly: I thank my daughter, Catherine Rose Martin, for her wonderful influence which has always given me courage. She is a daughter rare in compassion, unselfishness, and endless understanding.

Secondly: My grandson Matthew Martin Godbee's love for history and interest in wanting to learn about my childhood in Germany sparked the flame within me to write.

Thirdly: for many years, my dearest friend and mother-in-law, the late Mrs. R. A., [Mary Lib] Martin encouraged me to write about my life. Mrs. Martin was my mentor, a woman I dearly loved, respected, and admired.

It is my prayer and sincere wish that, through the pages of this book, our readers will find renewed strength, courage, and hope.

February 1993.

"Ladies and gentlemen, this is your captain speaking." The pilot's confident German accent awakened the sleepy passengers of Lufthansa Flight #132. "We will be landing in Frankfurt in just a few moments."

The intercom crackled, and passengers began to listen more closely. "We are in a holding pattern at twenty thousand feet," the captain continued. "Weather conditions are not in our favor, but we will attempt to bring this machine down. At that time, we will find out how well this machine is built." His attempt to make light of the situation failed. Instead, his calm demeanor belied concern over icy fog and zero-visibility conditions.

Undisturbed by the captain's announcement, Anna sat back and closed her eyes. She felt her Christian friends in her Bible Study Fellowship class back home lift her up in prayer.

Traveling to Germany alone, especially during the winter months, was not something she wanted to do. But this time, she was responding to God's call as He directed her to go to her dying brother's bedside.

She felt comforted and at peace as she listened to the plane's engine struggle to regain altitude. God had lifted the old burden of fear from her. Her thoughts reached back to her family six decades ago. "You must write a book and share your story," her best friend and mother-in-law, Mary Lib Martin, had persisted over the years.

"Perhaps I will … perhaps I will," Anna had responded each time. *Perhaps I will someday write the book for my grandson Matthew Godbee,* she continued to contemplate as the plane slid onto the runway and came to a screeching halt.

CHAPTER 1

Mid 1930s … Living the good life.

A blanket of snow covered the quaint old city at the southern foothills of the southern foot of Germany's Taunus Mountains, the place Anna called home. The neat and tiny figure of Anna's mother moved swiftly around their cozy apartment. Busy applying a fresh coat of wax to the old wooden floor in their kitchen, she stopped briefly to stir a pot of steaming hot chocolate on the kitchen stove. Lost in her thoughts, she smoothed out the tablecloth on the breakfast table. She cheerfully muttered to herself, "This is Christmas Eve, the most special evening of the year, and everything must be perfect."

The scent of the Christmas tree Anna and her brother Guenter had decorated earlier filled the air. Anna reached for one of the cookies their grandmother baked, which now decorated the tree.

"Hands off," her mother demanded from across the room. "You must be patient."

"All right." Anna clasped her hands behind her back.

"After all, this is the night the Christ child will send the angels to deliver the presents to all the children," her mother continued in a soft tone.

Earlier in the day, the postman had delivered a postcard from a cousin in the Black Forest. The picture of an Alpine winter scene caught Anna's fascination. Her cousin Eric—mild-mannered, tall, handsome, blue-eyed with blond hair—had promised to take her there by train sometime, but this evening he would take her to their grandmother's house to celebrate their traditional Christmas dinner.

The bells of the cathedral nearby broke the silence as Anna opened the window of her tiny bedroom to look for Eric. Across the rooftops, she saw the balcony of his apartment. She became especially anxious to see Eric's new wife, Emma, later that evening. Emma, a welcome addition to the family, had been reared in a little village near the Rhine, so this was her first experience in the city.

Snowflakes shimmered in the light of the old street lantern below as Anna patiently waited for a sign of Eric. Her long pigtails bounced as she jumped off the stool her mother had placed near the window.

"Where are you, Little Chubby?" Eric called from the entrance hall. As she ran into his arms, she began to sob. "Why the tears?" Eric asked.

"It's nothing," mumbled Guenter as he reached for Anna's coat. "She cries over nothing!"

Anna glanced at Guenter's big brown eyes and mischievous smile as he gently led her out of the apartment.

As they approached the street, a gust of icy wind pushed them back into the entrance.

"Jump up!" Eric smiled as he bent to lift Anna over his head and onto his shoulders.

"It's like riding on your rocking horse, Guenter!" cried Anna. She delighted in Eric's bouncing gait as they pressed onward toward their grandmother's house.

Their grandmother, small in stature, dressed in black, with her silver-grey hair neatly braided and gently framing her pretty face, greeted everyone with open arms. "I was concerned about you! Let me take those wet coats. Did you know I have been baking all afternoon?" she teased.

"We can tell," Eric said, smiling. "It smells wonderful! We love coming to your house for dinner because you are the best cook!"

She shook the snow from their coats and said, "My love for cooking and baking began with your grandfather. People in the restaurant business recognized him to be one of the finest chefs in the region. And he loved his instrument." A warm glow came over her face as she walked over to touch their grandfather's zither that rested in one corner of the room. "Heat stroke took his life in Baden-Baden during a competitive cooking event," she reminded the children.

Anna's mother stood close to his favorite zither and nodded as the grandmother placed the coats near the stove to dry.

"Now you may light the tree," she instructed her grandchildren. One by one, Anna and Guenter lit each candle that decked their grandmother's Christmas tree. The soft light of the candles illuminated the room. "I hope this rabbit is done soon. I know all of you must be starving," she called from the kitchen.

"For the last few months I helped feed that rabbit, and now we are having him for dinner?" Guenter shrieked as he shook his head in obvious displeasure.

As always, Christmas Eve was indeed a joyful event. Anna reclined at Eric's feet and sang as he played his mouth organ. Everyone was present except the children's father. No one questioned his whereabouts, but Anna's mother paced the floor in front of the French doors that led onto the balcony. Here she had a clear view of their grandmother's neighborhood.

A gentle nudge woke Anna from a short nap. "Wake up! It's time for midnight Mass. Your brother is spending the night with your grandmother. The two of us will go to midnight Mass," ordered her mother.

The chill of the midnight air came over Anna as she watched her mother lock the heavy wooden door of their grandmother's apartment house. "I am thankful the wind has calmed," she told Anna while pulling her hat over her ears.

Thick layers of snow made the walk up the steep hill to the ancient Catholic church difficult, but the sounds of the organ coming from atop made the walk pleasant. Anna held tightly to her mother's hand as they approached the church.

"This is exciting and more fun than sleeping," Anna giggled as she attempted to remove the snow from her boots before entering the church.

Catching her breath from the mile-long walk, Anna stood silent with her chin pressed against the wooden fence that surrounded the life-size nativity. Distracted for only a moment, she watched her mother kneel close by. She fixed her eyes on the figurines. "Everyone is smiling," she whispered. "Even the little lamb curled up near the baby Jesus seems to smile. We came to the birthday celebration just like the shepherds and wise men," Anna whispered.

Anna pushed her featherbed away and pulled her doll out from underneath. "Come on, Puppchen," she said, cuddling her doll tightly against her chest. "It's Christmas morning! We must find Guenter so that we can go into the living room and see what the angels brought during the night." St. Nicholaus had made his rounds three weeks earlier and left treats outside their door.

Guenter had come home from their grandmother's home and was patiently waiting in the kitchen. Hand in hand they opened the door to take a look in the living room. Anna stood speechless, with the back of her hand pressed against her face, and smiled. "How can this be, the little Baby Jesus sent all of these presents?" she uttered in amazement as she walked toward the dollhouse.

She had no idea that Eric had spent many weeks designing the tiny wooden structure, which included miniature farmhouse furnishings. "Guenter, look, even new skis for both of us," she shouted. Guenter rejoiced over the new books and art supplies for his hobby. Thrilled with their Christmas gifts, the children spent hours playing and waxing their new skis for a trip to the slopes.

Their mother seldom failed to remind them of the source of their gifts. To remember the reason for this special season was her message. While limited in skills of teaching about God, she had a deep love for Jesus that was evident and sufficient for planting the seeds.

Anna had a special love for Eric. He was the only adult male in her life. Her father was never around, and she had no memory of him. His name and whereabouts were spoken only in secret. From looking at the wedding photo on her mother's dresser, she knew he was handsome. Relatives referred to him as smart, hard-working, kind, but stubborn—a man who refused to join the "new movement of Hitler's party."

Sadness marked the face of Anna's mother, who had accepted the daily struggle of caring for the two children. They were her life and her number-one priority. She managed to stretch a small income earned by taking odd jobs in the neighborhood bakery and grocery store, and she was grateful for their grandmother's willingness to share cooking skills.

Anna and Guenter spent much of their time attending religion classes at the Catholic orphanage and convent. Each day there was a special day. The priests and nuns became part of the family—they were strict, but fun to be with.

A long winter brought its usual harsh periods of freezing temperatures, snow, and ice, but this did not seem to bother Anna and Guenter. After school, their sled, skates, and skis were ready for action. It was a fun-filled and exhilarating time for both, but not for their mother. Because of Anna's high energy, her mother lived with constant concern for her. She recalled an event that happened when Anna was a toddler—a story she often shared with family and friends.

With her voice trembling in her soft and caring manner, Anna's mother described the incident to a neighbor. "I asked our friend Anneliese to come over to help me with some alterations. While we were chatting, and before I turned my head, Anna reached for the scissors and started out the balcony door to look for Guenter. She fell and one of the blades struck in her right eye. It was a frightening sight because the eye was protruding! I carried her up the hill to the hospital. A young Jewish doctor, who was on emergency call, saved her eye!" There was no doubt in her voice as she pointed out that this young doctor was an angel put there to save Anna's eye. Gently touching Anna's cheek, she smiled, saying, "See? Her dimple will always be a reminder."

As the sun began to peek through the clouds and snow began to melt, the somber atmosphere that hung over the city slowly dissipated. Sounds of music from within the elegant sidewalk cafés pointed to the coming of an exciting spring. The waterfall in the center of the pond in the Kurpark once again began to glitter in the sunlight as the ice slowly melted. Feverishly, workers began their cleanup efforts in parks around the city. Beer gardens appeared along the narrow streets leading into the old city that Eric and their grandmother called home began to sparkle as fresh coats of paint and flowers emerged.

Because of her love of culture and the arts, Anna's mother chose a new apartment a short distance from the Kurpark, the famous Opera House and the Concert Hall. Elegant hotels and specialty shops lined the fashionable avenues that led through their neighborhood. There, along the narrow streets, bakeries and butcher shops proudly displayed their scrumptious pastries and sausages. Baskets of fruits and vegetables hugged the entrances of the corner grocery stores. From as far back as the time of the early Romans, people from around the world had come here to bathe in the hot mineral springs. This history made the ancient city one of Germany's most notable resorts.

For Anna and her mother, the Kurpark was an exhilarating place, and it was here that they spent Sunday afternoons. A choice bench surrounded by flower gardens became Anna's favorite spot to observe the visitors. Often, she counted the people who entered the stage entrance of the Opera House. "If I could just go there and meet some of these people! They look so interesting," Anna begged her mother.

"That is impossible," her mother firmly explained. "These people are members of the opera, and some are quite famous. No one can go there without special permission!"

Guenter, meanwhile, had other interests. He developed a love for nearly every sport. Anna could always find him on the athletic fields or at the Olympic indoor pool. His greatest passion was riding his bike with his friends through the trails of the nearby Taunus. Because of his love of sports, Anna too became involved in swimming and skating.

While Guenter had no desire to visit the Kurpark, he was always ready to hop on a bus heading to the Rhine for a Sunday afternoon cruise on one of the riverboats. These were rare and special occasions he and Anna shared. The scenery through the Rhine Valley was breathtaking. Anna and Guenter were fascinated by the vineyards clinging to the steep valley sides. Villages that rested along the riverbanks favored small houses that looked like toys. Guenter loved telling Anna the history of the castles built in the Middle Ages as they floated past the ruins.

Alone but content, their mother watched from the deck above, outside the boat's coffeehouse. She delighted in listening to the music played by a Gypsy violinist who moved among the people. With her usual faraway look, she frequently waved to the children.

Wine and beer festivals were celebrated regularly around the "old city." Anna's mother saw little enjoyment in attending these events. She preferred a quiet sidewalk café. Sitting in a crowd of beer-drinking people, whose conversations quite often got out of control, was to her wearisome and boring. She especially resented wine and beer festivals held on Sundays.

Anna's mother worked hard but never complained. Their tiny apartment sparkled. Fresh flowers, especially lilacs, welcomed friends and relatives, who enjoyed her company because of her sunny disposition. Her courage amazed many. She was, however, unable to hide frequent tears caused by her heavy burden—a burden she was too afraid to share with anyone. Oftentimes she arose during the night and quietly tiptoed to their bedroom window to listen for footsteps on the cobblestone street below. The squeaking of the window lock and the chilly night air awoke Anna, but she lay silent pretending she was asleep for fear she might add stress to her mother's mysterious sadness. She peeked from underneath the featherbed and watched as her mother clutched her father's picture to her chest. Although Anna felt sadness and confusion, she always knew she was loved and secure with her beloved family by her side.

CHAPTER 2

1936-1937 … Changing times … A first close-up look at Adolf Hitler.

Palm Sunday. Anna fixed her eyes upon a bunch of fresh flowers resting in the earthen washbasin in their tiny kitchen. A purple silk ribbon tied onto a basket hung from the faucet. She watched as her mother separated each petal, placing them into the basket. Her mother gently combed Anna's long dark brown hair and twisted it into curls with the old curling iron heated on top of the wooden stove.

Guenter burst into the kitchen, startling Anna. "Why the somber face?" he asked with his usual mischievous smile. "Look at you! Do you have a reason to look so gloomy?" Reminding Anna of the new lavender lace dress Eric had given her for her birthday, he shouted, "You should be smiling! You should be smiling!"

Paying little attention, Anna's mother examined the basket and arranged the ribbon around Anna's neck. "Let us go down to the cathedral," she cheerfully ordered. Anna's new shoes and the waxed wooden stairs made skipping down the four flights fun. "She is at it again," whispered Anna's mother in despair. "She is always jumping and dancing!"

With her arms swinging above her head, Anna took a deep breath. The scent of early morning rain still hung in the air as dark clouds hovered over the city. In the distance, the bells from churches around the city once again began to toll. Chestnut trees that graced each side of the avenue leading to the cathedral confirmed that spring had arrived.

Anna's heart began to pound as she reached the square behind the cathedral. She watched intently as priests and altar boys handed out palm branches to the crowd of people that gathered around and now made its way onto the streets.

"You see? The sun is peeking through to us," whispered Anna's mother. Following the quiet procession through the old city, Anna joined other children by dropping her flower petals on the streets that had been swept meticulously for the event. What all of this meant was not clear to Anna, nor was it to Guenter. It was obvious that their mother's wish to honor, respect, and fear God must take root in their young minds and hearts.

Everyone else in the family paid little attention to Anna's mother's devotion to their spiritual growth. Some considered it a waste of time. To them, emphasis on Germany's new leader was far more important. It was Hitler, Anna's mother was told by their grandmother, that her children must follow.

Pressure of opposition began to mount, yet Anna's mother became more determined to prepare Anna and Guenter for their First Communion and continued the necessary groundwork. "Your First Communion is only about three weeks away," reminded their mother as she watched them leave for school. "Watch out for Anna," she cautioned Guenter as they made their way across the busy intersection near their home. "This afternoon we will go shopping for her dress."

Later that day, Anna gingerly touched the white lace dresses on display in their mother's favorite boutique. Inside a glass bookcase, she spotted a small prayer book. "Look at the colors, the shepherd with one of his little sheep slung over his shoulders," she whispered. She could tell her mother was concerned about something. "May I try the dress on?" Anna pleaded.

"I am afraid we can't shop here," her mother responded. "It is too expensive. We'll ask Anneliese to make a dress for you."

Anneliese, a woman highly respected for her gift of sewing, was thrilled and accepted the challenge to reproduce the dress Anna had fallen in love with. Anna's mother was disturbed by Anna's disappointed look. "No one will know the difference," she assured her daughter. "I'll even ask Emma to come over to curl your hair."

Anna was relieved to see Emma arrive early the morning of her First Communion. "Let's see what we can do," mused

Emma, placing a bunch of pink roses from her flower garden into a vase. Using a hot curling iron, she painstakingly curled Anna's long dark brown hair. "Sit still," she urged as she placed a crown of silk daisies and laurel leaves upon Anna's head for the final touch.

Anna held on to Emma's white apron and peeked around her to watch as her mother walked into the room and said, "I have a surprise for you!" Clasping a tiny package wrapped in white tissue paper, Anna shouted, "Look, it's the shepherd with his little lamb! Thank you, thank you, now I have my very own prayer book!" She embraced her mother.

"Are you coming with us?" Anna begged Emma.

"No," Emma answered. "Eric and I have a meeting to attend. Maybe we'll go another time."

With her hands dropped on her waistline, Anna cried in despair, "There won't be another time! This is my First Communion!"

Emma remained silent.

Anna clutched her prayer book during Mass. "Everyone looks especially beautiful today," she observed. Several girls wore dresses similar to the one she had seen at the boutique, but now she felt her dress was even more special. Several rows behind, she noticed the boys dressed in black suits and white shirts. She grinned in response to a quick wink from her brother.

Sounds of the organ broke through Anna's thoughts. *Why can't it be this peaceful in other places?* she wondered. Increasingly,

Anna and Guenter were puzzled as the relaxed atmosphere within the family was constantly interrupted. Conversation about hunger and unemployment became commonplace. Cozy quiet evenings at their grandmother's house were replaced by loud and confusing conversations. Adults gathered around the radio. Backed up with music by Wagner, they listened to the shrieking voice of a man thought to be the one who could put their country back on its feet. Anna's grandmother generally led the heated discussions that followed. She became mesmerized by and at times hysterical over Hitler's emotional speeches. "Hitler rescued our *volk* from the deepest need," she repeated over and over.

"Who is this man everyone is so captivated by?" asked Anna's uncle Adolf, a tall, slender, soft-spoken gentleman.

"He is a man who three years ago had the audacity to establish his dictatorship," replied Adolf's wife, Paula, in her well-informed and aristocratic Berlin accent. "He is now head of state and commander-in-chief, thus taking complete control of Germany. They call him the führer."

"Those close to him say he is a man who spends hours at his retreat in Berchtesgaden meditating while staring at the moonlight-bathed mountains of Bavaria," Eric added.

"Is it possible, then," wondered Anna's mother, who bitterly opposed Hitler, "that in this atmosphere, his imagination of controlling the world is beginning to grow?" She glanced at Anna's grandmother, whose face turned red from anger.

"So why is everyone determined to follow this man who shows indications of vicious behaviors?" wondered Brigette, a close friend and neighbor, who sunk her head as she spoke. She was still dressed in black to mourn the recent death of her husband. "Some people call him a man with two faces. He is known to swear that the Ten Commandments are a code of living to which there is no denial. Yet he is vocal about the fact that he is not impressed with the strict teachings of the Catholic Church. He is critical of the morals of others but shows little self-respect. Does a man like this have respect for life?"

Anna's grandmother sat, arms folded across her chest, no longer able to hide her anger and disgust. "Let me tell you something!" Her voice reached a high pitch. "I am convinced that following 'this man'—whose name, by the way, is Adolf Hitler—is not only the right, but the only thing to do." No one dared to answer. She would not give in, and these discussions would last until the early morning hours.

Anna's mother became more fearful with each day that passed. She knew those who opposed Hitler had no chance of getting ahead. But she could not comprehend why nearly everyone believed in the führer's political platform. "There is evidence of bad things happening already," she shared with Anna. Both felt concern for their friend Karl Herdling and his family, and the humiliation they endured. Because he opposed the Nazi Party, he had lost his job as a senior banker only two days earlier.

Regardless of inclement weather, cloudbursts, or freezing temperatures, each school day began with the ear-splitting sounds of music through one of the loudspeakers. The lyrics were the same: "Today, Germany belongs to us, and tomorrow, the whole world!" As students lined up in the schoolyard, teachers carefully observed each of them, making certain their right arms were raised straight forward in the Hitler *gruss* (greeting), and with eyes fixed upon the new German swastika flag. This became their most important lesson for the day, a requirement of the new system. The message: to teach the children they must be strong and committed to the new leader.

Anna's teacher, Herr Dietz, a heavyset man who always walked around with his coat slung over his shoulder, let everyone know that he was a leader in the local party, and that he was an ardent Nazi. "I am trained in National Socialist principles, and I am determined that all of my students will be as well," he announced daily. He steadily urged students' parents to join his group. When Anna was unable to produce a paper signed by her father to confirm his attendance at a meeting, Herr Dietz became outraged. "Just tell your parents that participation in the party is for your own good. Otherwise … Oh well, they will learn," he shouted in anger.

Anna's mother became distraught over all of this, and so did Guenter. Although he was only five years older than Anna, he had taken on a fair share of fatherly responsibilities. She was afraid of Herr Dietz, and she dreaded going to school. The distractions hindered her ability to concentrate on her studies. Guenter spent much of his time helping Anna with her homework, but this was not good enough. No matter how hard she tried, she was unable to please Herr Dietz. He humiliated her, losing his temper in front of her classmates for no apparent reason.

Severe weather conditions brought on by freezing rain and snow contributed to an outbreak of flu and scarlet fever. Although Anna's mother feared grave consequences, she kept Anna home from school because of high fever and a dreadful sore throat. Mid-morning, she heard Guenter's footsteps running up the stairway. "He has only been gone an hour, surely he is not sick also," she whispered to Anna. She felt her heart pounding as Guenter opened the door.

His voice quivering, he spoke to Anna: "Herr Dietz sent me to tell you to come to school now, or he will tell the police to come and get you!"

"Didn't he get the note I sent him?" their concerned mother asked.

"Yes, I gave it to him, but he crumbled it up," Guenter replied, quivering.

"It's okay," Anna responded. "It's only until one o'clock, and tomorrow is Sunday. I'll make it."

The walk up the hill to the schoolhouse was frightful. Guenter held on to Anna, who was sobbing. "Mutti is going to worry about me all morning," she cried.

"I know, Anna," Guenter agreed. "I just don't know what to do. Don't say anything, but I wish father would come home."

In the schoolyard, during morning breaks, Anna often hid behind a tree and cried. She watched Herr Dietz as he strolled up and down, peeling his apple and hanging the peelings on a tree for the birds to feed on. "How can he be so mean and still care about the birds?" she asked Guenter.

"Because," he answered, "the birds have nothing to do with politics."

"I don't understand. Why does everything become more and more difficult?" Anna's frustrations accelerated, leaving her at a loss. "Perhaps I shall go up to speak to the nuns—they may have a solution."

Anna's mother expressed concern to Eric, who stopped by to look in on them. But Eric, too, had problems. "There is talk at work that I may be sent to Berlin. I don't know if can stand to leave Emma and the baby. We are told they are in desperate need for draftsmen at Hitler's headquarters." Eric's voice was dismal. Anna had quietly listened to the conversation while looking at a picture book he had brought her. He gently stroked her hair as she climbed on his lap. "You'll see, Anna, everything will be all right, you'll see, you'll see!"

Time and again, Anna's mother put forth the politically correct efforts. Disheartened by the relentless and hostile surroundings, she complained to their grandmother, "Instead of singing hymns, my children are forced to sing about Hitler—that's all we hear! Thank God we can still go to church where people talk about God."

It became more and more obvious that their once tenderhearted grandmother had fallen victim to the new system. At the very beginning, she was critical about everything, but as unemployment eased and living conditions improved, she began to weaken. "He will save our people from starvation," she proudly acknowledged. "It will be good to take the children to some of the events when he comes to the city! Besides, we would all be better off if you get this into your husband's stubborn head."

"I am afraid that's not possible. I haven't heard from him in several months!" Anna's mother responded. This began a tug of war between the two women.

One summer Sunday morning, Anna peered from the window of their apartment at the golden dome of the Russian chapel perched upon the edge of the Taunus Mountains. Everything seemed calm and serene. The aroma of freshly brewed coffee coming from the kitchen reminded Anna that she needed to talk with her mother.

Anna found her mother sitting quietly sipping a cup of coffee, eyes welling with tears. "What is wrong?" Anna asked.

"Your grandmother insists you and Guenter must go with her to the big rally in the park today." "And what about you?"

"I will go to church alone," answered her mother. Moments later, Anna sadly watched her mother's slow pace as she walked away.

The children found their grandmother nervously sorting through a stack of old paper bags. "I baked some cookies for you. We'll have a picnic in the park." Their grandmother smiled and placed the cookies into a basket. "We are late," she nervously snapped while instructing them to put on their coats. "We must hurry! We don't want to miss seeing him!" The grandmother was becoming somewhat bothered by the children's lethargy.

"Who is *him*?" Anna asked.

"It's a surprise!" exclaimed their grandmother.

The sounds of the marching band roared through the streets several city blocks away. "Where did all of these people come from?" asked Guenter as they approached the park.

Anna shook her head in amazement. "Look at the flags on both sides of the boulevard, there must be thousands of them! I can't see anything but flags!" She looked at Guenter and began to make her way through the crowd of people, leaving her grandmother and Guenter standing behind.

A man dressed in a brown uniform, one of many of Hitler's *Sturmabteilung* who lined the streets, took her by the hand and led her to an opening. "You can sit here on the curb if you like, but be careful that no one will step on you!" He pressed a small swastika banner into her hand. "When the big limousine with 'Herr Hitler' passes, I want you to wave this flag with enthusiasm real hard," he commanded as Anna nodded.

Anna could see Guenter and their grandmother through the crowd. The smell of leather boots worn by the men in the parade overwhelmed her. Dressed in brown uniforms, each wearing a swastika band around one arm, stern and proud expressions on their faces, some carrying flags, they stomped to the beat of the marching band.

Suddenly, loud screams erupted as people pushed forward. Guenter, panic-stricken, made his way through the crowd and took Anna by the hand. "You'll get run over, dummy, if you don't watch it." He pulled her back and sat down with her on the curb. Some of the men in uniforms pushed the crowds back.

"Here he comes!" a woman shouted.

"He, who?" Anna pressed Guenter for an answer.

"I think it's Herr Hitler."

Anna was fascinated by the entourage of horses approaching. "This makes it all worth it," Anna murmured, admiring the riders' ability to keep the high-spirited horses in line. All at once, everything got quiet. Anna looked over her shoulder at the people behind her. Everyone stood at attention, right arms raised just as she and Guenter were commanded to do each day at school. Only the sound of the horses' hooves could be heard.

Guenter whispered to Anna, "Have you ever seen such a big convertible?"

Anna shook her head. She stood up from the curb to get a better look at the men in the convertible. On the back seat, the führer stood waving to the crowd. Anna noticed his special attention to a group of children. One of the children handed a bunch of flowers to one of the men in uniform walking along with the convertible. He then handed it to the führer, who acknowledged the girl with a smile. Hitler's deep piercing eyes flashed across Anna and Guenter, who watched the entourage until it was out of sight.

Anna looked around and was amazed to see the people had so quickly dispersed. "Let's go and find a bench in the park for our picnic," their grandmother instructed. "The führer is going to speak in the park, and I want you to hear at least part of it!"

It's so different when Mutti and I come to the park, so very peaceful, Anna thought. *I wanted to go with her to church, but grandmother insisted we come here. Wonder why Grandmother never goes to church?*

Anna's grandmother spoke in a firm voice. "I want you two to sit and listen and whatever you do, do not make a sound while the führer speaks."

The crowd of people pushed forward to the speaker's podium. The music through the loudspeakers stopped, and the crowd set off a scream of "*Heil, heil, heil!*"

Anna leaned on Guenter's shoulder and covered her ears. Not only was Hitler's voice loud, it also sounded threatening. *Who is he so upset and angry with?* both Anna and Guenter wondered.

Finally, he stopped speaking, but the people once again erupted with loud screams, "We want our führer, we want our führer. *Heil, heil, heil!*"

Reluctantly, because of their grandmother's help in supporting the children, Anna's mother gave in to the children's involvement with their grandmother's activities. She rarely attended the meetings but remained steadfast with her own priorities by following her heart. She reminded the children each time she sent them off into their grandmother's care "not to forget 'Herr Jesus.'"

Anna and Guenter were constantly pulled between the two women. Herr Dietz treated Anna more kindly since he ran into Anna and her grandmother during one of the party rallies. She looked forward to her weekly religion classes at the Catholic orphanage and convent, and went to confession regularly. No one looked down at her there because she couldn't speak about her father. Some of her playmates were without both parents.

Anna cherished her intimate conversations with Sister Renate, who had grown fond of her. She could relate to Anna because she became an orphan during World War One. Helping Sister Renate with all kinds of chores around the orphanage was a delight. On special occasions, Sister Renate invited Anna to go on nature hikes with the children in the Taunus forest. It was fun, singing as they walked, gathering chestnuts, and learning to identify mushrooms so bountiful in the Taunus forest. Sister Renate always kept a small basket on hand for Anna to share and take to her grandmother.

"Would you please take this note to your mother," Sister Renate requested one afternoon as Anna was leaving the orphanage.

Anna's mother was pleased to hear from the nun. "Oh, how nice. I'll make a point to see her right away! In fact, I'll just come and meet you, and we will walk home together on Friday."

When her mother came on Friday, Sister Renate told Anna, "Take this note over to the priest. Your mother and I will chat for a while." The soft-spoken sister wrinkled up her nose and smiled at Anna, who returned her smile and skipped toward the rectory.

The meeting between the nun and Anna's mother was jovial and lengthy. "I want you to take Anna down to the Opera House on Monday," suggested Sister Renate. "They are testing gifted children for their ballet programs."

"I don't know how I can afford this," replied Anna's mother, somewhat distressed.

"I am not certain, but I believe there is a new program for children whose parents cannot afford this training. You must look into it! I have observed Anna for quite some time. She adapts quite well to our athletic programs—I truly believe she can qualify," insisted Sister Renate. "The new program is designed by one of the führer's new spearheads, Dr. Joseph Goebbels. Dr. Goebbels himself comes from a family of devout Catholics right here in the Rhineland," she explained. "Born with a club foot and one leg three inches shorter than the other, he beat tremendous personal odds. A number of Catholic scholarships enabled him to attend several famous German universities. He is a man interested in the arts. After writing unsuccessful plays, he was discovered to have a gift as a public speaker.

"The führer is wasting no time to put him to work. He is now in charge of taking the message of Nazism to Germany's youth. It is Goebbels' responsibility to explore the gifts and talents of our children, all at the cost of the new regime," explained Sister Renate. "Besides," she continued, "ever since the Olympics last year, the führer has been entranced with giving Germany's children every opportunity to develop into tough, well-formed men and graceful women. This is where Anna comes in!"

With this glimpse of hope, Anna's mother wasted no time and arranged a meeting with Herr Kummel, director of the youth program at the Opera House. "I will do what I can and hope for a perfect meeting," she gratefully reported back to Sister Renate.

"We'll have to get some new silk ribbons for your hair," Anna's mother enthusiastically suggested. "The little jumper Emma just made for you will be perfect." Inspecting Anna's black patent-leather shoes, she instructed Anna to take them to the neighborhood's shoemaker. "See if Herr Mayer can put new soles on these shoes. But tell him we must get them back by the end of the week."

Fascinated with the bell that hung loosely at the entrance, Anna entered the shoemaker's shop.

"What a nice surprise!" said Herr Mayer, bent nearly double from arthritis, as he came out from behind the counter.

"Could you repair these for me by this weekend?" Anna asked politely.

"Of course," he answered, observing Anna from underneath his bifocals. Because she frequently delivered repaired items to his customers, Anna believed he had a special place in his heart for her, and she wanted to share her excitement. Instead, she pressed her lips together. She felt the event she was about to take part in was too good to be true.

With great anticipation, Anna counted the days before the interview with Herr Kummel. "Please don't forget to curtsey," Anna's mother reminded her as they walked down the breathtakingly beautiful avenue toward the Opera House. Anna glanced at the bench the two shared on Sunday afternoons. She recalled her earlier desire to have a close look at some of the people she was about to meet. "Is this for real?" she whispered.

On the veranda, Herr Kummel awaited their arrival. He walked toward them, both hands stretched forward. "You must be Anna," he said, reaching for Anna's hands. "Thank you for coming." He bowed politely. Herr Kummel was a theatrical-looking man. His thick and rather long gray hair was neatly brushed, overlapping the collar of his dark jacket. His eyes sparkled from beneath his bushy eyebrows and the deep lines in his face.

"I will give you both a tour of the Opera House, but first I want to know all about you, young lady!"

Anna noticed her mother nervously twisting her embroidered handkerchief. No doubt, she was nervous about the outcome of this meeting. *Will Anna be disappointed once again?* she wondered. She waited until Herr Kummel finished questioning Anna before she felt confident enough to comment, "I am not sure if we can afford Anna's training here."

"Let's not be concerned about this right now!" Herr Kummel interrupted with a smile. "We are beginning a six-week training and testing session next month. I would like for you to bring Anna to the introduction, and we'll go from there. Besides, I want to see if Sister Renate observed correctly. And, I might add, there will be no questions asked about you personally should she be accepted."

With a sigh of relief, her mother elected to wait in the plush theater cantina. Herr Kummel gave Anna the grand tour. From a distance, she and her mother had been intrigued with the structure of the stately Opera House. They wondered about the significance and admired the sculptures of the panther teams pulling two-wheel carriages located on each corner in the roof garden high above the surrounding parks and colonnade. Now, Herr Kummel enlightened Anna by pointing out its history.

"In 1892," Herr Kummel explained, "two of the most respected and experienced theater architects from Vienna began construction of this famous landmark. For the finishing touches, they selected our very own sculptor, Herr Eberlein from Zinkblech, to create these magnificent works of art." Looking down to the park from the roof garden, Herr Kummel pointed to the monument of Friedrich von Schiller. "I find having my favorite poet in this location delightful. Are you familiar with the poet?" he asked Anna.

"Oh yes, he is my mother's favorite poet as well," she responded, "but Herr Goethe is mine."

They climbed and then descended the six flights of stairs, carefully observing each floor and its designated function.

"The top floor is our storage area. All of the costumes are carefully cleaned before they are put into storage. The fifth floor is occupied by our costume designers and shoemakers. This is where they will fit you for your toe slippers when you are ready for them." He spoke as though Anna had already been accepted.

"You will begin on the fourth floor," explained Herr Kummel. "Now, if you become famous and important some day, you will move to the main floor. It is the floor of the stage area. Before then, there is lots of work and practice to be done. And this is the reason the remaining floors are designated for music, voice, dancing, acting lessons, and rehearsals.

"I have kept the best for last," he said, watching Anna's expression as he led her onto the stage. "The stage is set for *Saison in Salzburg*," Herr Kummel proudly explained. "It's a fairly new operetta, and we are getting the kinks out of it in preparation for the führer's visit. You will like the music."

"It's just like being in the Alps!" Anna sighed with amazement as she finally had the courage to speak. She watched the painters on their scaffolds high above the stage put the final brushstrokes on the gigantic backdrop.

After the grandiose tour, Herr Kummel gingerly pulled her through the massive red velvet curtain for a glance at the auditorium. "You see the center of the third balcony?" he asked. Anna nodded. "This is the Kaiser Balcony. All the dignitaries occupy those special seats."

At the moment, Anna was more entranced by the priceless artwork that graced the rotunda. *This must have cost millions*, she pondered.

She watched Herr Kummel as he disappeared through the revolving doors that led into the Opera House from the elegant colonnade. She stood enchanted by this stranger who all at once became a friend. His gentle manner as he walked her through the corridors of this magnificent building, the sounds of the various rehearsals in progress, and the fascinating people stirred the desire within her to be a part of this exciting place.

A few weeks later, a simple postcard placed beside a small crystal vase holding three pink roses awaited Anna after school. "We are looking forward to your daughter's orientation at the Opera House, April twenty-second at three-thirty pm," signed Leon Kummel. Anna pressed the card against her chest and ran to share the excitement with Guenter. "It's only five days away, and three days after my seventh birthday!" she announced.

"Okay, okay, I'll go with you the first time so that you don't get lost," he responded with authority.

On that first day, nearly a dozen children listened in suspense to directions given by Herr Kummel. His last words were, "Remember, children, we will keep you busy for the next six weeks."

Guenter was afraid I might get lost, Anna thought, *how will I keep from being lost in this gigantic place? It's many times larger than the schoolhouse.*

"Make certain you are there with time to spare," was her mother's instruction.

Five girls chosen to demonstrate their talent for ballet stood nervously outside the rehearsal auditorium. Anna stretched her neck for a quick glimpse of the members of the School of Ballet in action. The accelerating sounds of Chopin coming from the piano, mixed with the thumping of footsteps, produced in Anna a mixture of fear and excitement.

She was last to enter. Afraid and intimidated by the others, she held on to the bar and watched until the instructor's call for her turn. "Loosen up and just follow the rhythm of the piano," commanded the radiant ballet teacher, Frau Hanze. Anna followed her graceful moves as she stole a glance at her own reflection in the wall-sized mirror. Frau Hanze offered no special praise as she had for the others. Anna felt clumsy and disappointed. Until the last girl's turn, she felt defeated—but watching the frail and tiny girl perform gave her new assurance. Anna's thoughts again reflected on her conversations with Sister Renate. From here on, she would practice to keep up with the experienced and fluent dancers.

Conditions within Anna's family worsened. Nearly everyone joined the Nazi Party. Some became quite pushy.

Torn between two women, one who followed her heart and the other who followed her head, the children coped.

At school, Guenter began to experience intimidation, but remained an outstanding student. Taking care of his daily chores before heading to the soccer and athletic fields showed his willingness to obedience. Occasionally, he delighted in treating Anna to a bus ride to visit the zoo in Frankfurt. Both children had an incredible love for animals. "That's how I know God, through the eyes of His beautiful animals, especially the little lambs," Anna often professed.

Their grandmother favored Guenter and insisted on controlling him, while their mother held on tightly to rearing Anna. The whereabouts of their father continued to be a mystery, and any conversation about him resulted in their mother breaking down in tears. Anna and Guenter were quite skilled at eavesdropping whenever adults spoke in whispering tones.

"I hear you had a little visit with the children's father near his former workplace?" Anna overheard Emma questioning their mother, referring to one of the upscale hotels near the Bahnhof. Mother offered no information, but quietly abandoned both company and questions.

Eric and Emma had many conversations about Anna's father. Rightfully so, since both contributed to the children's welfare. Emma's short and stocky figure seldom slowed down. Her comical personality put an end to most somber moods. When it came to Anna's well-being, she was serious and thoughtful, especially concerning Anna's appearance. "I was reared in the vineyards down the Rhine, and I don't know much about your customs here in the city. I do know that we must do something about Anna's wardrobe," Emma insisted. "You can't let her go to the Opera House and mix with high-fashion people dressed so plain. Her dresses are much too long!"

"That's fine," Anna's mother agreed with a distraught look on her face. "Just don't mix up her head with politics! She hears enough about that at school and from her grandmother."

Anna's mother and father.

Anna's family church adjacent to the orphanage.

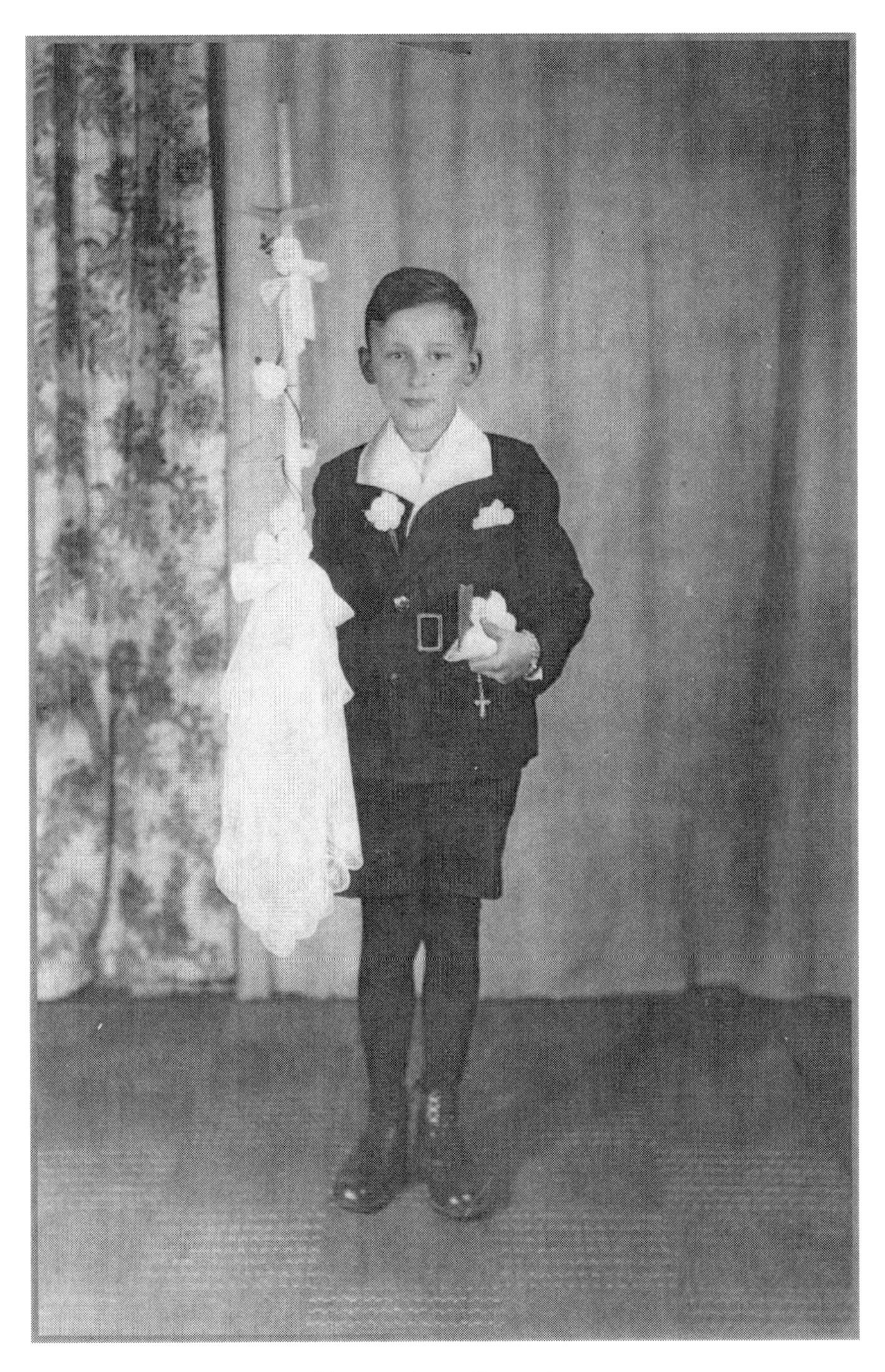

Guenter's confirmation.

Anna's confirmation.

Chapter 3

1937-1938 … The struggle begins.

Why won't anyone explain to me the whereabouts of my father? Anna wondered. She searched for an opportunity to ask Eric.

"Easy, easy," he cautioned her as she jumped on a high stool placed amidst his paint and brushes in a corner of his living room. With fluent and delicate strokes, he applied the finishing touches to the canvas while Anna delighted in the scenery of the Rhine Valley.

She tilted her head. "Please, tell me what our father is like?" she continued to plead.

"Oh," Eric carefully answered, holding one of the brushes between his teeth. "He is well-traveled, and did you know he fluently speaks several languages? I remember he is kind and loves people, but his stubbornness can get him into trouble. Just like you if you don't stop asking so many questions!"

Almost tossing over his easels, she climbed on his lap. "Is he smarter than you?" she pressed on.

"Probably so, but not much," Eric laughed.

"It's not funny!" she cried. "Other children are asking me questions about my father. I don't know what to say. They even make fun and talk about me." She once again tilted her head, looking at his painting, admiring the way he captured the depth and ambience of the scenery along the Rhine.

Eric held her close. "Shhh, I know it's hard for you to understand, but there are just some things we can't talk about these days." His warmth calmed her fear.

Anna wished the six-week testing period at the Opera House would never end. Her mind wandered as she made her way along the elegant avenue and through the park to the Opera House. A few weeks ago, Guenter had helped her memorize the flags from all different countries that lined both sides of the colonnade. *They are no longer there,* she noted to herself, shading her eyes from the bright afternoon sun. *Now they all look alike—all are the same—all have swastikas now! Guenter will be surprised and disappointed.*

Herr Kummel's note, addressed to their mother, arrived with good news: "Anna may begin her studies in ballet at the Opera House." In addition, "We would like your permission to give her an opportunity to perform with the children's choir in our upcoming events. We will welcome her into our supernumeraries as well as small parts in acting and dancing.

Rehearsals will be scheduled during the week, at which time she will be excused from school. Of course, she will be compensated for all performances, but you will need to make arrangements for a private tutor."

Anna felt her heart pounding as she ran up the steep hill toward her grandmother's house to find Guenter, who was busy helping their grandmother clean a rabbit cage in her garden. Distracted for a moment, she shrugged her shoulders and asked their grandmother, "How can you take such good care of the rabbits and then kill them for food?"

Grandmother looked stunned at Anna's question. "Because," she replied in a somber tone, "our butcher's supply is getting scarce."

Guenter interrupted. "Let's go down to the ice-cream shop. We'll celebrate the good news from Herr Kummel, jump on!" He pointed to his bicycle.

Guenter continued to cheer Anna on in her newfound activities, while their mother welcomed the diversion. Herr Dietz's unpredictable moods continued to deprive Anna of her enjoyment of school and the ability to make friends among her classmates. He discouraged her from attending religion classes at the orphanage and convent, saying, "Those nuns and priests can do nothing for you but mess up your head." It became apparent that he singled her out for punishment.

Following instructions from the schoolmaster, Herr Dietz selected so-called volunteers to take part in dental examinations designed for schoolchildren. "Just tell your mother to sign this paper," he demanded, pushing a form under Anna's book satchel as she left the classroom. Afraid once again of reprisal, her mother signed the note.

Anna entered a huge well-lighted room divided into narrow sections that contained reclining chairs. A strong odor of antiseptics hung in the air. A heavyset young woman dressed in a white coat motioned Anna to one of the chairs. Rudely mannered, she began to prod around Anna's mouth. She swiftly stepped aside to confer with a much older woman, who nodded approval. Then she began to drill on one of Anna's teeth she claimed needed filling. When the pain became excruciating, Anna begged her to stop, but the woman ignored her plea to stop drilling. The treatment was humiliating. As the woman stepped aside, Anna leaped out of the chair and dashed out of the building. Sapped of energy, with a hole in her tooth, she arrived at home and fell asleep, keeping the incident to herself.

Whenever possible, and because of concern for her mother, she began to keep Herr Dietz's tactics to herself. Soon, the teacher's cruel intent became overshadowed by the excitement of being part of one of Germany's finest Opera Houses. Ecstatic and as though walking on air, she looked forward to her ballet lessons, practice, rehearsals, and just being with the people.

She also looked forward to her daily walks to the Opera House that took her by the fashionable and famous shops along the picturesque, tree-lined avenue. She stopped frequently in front of an elegant beauty salon. With her eyes closed, she stood and delighted in the fragrance that came from within. *Perhaps someday, I will buy a gift for Mutti here*, she secretly wished.

"You are the little girl who performed with the children's ballet in the *Puppenfee*," a refined gentleman said, interrupting her thoughts as he walked out onto the sidewalk to roll back the canopy that shaded the display window of his elegant styling salon. "Would you mind taking some samples of our 47/11 cologne to share with your friends at the Opera House?" he insisted.

Anna returned his smile as she followed him inside. She watched as he thoughtfully wrapped tiny bottles of cologne in a colorful paper bag. "May I take one of these to my mother?" she asked.

"Yes, of course, I will give you a larger size for her."

Anna curtsied while reaching for his hand. "Thank you. I am Anna," she said with a smile.

"Yes, of course, and I am Frank Goldstein. My wife and I came here from the Netherlands several years ago, and we are both fascinated with the exquisite performances at the Opera House."

Overwhelmed by the delightful scent and enchanting surroundings, Anna glanced over the posh salon as she shyly walked out onto the street.

At age eight, she became the youngest member in the School of Ballet. She enjoyed special attention from the older ballet students. Adult performers delighted in her impersonations of their performances. She enjoyed all parts assigned to her, like the little boy begging for his wooden horse and trumpet in *La Bohemia*, and dancing as a soldier or chimney sweeper in *The Christmas Story*. She loved singing and being part of the crowd in *Carmen*, *The Gypsy Baron*, and even the more serious operas like *Tosca*.

Anna took her training under the well-respected ballet master, and soon became well-versed in the history and terminology of ballet. On the elegant terrace outside the stage door, Herr Kummel stopped Anna on her way to practice. “Anna,” he said, touching her shoulder, “would you like to be in Wagner’s *Meistersinger von Nürnberg*? It is one of the most beautiful operas ever written and very lengthy, about four hours. There will be many hours of rehearsal,” he continued, “but you will derive great joy, I am certain, from being part of it. And besides, we will welcome your personality.”

Anna hung her head. “What about school?” she questioned.

“We will send a note to your teacher and arrange a tutor,” he confidently responded to Anna’s concern.

The first performance of Wagner’s *Meistersinger* fell on a bright Sunday afternoon. Anna’s mother accepted Herr Kummel’s invitation, but did not feel that her wardrobe was fashionable enough for the event. Although her part seemed insignificant, Anna had never experienced such exhilaration.

Lost in the multitude of talented performers, she stood offstage enthralled by the thundering sounds, the overture of Wagner's masterpiece.

"Would you like to see what the excitement in the audience is all about before the curtain opens?" the broad figure of the lead male soprano leaned over and whispered to Anna.

"Yes," she nodded. Her hand absorbed in his, he led her onto the stage and gently lifted her above his head. "Here we are," he said, pointing to one of several peepholes in the massive velvet curtain. "I'll hold you up while you fold back the cover."

She noticed the people in the audience focusing on the Kaiser Balcony. She spotted two men both dressed in brown uniforms, surrounded by several men dressed in black uniforms. "Do you see them?" the soprano asked, looking up at Anna.

Anna nodded, looking down at the bearded and heavily made-up face. "It's Herr Hitler and his friend Dr. Goebbels. May I take another look?" she gasped.

Unlike the people in the park, the people in the audience sat silently. Only the powerful sounds of the orchestra filled the air. Anna's new friend gently put her down and, after a pinch on her cheek, walked offstage. "See you!" he shouted as he disappeared behind the heavy curtain. His Bavarian dialect rang in her ears.

I can't wait to tell Guenter, she thought as she listened to her new friend's artistic voice bellow throughout the performance.

Seeing Hitler and Dr. Goebbels in the audience was not nearly as exciting as pretending that the opera was real life. The stage setting and customs from an era long ago helped Anna with this illusion. Escaping her real life at home and at school made pretending worthwhile. She concentrated and looked forward to her daily ballet lessons. Every handrail she passed became a bar. Whenever space was sufficient, she practiced her large traveling steps, turns, leaps, and pirouettes.

Sharing these feelings over dinner with other family members proved to be a mistake. "If it were not for Dr. Goebbels, you ungrateful little girl, you would not even have been there," charged a neighbor who came to visit for dinner.

Anna caught her mother's eyes welling with tears as she quietly left the room. Perplexed over the ordeal, Guenter held back tears as he asked Anna, "Why are the adults in our family constantly arguing over who is right? No one can always be right!"

Who the majority of people believed to be right became more and more obvious. Portraits of Hitler soon replaced religious artifacts displayed in homes. Toy shops were filled with toys decorated with the popular swastika. To gain popularity, courteous greetings like a simple "hello" were replaced with "*heil* Hitler!"

Familiar faces Anna looked forward to seeing regularly at the Opera House suddenly disappeared. Here, too, the etiquette of daily greetings changed dramatically. Herr Kummel somehow remained neutral, but he was forced to call a meeting with the children in order to re-educate them. "From now on," he explained while rubbing both hands nervously, "please announce your presence as you come through the stage entrance with '*heil* Hitler.' And kindly do the same when you leave." Anna knew she was not alone in having to overcome this awkwardness.

Mystified by the changes, she felt drawn to talk with Sister Renate. She rarely skipped her ballet lessons, but on this day, making an exception was important. Frau Hanze excused her provided she practiced prior to the next session.

She rushed home to pick up a surprise for Sister Renate and the children. Disappointed to find no one at home to talk to about her frustrations, she crawled under her bed to retrieve a small wooden box. Peter, Guenter's cat, happily crawled under the bed with her but was unable to distract her.

She ran until she reached the orphanage and convent. Astonished over most unusual traffic surrounding the building, she stopped across the street and watched a group of men in uniforms unload boxes from trucks parked on the median and carry them into the building. For the first time in many weeks, she felt a nagging sensation in her stomach—the kind that often occurred when her teacher walked into the classroom.

"I don't want to leave here until I see Sister Renate. I must see her!" she mumbled. Additional trucks arrived and uniformed men continued to carry stacks of boxes into the orphanage. "I'll just sit on the playground until everyone leaves. But I wonder where the nuns and children are," she continued to mumble. Her stomach tightened as she noticed a group of men carrying the children's tiny white iron beds out into the street. She covered her ears from the sound of iron against iron as she watched the men carelessly throw the children's beds into the trucks.

Finally, the trucks drove away and there was silence. Anna got out of the swing she had been sitting in, brushed the sand from her shoes and dress, and started toward the front door to ring the doorbell. She stepped back and looked up and over the two-story building when she heard unfamiliar footsteps.

A tall young man dressed in black riding boots, pants, and shirt with the familiar swastika band around his right arm opened the door. "I am looking for Sister Renate," she told him.

"Who?" responded the impatient young man.

"Sister Renate," repeated Anna.

"Oh," he laughed sarcastically, "you're looking for the nuns! They have been moved to another location and so have the children. Somewhere in the Black Forest, I believe. That's all I can tell you! Go home, your parents must be wondering where you are," he yelled as he slammed the door shut.

Bewildered, she pressed her hands against the massive stone building and pushed her face onto her arms. She wept until she felt a tapping on her shoulder. "Guenter," she cried, "how did you know I was here?"

He gently pulled her head against his shoulder. "I just came from the tracking field. I wanted to confirm rumors I heard a while ago, about the nuns having to get out of the orphanage. The building, they say, belongs to the local government and not to the church, so they were asked to move out without notice. But Anna, you must not talk about it, do you hear?"

She detected the usual urgency in his voice. "But I must see Sister Renate," she cried.

"That's not possible right now!" Guenter was unable to comfort Anna, and instead became frustrated himself.

She held on tightly to the small wooden box as they started their walk home. "What is in the box?" probed Guenter.

"It's some money I saved from my allowance. I wanted to surprise Sister Renate and buy some treats for the children."

Guenter showed an urge to pry. "And what allowance are you talking about?"

She kissed him on the cheek. "It's the money Herr Kummel pays all of us for performing at the Opera House. Remember, I give it to Mutti to use for the three of us."

With a big grin, he responded, "Hurry up and make lots more!"

Anna was too distraught to be amused. She quietly retreated to her room and clutched her prayer book while staring at the shepherd and his tiny lamb. Exhausted from crying, she fell asleep.

Not knowing Sister Renate's whereabouts left Anna depressed. She was indebted to the nun for her wonderful world at the Opera House and vowed to continue to do her best there. On her way to practice, she sat down on a park bench and removed the heavily knitted kneesocks her mother insisted she wear, even though none of the girls in her ballet class wore them. She placed them in the tiny suitcase that held her ballet slippers and action wear. *I am early*, she thought, as she leaned back and glanced at the view she and her mother had enjoyed during earlier times.

She recognized her friend Sabina, whom she'd met on their first day of ballet, standing outside the stage entrance. Anna ran toward her.

"Oh, I am so glad I found you," Sabina said with a smile, her voice filled with excitement. "I didn't know where you lived, so I was unable to look for you elsewhere."

"Where have you been?" Anna asked.

"They wouldn't let me continue after the six weeks. Now I take private lessons, and they are very boring." An elderly woman dressed in black approached them. "This is Frau Schmidt, our housekeeper," Sabina said as Anna shook the woman's hand and made a quick curtsey.

"Could you come and visit us?" Sabina begged.

"Oh yes!" Anna hastily replied. She waved at Sabina and watched as she was driven away in an ebony-colored convertible.

Anna had often wondered about the whereabouts of Sabina, who had become a friend when Anna felt lost and deserted. Both were without the company of a father. For bureaucratic reasons, Sabina shared with Anna during their first intimate conversation, her father was forced to flee to another country. Her grandfather insisted they live here because he needed help with the family hotel and the villa located on the fringe of the Kurpark.

"At least you know where your father is," was Anna's reply.

Every day she walked by Sabina's grandfather's hotel. The hotel was located only a few blocks from the Opera House. It was a beautiful structure built to last and took up all of a city block. Five stories to its roofline, with dormer windows indicating two more stories above that. Her spirits were always lifted by the sound of violins from within. She was intrigued by the refined and well-dressed headwaiters serving the hotel's noble guests in the terrace gardens.

Sabina's mother welcomed her daughter's new friend and encouraged frequent visits. So far, Anna's social graces had been limited to her mother's simple ways. From this modest lifestyle, she needed to adjust to new ways in order to fit into the company of the most affluent. But she felt accepted and appreciated in the presence of one of the region's most respected families. Their villa resembled the castles she and Guenter had seen only from a distance along the Rhine. Servants formally dressed in black and white treated Anna as a member of the family.

"They refer to me as 'Fraulein Anna,'" she cheerfully informed Guenter. "I feel that I am part of a fairy tale."

Their mother listened with amazement, unable to take it all in, but her daily struggles continued to escalate, always fearing for letdowns her children might experience.

Guenter, though, quite the opposite, enjoyed teasing Anna. "Must I make an appointment with you, Anna, when we want to do something together?"

Anna's increasing popularity and her activities in the Opera House seemed to mellow Herr Dietz. From time to time, he grumbled about her absence from school. But he respected the connection between the people in charge there and those who contributed to its functions. Therefore, he was afraid of stepping over the line for fear of creating problems for himself by interfering with Dr. Goebbels's goals. Anna's time was now filled with practice, rehearsals, and visits with Sabina's family.

She was amazed to notice that there were no Nazi artifacts in Sabina's home. Only expensive art adorned the walls of the magnificently decorated villa. No one used the new German greeting of "*heil* Hitler." Though somewhat puzzled, Anna found this to be a breath of fresh air.

"I am not allowed to attend public school," Sabina shared with Anna. "My tutor comes here to the villa every morning. Would you like to have her help you also?" Her lovely face revealed concern for Anna.

"Yes, this is too good to be true," Anna told her. "How can I thank you?"

A mischievous smile came over Sabina's face. "Would you give me your old toe shoes when you get new ones? My new dancing teacher says I am not ready for toe shoes yet."

"Sure!" Anna was elated. "Herr Kummel said I should go to have new slippers fitted right away. You may have my old ones—they are really almost like new."

Sabina soon caught on to her new friend's needs. Unspoiled, unselfish, and caring, Sabina looked for opportunities to help her. She insisted on helping Anna with a complete makeover, with the help of her older cousin who was thrilled to pass on to Anna fine quality clothes she had outgrown.

Sabina's mother delighted in inviting Anna to her afternoon tea parties. "She is such a clown," she told her friends. "I like having her around because she always gives Sabina such a lift."

One day, while instructing one of the servants on how to polish the hand railing on the circular marble staircase in the entrance of the villa, she asked her daughter, "Would you and Anna like to perform for our special guests on Saturday?"

"Are you serious?" Sabina looked at her mother with the familiar sparkle in her eyes as she twisted her long black hair.

"Of course I am serious. You play 'Brahms Number Seven' on the grand piano very well. Anna loves all of Brahms's music. She can dance, and you may want to ask one of your cousins to be master of ceremonies. I'll even take the three of you to our hotel restaurant next week for a special treat."

Anna felt sad that her mother was unable to take part in the social life of Sabina's family. There were times when Anna's mother felt lonely and left out. She accepted the fact that, because of her simple ways, she could not relate to Sabina's mother, but she was thankful for every moment Anna spent with this compassionate family. She found contentment knowing that her daughter was in the company of educated people and away from the Nazi influence she fought against on a daily basis.

"I wished that you could come to Sabina's mother's tea party," Anna told her mother while sharing her excitement about the upcoming event.

"It is all right, there is a lovely bench in the park behind the villa near the tennis court. I'll go there and sit. From there, I can watch the guests arrive, and I will be very pleased that you are there having a wonderful time," responded her mother.

Anna stroked her mother's soft hands and embraced her. "Thank you, Mutti," she gasped as emotions overwhelmed her.

It turned out to be a picture-perfect afternoon. Waiters passed trays of mouth-watering pastries and a variety of sparkling drinks among the guests. No politics were mentioned. Hunting, music, and horses dominated their enlightening conversations. Anna became enchanted with the elegant tea party. She sensed a carefree and refreshing atmosphere, and the girls' performance fit perfectly into the setting.

Without a single flaw, Sabina's tiny fingers moved across the keyboard of her grandfather's grand piano as Anna demonstrated her skill in dancing. Even Sabina's shy cousin Barbel, to every one's surprise, elegantly played the violin.

"I would like for you to bring your friend as our guest to the Riding Academy on Sunday. My son Erwin will be riding his stallion, Ben. Will you come?" a handsomely dressed gentleman asked as the guests dispersed. He slipped on his alpine coat with the help of one of the servants.

"Of course, thank you!" Sabina quickly responded, giving Anna a wink of approval. Anna felt her face flushing from all the excitement.

She had not forgotten her mother as she slipped away to Sabina's room. Carefully pushing aside the sheer curtains that graced the French doors, she stepped out onto the balcony. Her mother's tiny figure sat on a park bench near the tennis courts waiting patiently for Anna and their joint walk home.

The girls continued to enjoy their friendships and had much in common. Neither spoke about her father for fear of unknown repercussions. Everyone in Anna's family was amazed at her stylish new look, especially Emma. Her mother, however, showed concern over their lack of ability to appropriately reciprocate.

For Anna, concentrating on her studies became increasingly tough. Herr Dietz continued his cruel behavior toward her. Quoting the führer, he frequently reminded the children, "All people who have German blood running through their veins belong to the National Democratic [Nazi] party." He was thrilled when it became mandatory to conclude each school day by singing the national anthem of the new movement.

To saturate the children's minds with the lyrics of "Adolf Hitler we must follow, him we must obey, he is our savior, for Hitler we live, and for Hitler we must die" became the movement's number-one goal. Herr Dietz supported this goal wholeheartedly. Becoming a member of the Hitler Youth seemed more important than the children's academic studies. Admittedly and proudly, Herr Dietz was happy to teach Nazi ideology.

Anna's grandmother wholeheartedly supported Herr Dietz's ambition. "Herr Hitler will take care of the ordinary working people," she contended. Now able to draw a small pension from her deceased husband, she spent much of her time as a volunteer for the Nazi Party.

Anna kept her frustration and painful experiences to herself and spoke only about her fun adventures. She watched her mother, whose tolerance astonished her. As she listened to their grandmother's demands to have the children join the Hitler Youth, she watched her mother's tiny physique tremble. She knew that the purpose of the Hitler Youth was to indoctrinate boys and girls into the Nazi Party's politics and culture. Furthermore, she sensed Hitler's goal was to brainwash the German youth to become unsympathetic and unfriendly toward Jews and other minority groups, such as Gypsies and the disabled.

Guenter did not resist, for he felt his grandmother's intentions were good, and he wished to please her. "Besides," he explained, "I am looking forward to joining, because I can spend more time in my favorite sports."

"You do not understand, nor do you seem to care, that joining the Hitler Youth means preparations for more serious commitments in the children's adulthood," argued their mother.

Their grandmother, on the other hand, questioned her daughter's source of information. "What basis do you have, and who gives you reasons to be so opinionated?" she maintained.

The lack of security of her father's presence, abuse from Herr Dietz during school hours, loss of Sister Renate's friendship, and the absence of the children in the orphanage left a void in Anna's life. She remained close to her brother, but she missed their special times together. Her mother's love, Eric's paternal influence, her friend Sabina, and the wonderful people at the Opera House, however, filled this void.

Anna found comfort in Eric's promise that he would be there for her always. While Anna's mother's words were few and her teachings awkward, she had the gift to successfully teach her children appreciation for the bare necessities in life and faith in God.

Anna with her mother during her first visit to the Opera House.

Chapter 4

1938 … Tension continues to mount.

Underneath Anna's favorite park bench lay a lone bright red flag. She reached to pick it up but quickly pulled back as her mother sternly commanded, "Please leave it—this does not belong to you!"

Shocked by her mother's stern tone, she asked, "Why don't you like swastikas?" Her mother's only reaction was a shrug of the shoulders.

Earlier in the day, Anna had observed her mother standing like a helpless child among the sea of people and banners to watch Guenter, one of thousands, march in the May Day parade. Sounds of regimental drumming and feet pounding against the pavement rang throughout the area. Members of the Nazi Party, some dressed like characters in a musical comedy, proudly demonstrated the goose step while leading the way.

Dressed in brown shirts and black pants, new members of the Hitler Youth carried swastika banners. "Our flag is the new future," they sang, "and into the future we are marching side by side." Choirs of white-bloused girls, members of BDM (a Nazi-led organization of German girls), lined the streets and chanted, "Führer, Adolf Hitler, we follow you, *heil, heil, heil*!"

Thousands of onlookers gathered in front of Sabina's grandfather's hotel and focused on one of the large balconies embellished with swastika flags. Then the tall French doors opened and Hitler stepped out and waved to the crowd. The crowd burst into loud screams. Then there was silence until the voice of the führer began to bellow: "Today we rule Germany, but tomorrow we will rule the world. Stop thinking for yourself, I will do the thinking for you. Just obey and I will make you rulers of the world!"

The crowd again began to scream, "*Heil, heil, heil*!"

Hitler stopped and for a moment stood silent. His right hand extended over the mass of young boys. He smiled and looked over the crowd. He raised his voice to the familiar high pitch and continued: "Look at Germany's magnificent youth. Look at these fine young men and boys. With them, I can build a new world!"

Again he paused. "Yes, my teaching will be strict. I want my youth to grow up as a violently active, dominating, fearless youth!" Again silence. Then he went on in a shouting voice, "No weaknesses or tenderness will be allowed!" He banged his fist on the podium. "With that I shall create my new order. The world around us will bow down to them!" With both hands he pointed again to the mass of youth. "They will be the god-men of the new world!"

The banner waving crowd began to cheer, "*Heil, heil, heil*!"

Hitler's message was clear. His statements became the law of the boys' young lives. They were sworn to never forget the name "Hitler." Not only had they become the bearer of Hitler's banner and symbols, but also of his faith. They were ready to fight and, if necessary, die for their führer, Adolf Hitler.

It was clear to Anna's mother that Hitler's speech played on the emotions of the youth. She was convinced of this when she saw her son and those who took part in the indoctrination cry in broad daylight. She knew he was too young to understand the meaning of taking the solemn oath of the legions, all out of love for Hitler. She tried hard to remain unaffected by the commotion and anxiously began to pull Anna through the shoving of the people.

"Let us go over to the park and wait for Guenter. We'll sit by the fountain and watch the swans for a little while," she affectionately suggested.

Anna impatiently twirled a rubber ball given to her by one of the storm troopers during the parade. She looked across the lake and pointed to the entrance of the Opera House. "I can't wait until tomorrow!" Her voice revealed anticipation and desire to be there.

Turning toward Anna, her mother pleaded for her full attention while removing the straw hat that shaded her eyes from the bright sun. "Please listen carefully to what I am about to tell you. From now on, you must be sure to be discreet in whom you are speaking to and what you are saying. And please, do not ask questions. Things are changing and mysterious things are taking place. People are afraid. Do you understand, Anna?" Her voice trembled as she spoke. "And whatever you do, remember there are spies all around us. Be careful what you say, especially around your schoolmates."

Anna let go of the ball decorated with swastikas and watched it roll into the lake. She reached for her mother's trembling hands. "I promise to be careful," Anna assured her. Nevertheless, Anna again hoped for an explanation of her mother's frustrations. Again, she yearned for an explanation of her father's mysterious disappearance.

With a deep sigh, her mother pointed to the fluffy white clouds that traveled across the sky. "And please, please, always remember what you have learned in your religion classes." Anna noticed an unusual sternness in her mother's voice.

Exhausted from the three-mile march through the old city and the frustration of searching for Anna and their mother, Guenter ran toward them. "Look at my new dagger," he shouted. Unaffected, their mother looked at the golden letters carved into his new dagger that read, "Blood and Honor." Guenter took a deep breath. "I am glad I found you. I figured I could find you here in Anna's favorite spot!" He lifted his backpack off his shoulders and emptied its contents into his mother's lap. "You may have the cakes and candy," he cheerfully announced. Then he added, "Grandmother is waiting at Jaeger's cafe. I am spending the night with her, but I will see you tomorrow."

"Will you go with us to church?" Anna looked him over as she spoke. He looked handsome.

His large brown eyes pierced Anna's. Then, fearful of hurting their mother's feelings, Guenter turned away. "No, I am sorry, I cannot! My youth group is meeting early in the morning. I must attend or else I will get myself into trouble with my squad leader!" Their mother sat quietly, stared into space, and shook her head in obvious displeasure.

Anna understood her mother's previous remark. Guenter's special time with Anna and their mother, and attending Mass on Sundays, had ceased. Activities in the Hitler Youth had taken priority.

Anna's mother feared that the words of his sing-along with the Hitler Youth, "Heavenly grace gave us the führer, our life is worthless unless we give it to the German flag," had taken hold of his young mind. She knew that the leaders represented Hitler as God. Anna's mother knew that she had no choice in the matter, for fear that she might run into trouble with the Gestapo. Parents gave up their rights once a child joined the Hitler Youth.

Hitler's people began to round up healthy and "perfect" young German men for the service. Eric did not qualify, although his tall, slender build, blue eyes, blond hair, and talent as a draftsman-artist fit their bill. Because of an athletic injury and unsuccessful surgery, he was unable to bend his left leg. Eric loved his job with the local town government, and therefore felt secure and unafraid of being drafted.

But Hitler's people had other ideas. Within forty-eight hours, his presence was demanded at Hitler's headquarters in Berlin. Emma was expecting their second child, and this was unwelcome news. Eric immediately called the family together. Anna listened quietly as he explained, "I will not be able to write to you or make contact for six weeks. Please do not ask why," he pleaded. "I do not have the answer." His voice began to tremble as he continued, "And please, look after Emma and our little Lothar. The baby, you know, is due in two weeks." Anna clenched her fist. She wanted to cry, but she was afraid of upsetting Eric. She knew he needed everyone's support.

"You and Anna may see me off at the train station, if you like," Eric suggested to Guenter. "The trip to the train station will be much too strenuous for Emma." Anna nodded, fighting back her tears.

Two days later, Eric's message for Guenter floated over the screeching of the locomotive's steam engine: "Take care of the family, and be good to your sister! You are almost fourteen. I am asking a lot from you, but I know you can do it!"

With a subtle move, Eric pulled his injured leg upon the platform while the conductor made his last call. Slowly the train began to inch along as other passengers scrambled to get on. Eric stood stone still, then reached for a handkerchief in his coat pocket and began to wave.

"Stay here!" Guenter yelled at Anna as the train began to inch along. But she ignored his plea and started to run as the train increased its speed. Out of breath, she stopped and watched Eric bury his face in his handkerchief. "I won't cry"—the train whistle drowned out her voice. "I won't cry," she repeatedly shouted until Eric disappeared behind the steam of the engine along the seemingly endless track and into the distance.

At a loss for words, Anna and Guenter sat silent during the bus ride back home. Speaking in a somber tone, Guenter assured Anna, "Things are changing, but we are not alone."

"I know," she agreed, noting the change of scenery along the fashionable avenue. Huge billboards that once displayed the region's picturesque vineyards had been replaced with portraits of Hitler. Nazi banners draped government buildings and well-known hotels. Lost in her own thoughts, she felt Guenter's nudge. "Come on, we get off here!"

The children found their mother, pale and visibly shaken, sitting on the stairway in front of the apartment. "Who was the stranger dressed in a black leather trench coat we just passed in the entrance?" Guenter asked. "And why did he hide his face with such an ugly hat?" Guenter continued as he leaned over to kiss her.

"I have no idea," answered their frustrated mother. "He wanted to speak to the man of the house, and I told him there is no other man of the house except you, Guenter." Unannounced visits from this mysterious stranger continued.

Guenter was right, and indeed, Anna's family was not alone. Those who accepted the leadership's slogan, "Get right with Hitler, and your needs will be given you," had nothing to fear. Who was paying the price, however, was not clear. Like a fox sneaking up from behind a henhouse, Hitler's propaganda began to sneak up from behind and into the minds of people.

Herr Dietz, as always, wasted no time by adding hate attitudes to his agenda. "Gypsies and Jews," he shouted, "do not have our blood. Their blood is tainted. Stay away from them, for they do you no good!"

Puzzled by this new warning, Anna stared through the classroom window and across the park to the hospital. Her mother often spoke about the young Jewish doctor there who saved Anna's right eye. She continued to have difficulty understanding Herr Dietz's hateful attitude.

Moreover, how would this affect little Ellie, her neighbor, with whom she occasionally played on weekends? Not to mention her music director at the Opera House who so patiently worked with her during rehearsals. She recalled the little shoemaker on the fifth floor of the Opera House who so thoughtfully fashioned her first ballet slippers. What about Herr Goldstein? A sudden chill came over her.

She had no one with whom she could share this. Hopes about her father had faded, the nuns including Sister Renate and the children at the orphanage had left without an explanation, and Eric too was out of reach. Upsetting her mother was out of question.

The priests at the Catholic church, who had always been accessible, were now only available for Mass and confession. Religion classes were cancelled, and rumors spread that one of the priests had been sent away. His location was kept secret. These thoughts began to haunt Anna's young mind. She recalled Sister Renate saying during one of her religion classes, "Whenever you are confronted with challenges, you must rise above them, and always do what is right." Anna pledged to always remember the nun's advice.

Guenter rarely complained, but the many added responsibilities overwhelmed him. Joining the Hitler Youth was a great disappointment. Extra activities in sports, the exciting outings on weekends, soon turned out to be weekend labor. Physical fitness and training in toughness turned out to be the order. To be accepted by the squad leaders, the boys had to prove their strength. Hitler's leadership decided to use their young boys to build bunkers around the city in case of war and possible enemy attacks. Leadership stressed this free labor and referred to it as "obligation."

Guenter was always careful not to hurt Anna's feelings, for he knew with the constant changes she had become extremely sensitive. He dreaded confronting her with changes of any sort. After being told by his Hitler Youth leader of additional after-school meetings, he worried about disappointing Anna again.

Hysterically, Guenter ran across the schoolyard after school, looking for Anna. "From now on, you must walk home alone!" He pressed the key of their apartment into her hand. "Make sure you lock the door behind you!" His eyes welled with tears, and his stressful behavior startled her. She slung her book sack over her shoulders and alone began her walk home. She looked forward to their joint walks every day, for Guenter's attentiveness was comforting after the unpleasant hours in Herr Dietz's classroom.

The tempting pastries displayed in a window of the neighborhood bakery brought hunger pains to her attention. "Maybe Mutti left a snack in the kitchen cupboard," she muttered. Guenter's cat, Peter, let out a loud cry as she reached the top of the stairs. "Are you hungry too? I'll share my milk with you! Oh well, you may have it all!" She leaned over to pick him up and closed the door to the kitchen cupboard. Peter watched her move around the room. Once fed, he curled up in his basket to take a nap. The fire in the small wooden stove continued to burn. "Let's add some coal, we will keep it nice and warm until Mutti gets home."

Peter remained undisturbed. Carefully, she added a huge coal nugget to the simmering fire.

Anna was unable to ignore her hunger pains. She longed for Guenter's presence and felt lost without him. Concerned about her school assignments, she sat down at the kitchen table and began her homework. The tiny kitchen was the only heated room in their apartment now, since conservation with heating coal had become mandatory. Her mind wandered. She missed Eric and realized that everything had become more difficult since he left.

Unable to concentrate on her homework, she closed her books and wrote a note to her mother. "I will be at the Opera House and from there to Sabina to play. I miss you!" She skipped through the park, across the veranda, and into the stage door.

"Can't you wait until you are upstairs, Anna?" The stage manager teased her with a smile. "And, *heil* Hitler!" he reminded her.

"*Heil* Hitler," she responded. She recalled Herr Kummel's plea about the greeting. After a two-hour dancing session, she quickly changed and neatly placed her action wear into her locker in the dressing room she shared with several of the ballet students.

Hunger pains continued to distract her as she skipped through the park toward the villa. Frau Schmidt, the family's housekeeper, greeted Anna with a warm hug. Sabina's hurried footsteps pounding on the marble stairs let Anna know she had something exciting to share with her. "We are going to watch our friend Erwin perform with his stallion at the Riding Academy on Saturday! Will you come? My cousins and I are taking riding lessons from Master Karl after the event, and you are invited! Isn't that great? And isn't it exciting?" Sabina insisted.

Looking for an excuse, unsure and embarrassed, Anna looked away. "I can't go. We have rehearsal at the Opera House. Besides, I do not own appropriate clothes to wear for riding."

Frau Schmidt turned away from the dumbwaiter she was busy loading with the delicate tea service she used to serve Sabina's grandfather in his library. She peeked over her bifocals and suggested, "I bet the boots you girls have forgotten about in the storage closet will fit Anna. We'll shine them up just like new!" "Ushi may have some of her riding pants that no longer fit her," Sabina added.

With this unexpected challenge, Anna forgot the empty feeling she experienced earlier. She followed Sabina and Frau Schmidt down the stairs and into the kitchen, where the family's cook was busy preparing the evening meal. The aroma of brewed coffee and baked goods greeted them. "We will have tea and some of Frau Schmidt's yummy streusel kuchen," Sabina suggested in her enthusiastic and polished manner.

"Fine with me," Anna agreed. She did not want her friend to know she was hungry.

Cheered once again by her friends and their generosity, Anna skipped through the park, singing all the way home. Her mother was pleased about the invitation to the Riding Academy but wondered once again how she would be able to reciprocate her daughter's friends, people she had not even met. "I have been wishing that some day you and Guenter may ride one of the horses at the Riding Academy. I have watched the riders pass by many times."

Anna nodded. "I know, Mutti, I have seen you standing near the entrance of the Riding Academy stretching your neck to get a glimpse of the inside. Maybe now you will!"

Thanks to Herr Kummel, rehearsal for Anna and the three children who took part in *La Bohemia* was dismissed early. "Please do not break a bone and do not come back here smelling like a horse," he laughed, kissing Anna on the cheek.

Anna watched Erwin demonstrate his skills in riding, and admired the beauty of his gray Arabian. Much like the horses in Hitler's parade, rider and horse were in complete sync. She was amazed at the stallion's stamina and elegance, and Erwin's total control. Just as Sabina promised, she accepted the invitation of a first riding lesson. This proved to be embarrassing. Unlike Sabina and her cousins, who were experienced riders, Anna felt awkward and clumsy. Soon, however, she caught on and fell in love with the people, place, and every horse there.

Since the Riding Academy was less than a five-minute walk from her home, Anna visited the stables often. Riding lessons were out of the question, but she was content watching the activities around the stables and in the riding ring.

"Would you like to take one of the horses up into the ring and exercise him for a while?"

Anna looked up and into the thin and wrinkled face of an old gentleman. He wiped his hands on his leather apron and reached for her hand. His eyes scanning the long row of four stalls, he said, "I am the trainer for these critters. I am also their doctor when need be. And who might you be?"

"Anna!" she responded as she curtsied while reaching for his warm, but rough and weathered, hand.

"Just call me Master Karl," he cheerfully suggested. "That's what everyone calls me, and the horses know me by that name."

Anna watched her new friend gently place the bridle on one of the beautiful white Lipizzaners. He glanced over several neatly stacked saddles. "This one should do it," he said, winking at Anna, who followed her new friend up the ramp and into the ring.

"How comfortable are you up there?" He looked at the saddle while tightening the strap.

"I am not sure, and I am not even a member here," she sighed. "My family can't afford my coming here to ride."

"I understand, but I tell you what," Master Karl continued. "I will give you a job. Since you seem to love horses and you live close by, I will let you help me feed the horses whenever you find time before school. We have twenty-eight of them, you know." He ran his fingers through the horse's neatly brushed mane. "If you have time to spare in the afternoons, I will teach you how to groom the horses. And I promise to make a fine horsewoman out of you as well!"

He held the stirrup and motioned for Anna to mount. "His name is Rubin. Be gentle with him, and he will be gentle with you." Somewhat timid but excited, she looked down at her new friend and nodded. Even Rubin responded by throwing his head back as though giving approval, his shiny mane sliding across her hand as she maneuvered the reins through her fingers.

Patiently, Anna's mother continued to encourage her children, even though she herself became increasingly discouraged. She seemed troubled by the training Guenter continued to receive in his Hitler Youth meetings, and the constant nagging from nearly everyone around her added additional stress. "I am growing tired of listening to 'It is time for you to give up your religious nonsense,'" she shared with Anna. Arguing with their grandmother, whose intentions she felt were good in the past, was useless. Besides, she depended on her for the children's daily meals. "It's tough to hold on to our principles, Anna," her voice quivered, "but we must try!"

Schneewittchen und die 7 Zwerge

Märchenspiel in 10 Bildern von Friedrich Forster.
Musik von Hugo Herold
Inszenierung: Max Müller — Musikalische Leitung: Theo Bach

Personen:

Der König	Hilmar Manders
Die Königin, seine zweite Frau	Traute Fölß
Prinzessin Schneewittchen, seine Tochter .	Donate Ruland
Trolla, Kammerfrau der Königin . . .	Dora Tillmann
Der Prinz	Kurt Strehlen
Fridolin, der Gärtner und Jägerbursche im Königsschloß	Gerh. Frickhöffer
1. Zwerg	Eva Gabriel
2. Zwerg	Elsbeth Eng
3. Zwerg	Gerda Gaßmann
4. Zwerg	Marianne Bechthold
5. Zwerg	Gisela Schroth
6. Zwerg	Hildegard Bunck
7. Zwerg	Karoline Freimann

Glühwürmchen: Ingrid Sturhan und Mathilde Bunck
Im Königsschloß und bei den sieben Zwergen im tiefen Walde
zur Zeit: Es war einmal
Bühnenbild: Magda Haas — Technische Leitung: Paul Barbeler
Pause nach dem 4. Bild

Program of city's famous Schauspielhaus.

RESIDENZ-THEATER
WIESBADEN

SPIELZEIT 1943

DIREKTION: MAX MÜLLER

Hettlage
Kirchgasse, Ecke Friedrichstraße u. Theaterkolonnade 5

Das große Spezialgeschäft
für *Herren-*
u. Knabenkleidung

Interior of Schauspielhaus, the place of Anna's first acting assignment.

Anna and friends during one of many make-believe rehearsals.

CHAPTER 5

1938 … Kristallnacht—the night of broken glass.

Nazi rallies continued in every public meeting hall on a regular basis. Along the tree-lined avenues, processions of thousands and torchlight parades became weekly events. Hitler chose Anna's hometown as one of his favorite retreats. With rare exceptions, he elected to reside at Sabina's grandfather's hotel. One of the reasons was that he enjoyed bathing in the mineral waters piped into the hotel from one of fifteen hot springs in the park across the way. Hitler enjoyed the hotel's relaxing and health-promoting atmosphere.

Accompanied by Dr. Goebbels and other high-ranking SS officers, he frequently made unexpected appearances at the Concert Hall and Opera House. This usually created quite a stir for the people who anxiously waited for an opportunity to get a glimpse of him. The rest of Hitler's entourage, the brown-shirted storm troopers (SA), flaunted their presence in upscale beer gardens nearby.

Hitler's broadcasts from Berlin became shorter but more frequent. The sound of his fist pounding on a podium divulged his anger. "There will be a greater tomorrow," he promised the German people as he began to make outlandish promises—especially to women, who became his strongest supporters. "You will soon occupy finer, yet more affordable apartments. Your children will enjoy better education and opportunities."

But for Anna's mother, things continued to get tougher. She was desperately afraid of rumors that secret police were closely watching their neighborhood. Visits from the stranger stopped, but she felt she was under constant observation.

Anna's mother often spoke about Sister Renate. Attempts to locate the whereabouts of the nuns and the children failed. She felt indebted to Sister Renate for the opportunities offered her daughter. Anna's affiliation with the Opera House, the affluent friends who contributed so much to her contentment, and her recent acceptance to the elite Riding Academy were all a result of Sister Renate's original influence.

Anna was determined to excel in her training at the Opera House, and her popularity grew. Onstage, her cheerful voice brought laughter to the audience, especially in her first acting part in *Snow White and the Seven Dwarfs*. She felt at home singing and dancing in all the popular operettas. Her name began to appear in programs and in the "Performing Arts" section of newspapers and magazines.

Even Hitler's close associates who had become regular visitors to the Opera House recognized her talent. After one of the performances and much to her surprise, a huge bouquet of flowers stood on a table in the dressing room she shared with several other ballet students. "To the little Marianne and friends, heartiest wishes from the führer's friends," read a note embellished by the eagle and swastika.

"I have never seen such a large bouquet of flowers, what must I do with it?" she excitedly asked Herr Kummel—who, as always, had a practical and thoughtful solution. "Why don't you take them to some people who are lonely?" he suggested. Following his suggestion, Anna and several ballet students delivered the flowers to a newly erected makeshift hospital just a short walk from the Opera House. But first, she gently placed a small bunch of roses in a jar of water for her mother.

Anna's mother was pleased and deeply appreciated these opportunities. She was comforted by the fact that her daughter's friends in the Opera House filled the gap of Anna's missing father and Eric. "Anna's enthusiasm keeps me going," she confided to her friend Monica. "I am grateful she spends her time in the company of nice people."

Whenever possible, she anxiously listened out for the riders passing through the streets to see if Anna was among them "You see my daughter?" she excitedly asked people passing by. "If it were not for your size, I could barely tell you apart from the other riders. I am so proud of you! I want to shout when I see you!" she teased Anna, knowing this would embarrass her. Anna confessed to being somewhat proud as she rode through her neighborhood on her way to the equestrian trails that led into the Taunus mountain range.

Unlike the other riders, whose parents paid for this luxury, Anna could only join them at Master Karl's discretion. He did everything possible to include Anna because of her willingness to care for the horses. But her mother found it difficult to believe that Master Karl, with the approval of the owner, Herr Ackermann, made this possible.

Anna's mother was afraid of jealousy that would result in gossip, and constantly reminded herself to be low-key instead of sharing her enthusiasm. Presence of Nazi Party leaders who lived in the area intimidated everyone, especially Anna's mother. "Be careful what you say, someone may turn you in," became a regular warning from the round-bellied and red-faced owner of the local pub. This caused added anguish.

It became extremely difficult for Anna's mother and her friend Monica to practice their faith. They listened with horrified fascination to radio announcements like: "Catholics and Protestants must be vanished!" Even more devastating and heartbreaking was the act of one official as he hung Hitler's portrait in the sanctuary of the church.

Although only a handful of women still attended the weekly women's group, Anna's mother fought to remain steadfast, taking advantage of the few opportunities still available through the church. Even the priest's regular visits to these meetings stopped. The women chose a small restaurant near the church, since meetings without connection to the Nazi Party were forbidden in public locations. The small meeting room in the priest's rectory was classified public. Gatherings in private homes were also forbidden. The restaurant the women had chosen for their meetings catered to the SS, who closely monitored their activities.

Blaring and disturbing conversations from the men kept the women from concentrating as they sat huddled together in a corner near the entrance of the restaurant. With the smell of beer and smoke filling the room, the women soon became discouraged and unable to cope with these unacceptable conditions. Like many others who wished to continue in their faith, Anna's mother and her friends were driven into isolation. They became discouraged and cancelled their weekly meetings. Shrugging his shoulders, the owner, a friendly and familiar face to the Catholic community, apologized and explained, "There is nothing I can do!" Even the bells of the old cathedral had fallen silent. This became a way of life.

Everyone seemed on edge. Neighbors began to tell on each other. Arrest followed anyone who stood in the way of the Nazi order. One of the neighbors who made routine visits to the neighborhood pub on his way home complained about the new system. He was dismissed from his job the following day. His wife, mother of three young children, was devastated. Unable to cope, her husband committed suicide several weeks later. It was apparent that the Nazis had started to take control over the people.

Loudspeakers began to patrol the streets encouraging the women to volunteer in service for the *Reich.* Anna's grandmother's petite and swift-moving figure dashed out of her home and into the streets whenever she heard a loudspeaker. "We don't want to miss anything," she proudly announced to anyone within reach of her daring voice. She filled the role of a self-admiring volunteer and vendor during the rallies. With a huge basket of pretzels, she worked her way through the crowds yelling, "For the cause of the führer!"

Pressure increased for women to replace men in the workforce. Because of this kind of pressure, Monica's daughter Ulli accepted a job as a railway conductor. Only days later, because of inadequate training, she was crushed to death while separating two rail cars. The cause of Ulli's death, read a statement in the local paper, was that "she died in service for her führer and the *vaterland*." This was no comfort for Monica, widow and mother of an only child.

In another change to the workforce, foreigners replaced men who earlier were taken out of factories. Every healthy sixteen-year-old boy was encouraged to join the army. Anna's mother lived in constant fear of this.

Only Emma and her friend Monica remained close to Anna's mother as her struggle continued. She was stubborn and refused to accept financial assistance from the newly established Nazi Welfare Organization. "They ask too many questions," she complained to the nagging grandmother who continued to put the blame for their struggle on the children's father.

Emma too experienced difficulty coping. Nearly a year had passed since Hitler's people had summoned Eric to Hitler's headquarters in Berlin. In his letters, he expressed concern for his family. His letters were censored because of his highly classified work. Reading between the lines, Emma knew he was homesick and anxious to be with them and to meet their new baby girl, Karin. She yearned for Eric's visit. To overcome her loneliness, she often visited her mother, who lived alone in their family's quaint old farmhouse near the Rhine.

"Those are tears from heaven," said Anna's mother, distraught and exhausted, as she pulled the covers under Anna's chin. The rain running off the slate roof outside Anna's bedroom added gloom to the troubled environment. Anna blinked to get the sleep out of her eyes. It was cold. She shivered, looking at the grayish-black sky outside as her mother pushed back the exterior shutters of her window.

Her mother's voice dropped to a nervous whisper. "I am not sure, Anna, I thought I heard strange noises during the night. It sounded like heavy vehicles a block away. I have a strange feeling, and I know that I did not dream this! Something is terribly wrong!"

Later that afternoon, her instincts proved to be correct. Local police discovered a hiding place that someone in the area had reported. More than a dozen men referred to as vagabonds were taken away during the night. Nothing else was revealed about the incident.

Anna watched her mother dust her dresser and gently shine a cherished figurine of the Blessed Mother. "It's one of the last gifts from your father," she whispered.

Anna gave thought to her mother's earlier remarks. *Tears from heaven?* She had no problem understanding what her mother meant. In her mother's mind, lightning and thunderstorms, for example, were warnings from the God she revered and feared. "He," she explained, "lets us know He is up there, and He lets us know that he is not pleased with us, always remember this Anna!" Anna sensed a combination of confidence and fear in her mother's voice.

An unexpected visit from Gertrude Osterbaum, a well-respected woman in the Catholic women's group, came late that evening. Still stricken with fear, Anna's mother peeked through the delicate lace curtain of their front door. She noticed Gertrude waving a yellow sheet in her hand as she impatiently knocked on the door.

"All right, all right," her mother said, quickly opening the door.

Gertrude took hold of her arm upon entry, her normally pale face flushed with anger. "How long have you known me, Lina?" she cried. "We were confirmed together when we were kids! Now the people up there in the government offices reclassified me as a Jew just because my grandfather was a Jew. That means my little Trudie is also a Jew. Do you know what this means? They are calling us *mischlinge* [half breeds]!" Her voice trembled. "Besides, how do they know all of this?"

Anna's mother stretched to reach her coffee grinder on a shelf above the stove and a small tin can of coffee she had saved for a special occasion. "I will make us a cup of coffee," she said, gently withdrawing from Gertrude's clutching hand as she watched her pitch the yellow paper into the burning flames of the kitchen stove. There was little chance to comfort her dear friend who for so many years encouraged and brightened the lives of the Catholic women's group.

Other instances followed. Frau Bauer, Ellie's mother, stopped Anna's mother in the stairwell of their apartment house. "Ellie can no longer skate with your daughter on weekends," she said, her voice sounding strange. "Some of the children made fun of her in the park. It is just too painful to see her get hurt. I hope you understand. Besides, we do not want to drag you into danger as well!"

Anna's mother was saddened by this change, but she too was afraid. Touching Frau Bauer's hand, she shook her head and turned away, but she was unable to keep from staring at the star which read *Jude* on little Ellie's jacket.

"We are in danger!" Ellie's mother cried. "She is only six!" She attempted to hide the star by turning over her lapel as another neighbor passed by.

Black clouds continued to hang over a city once wrapped in beauty and filled with music. Anna too felt the sudden change and tension at the Opera House. Her ballet master did not show up for rehearsal. As was the case with Sister Renate, he simply disappeared. Anna was crushed, knowing he would not leave without saying goodbye. She looked forward to his hugs before and after the rehearsals. No one knew anything about his whereabouts, and no one dared to ask questions.

Bewildered, Anna ran the five flights of stairs to the top floor of the Opera House to look for the little shoemaker. His thick horn-rimmed glasses and several unfinished ballet slippers lay on his workbench, and his leather apron was slung over his coat rack. He too was no longer present.

For many months and whenever possible, Anna had sat and listened to a talented young flutist practice his instrument in the orchestra's rehearsal studio. She was enthralled with his ability to bring forth the flute's unbelievably beautiful sound. He too was no longer present. His chair remained empty.

Walking her favorite route along the avenue to the Opera House, she noticed unfamiliar names on storefronts. She missed the chocolate ladybugs given to her by Herr Simons, the owner of the confectioners' shop. More than this, Anna missed his chats about the fragrance of flowers along the colonnade "Stop for a moment, Anna, and listen to the cheery chatters of the birds who nest in the old river birch in front of our shop," he often suggested. Frank Goldstein across the street, Anna was told, had gone on an extended vacation. All of this proved overwhelming and too much to grasp in Anna's young mind. She did not understand why people she loved continued to vanish from her life.

She felt desperately alone, having no one to talk to. Guenter's newly developed mood swings confused her. He quickly changed subjects whenever Anna began to ask questions. On one occasion, with his childlike intellect, he explained to her that Dr. Goebbels, Hitler's new propaganda minister, despised Jewish people and that he might hurt them. "Just do not talk about it," he insisted.

"If only our father and Eric could come home for a visit," Anna cried.

But her sunken spirits did not last. She remembered Maidlie, the old mare at the stables. Master Karl put the old horse in her care. "I must go to the stables and put compresses on her infected leg, maybe I can also take her out for a short ride. Master Karl says she needs to be exercised," she sighed. Besides, a thorough brushing of her gray coat, which had turned white with age, would be a welcome treat to the old mare. Anna recalled her conversations with Sabina. "We must always think about fun things, even if we have to pretend." Those, Sabina told her, were the words of her wise grandfather.

Until now, Sabina had not visited her at their apartment. Anna had avoided it because she feared losing Sabina's friendship. Besides, she felt awkward and embarrassed about her family's modest lifestyle. Anna's mother was much older than Sabina's mother and lacked her extraordinary social skills. Because of these awkward feelings, Anna made certain to meet her friend in other places and ahead of time. On this day, however, Sabina's curiosity changed Anna's strategy.

Returning from attending to Maidlie, Anna heard Sabina's laughter as she reached the landing outside their apartment. She hesitantly opened the door. Sabina greeted her. "Your mother and I have finally gotten acquainted, and we are having a lovely visit." She scrunched up her nose and giggled. "I bet I know where you have been. I believe you have visited the horses. I brought your mother some lovely fruit from the hotel garden, and I have a surprise for you, too. My mother has invited us for tea at the hotel this afternoon. She invited my two cousins also."

Embarrassed, Anna looked around the tiny kitchen. Her mind wandered. *I wonder if she has noticed the empty cupboard?* But Sabina was totally unaffected as she looked around and remarked, "How cozy." Her eyes caught the lone rose on the table. "We have pretty flowers in our hotel garden. I shall remember to bring some next time." She reached for the hand of Anna's mother, who sat content and motionless observing Sabina's charm.

"Thank you," Anna's mother responded in her typical soft manner. "I can't wait to see you again." Sabina waved as she retrieved the empty basket.

Curious neighbors looked on as Anna and Sabina strolled through Anna's neighborhood. Sabina appeared fascinated as she discreetly examined the buildings. Accustomed to the upper echelon location of her grandfather's mansion, she obviously was not accustomed to her friend's modest surroundings.

The dismal faces of foreign laborers and their pathetic appearance interrupted the girls' conversation. "These sad-looking people are here from Poland to build air-raid shelters for us," said Anna. "Guenter told me about the project when I helped him move our chairs into the air-raid shelter that accommodates all the residents of our apartment house." Anna remembered Guenter commenting, "I hope we will never have to use this place," as he placed gas masks and blankets in each chair.

"What is this commotion about?" Anna asked Sabina as they approached the hotel. A vapor of steam enveloped them as they passed the gazebo that housed the hot underground mineral springs. Sabina nervously fluffed her hair. "I believe Herr Hitler must be here. We will enter through the main entrance," Sabina giggled, "just like all this fuss is about our arrival!"

A tailored valet stood near the entrance. He smiled at the girls and nodded. Bright Turkish carpets led the way into the quaint old hotel. Tall windows along the corridor gave easy visibility onto the sweeping lawns and flower beds across the park. *I wish Mutti could see this place*, Anna thought.

A waiter passed with a tray of sandwiches. The aroma struck Anna's nagging hunger pain. "We'll look for my mother down in the kitchen, she is probably giving instructions to the personnel about now," said Sabina, leading the way to the marble staircase that went to the lower level.

Amused by the kitchen personnel standing at attention, Anna followed Sabina into the gigantic hotel kitchen. Dozens of cooking racks loaded down with assortments of baked goods stared at them. As always, Sabina's discerning mother noticed Anna's frantic expression. "Fertie will give you a sample!" Sabina's mother winked at the chef as she walked toward the girls. "Or perhaps we'll go up to the tea room right away. Anna is always hungry," she affectionately confided in Fertie.

Anna moved her hand across the gate of the brass elevator door as it ascended to the main floor of the hotel. Sabina quickly pulled her hand back. "We are not allowed to touch this," she fondly corrected Anna. A sound of heels clicking together startled the girls as two men in front of the elevator greeted each other. "That is Herr Hesse, one of the führer's most respected confidants," Sabina's mother whispered. "You girls must be very quiet so that you do not disturb our guests."

With the relaxing sound of a lone violinist in the background, Anna observed every move during lunch. Intrigued by the elegant surroundings and especially

Sabina's mother's genuine conversation, she realized that without Sabina's family, this moment would have been a mere fantasy.

Later on, peeking through the railing of the terrace outside the tearoom, the girls watched as Hitler's motorcade lined up on the edge of the park. Butlers and chambermaids from the neighboring hotels stood on the balconies hoping for a glimpse of Hitler.

Sabina's cousin Barbell lifted herself out of her chair as a group of men dressed in black uniforms walked out of the hotel and approached the motorcade. "Hitler and Goebbels," she said, pointing to them. Sabina's mother was quick to pull back her hand.

Anna looked at the clock on the wall. "We have rehearsal at the Opera House in half an hour. I must go." She remembered her mother's strict instructions never to be late, and to acknowledge people's kindness.

"We'll walk you to the corner," Sabina suggested cheerfully.

Several maids gathered outside the executive suite just vacated by Hitler and his people. Sabina took Anna and her cousin Barbell by the hand. "Let us go inside and have a look!" Reluctantly, the girls tiptoed into the executive suite as two of the chambermaids stepped aside. Anna recognized the scent of cologne that still hung in the air. It reminded her of Eric. "Isn't this interesting?" Sabina's mischievous expression showed excitement.

Everything was left neat except the newspapers that were strewn everywhere. Barbell picked up one of them and smiled. "Hitler must like his picture in the newspapers!"

A mild breeze gently lifted the sheer curtain in front of the tall French doors that led to the balcony. From this location, Hitler made his speeches to the thousands who took part during rallies in the park below. A serving cart sat undisturbed. Anna noticed two untouched boiled eggs still resting in the silver eggcups and several empty wrappers of Swiss chocolate. She touched the coffeepot after lifting the warmer. "It's still warm," Anna whispered. "My mother would enjoy a cup. Real coffee is a rare luxury for my mother." She spoke softy so no one could hear her. For a moment, sadness for her mother filled her heart.

Sabina's mother's uplifting voice interrupted her thoughts. Accompanied by one of the hotel managers, she walked into the suite. She expressed concern and reminded Anna of her rehearsal appointment. "Is your presence here by any chance Sabina's idea?" she asked with a smile.

Anna shared the afternoon's events with her mother. She was pleased to see her mother smile, as she described their adventure in Hitler's suite after his departure. And she was pleased to see her face light up as she handed her the small paycheck Herr Kummel had given her for a recent performance.

Chapter 6

1939 … Signs of devastation.

Because Anna and her family lived within one city block of the heavily populated Jewish neighborhood, they saw firsthand the pressure put on their Jewish friends and neighbors. It began with verbal slogans encouraged by the new party members. "Do not do business with Jews—do business with your own people," read posters nailed onto government buildings.

Soon thereafter, Jewish homes were looted of their personal and valuable possessions as family members helplessly stood and watched. They were forbidden to dine in non-Jewish restaurants, and were banned from theaters, movies, and even the beautiful parks around the city.

Routinely, the two-faced and ruthless SA, the Nazi Party's military force, swarmed through neighborhoods and threatened to arrest anyone who spoke out against them.

Members of the SS, the elite and heartless group of Hitler's *Schutzstaffel*, had free rein to do whatever they wished to anyone who showed favor to Jewish neighbors and Gypsies, or anyone who dared to challenge them by speaking out. No one seemed safe from a knock on the door.

For reasons no one seemed to understand, especially Anna's simpleminded mother, Hitler's anger exploded. "All obstacles will be overcome," he shouted in rallies and over the radio. The position of Germany's churches had become an obstacle, especially the Catholic Church. One of the Catholic bishops was quoted as saying, "If the so-called German faith movement succeeds, it will signify the end of religion." He became a personal target. His home was set on fire.

Almost overnight, and without warning, tension heightened everywhere. Violence erupted over trivial matters. Men in uniforms smashed the windows of Anna's favorite card shop across the street. There was glass everywhere. "Spit in their faces," yelled a Nazi leader's daughter to a group of young children roller-skating in the park, as the girl's mother looked on and smiled. "Don't be afraid, their blood is not like yours!" Cold chills came over Anna as she was reminded of Herr Dietz's earlier comments. Everywhere one looked, shops and restaurants displayed signs: "*Juden verboten.*"

Anna regularly ran errands for their grandmother, since Guenter's Hitler Youth meetings demanded nearly all of his free time. On her way to pick up a basket of pretzels for their grandmother's vending business, she passed by one of the area's most beautiful landmarks, the synagogue. She became fascinated with its unusual structure. "Just as our ancient Catholic Church up on the hill is God's house, so this house is God's house for our Jewish neighbors," her mother had recently explained. Anna smelled smoke nearly two blocks away and realized it came from the synagogue. She placed the basket of pretzels on a bench so that she could climb up to take a look over the massive stone wall that surrounded the synagogue.

Her eyes began to burn from the heavy black smoke billowing out of the building. She drew back as one of the five golden steeples tumbled to the ground. Dust enveloped her. Only pieces of stained glass around the slender arched window frames remained. In front of the building a huge pile of books burned. Pieces of black burned paper blew in the wind. "Guenter so loves books, he would be hurt to see all these books burning," Anna mumbled. Disheartened, she stood and wondered why no one was around to stop it. "I have always wanted to go inside, and now it is too late. Why doesn't some one stop all of this!" she cried.

Anna watched her grandmother dress for the rally that evening. She followed her into her bedroom and jumped on top of her grandmother's soft goose featherbed. With utmost precision, Grandmother tied a crisp white apron over her simple black dress. She swirled around in front of her mirror and smiled. To add a special touch, she painstakingly tied a silk scarf embroidered with swastikas to identify her role as a volunteer for Hitler.

Still disturbed over the incident at the synagogue, Anna asked her grandmother for an explanation, but her grandmother only shrugged her shoulders. There seemed little concern in her response to Anna's question. Through the kitchen window, Anna could hear her singing as she walked across her garden with her basket of pretzels under her arm, proud and enthusiastically looking forward to serving the führer.

Herr Dietz sat at his desk with his arms folded across his chest. Anna noticed a vacant seat in front of her. "Some of the children in our school have gone to camp," he snapped. With his measuring stick in hand, he pointed to the vacant seat. "You may move up!" he said, pointing toward Anna. His voice had changed. She was astonished to see him speak more gently than usual.

Anna bit the knuckles on her hand and stared at Herr Dietz. She felt a strange knot in her stomach. As she lifted the cover of the desk, she recognized a wrist brace belonging to the crippled girl who had occupied Anna's newly assigned seat. Too afraid to question her teacher, she gently closed the cover. "Maybe I will say hello to her at the park," she murmured.

"This morning," said Herr Dietz, "we will take a trip across the Rhine to Mainz. I have invited Fraulein Meier, our new history teacher, with whom I plan to share teaching this class from now on. She is well-versed in history and geography. We will take a look at Gutenberg's first printing press dating back several centuries and some of the old Roman landmarks," he added.

Anna felt elated with the news. From the beginning, she felt comfortable in the chubby, fair, and pigtailed young teacher's presence. Everyone enjoyed her Bavarian dialect. Her colorful dirndl suited her personality. At the last moment, Herr Dietz directed the new teacher to take total charge of the field trip.

Anna felt her heart leap for joy as she sat content in the front of the bus, soaking up the feeling of freedom among her classmates. With Herr Dietz's absence, she felt included in her class for the first time. For the first time after nearly four years she dared to speak, for the first time she could be herself as she joined in her classmates' conversations and singing. Her mind wandered as the bus made its way through the vineyards along the Rhine. From a distance, she recognized the towers of the Romanesque cathedral she had visited with her mother some time ago, and she thought about Guenter and their trips along the Rhine during more fun times.

A soldier at an intersection signaled the bus driver to stop. He boarded the bus and spoke, visibly exhausted. "I am sorry, but you must turn back. The British did a number on our city of Mainz last night during its first bombing. They estimate several hundred planes took part in last night's air raid."

Fraulein Meier turned toward the children. "We have planned this trip for weeks, can't you see their disappointed faces?" she persisted. After a lengthy discussion, the soldier gave in to the enthusiastic teacher. She winked at the girls as the soldier gave a final and stern okay. "Only provided you accept full responsibility," he announced once more. With a harmonized "yay" from the children, and a smile from the bus driver, the bus continued on its way.

Anna felt her love for history and geography come alive. Intently, she stared out of the window as the bus neared the port. Ships of all sizes hugged the shoreline. People were going about their business. The sound of an occasional ship horn blurted out. For all the children, this created excitement and appreciation for this moment. In the distance, however, dark clouds of smoke surrounded the smokestacks rising above the city.

As they neared the bridge, another soldier impatiently waved his stop sign above his head and signaled the bus driver to come to a halt. The matronly bus driver got out of her seat and volunteered to have a discussion with the soldier. Only moments later she returned and continued to drive on. Fraulein Meier encouraged the children to applaud the brave driver with an even louder "yay!"

No one paid attention to the bus as it entered the old city. Fire engines roared through the streets. *A different scene from that of the burning synagogue*, Anna recalled.

"The soldiers were right, we best turn back," Fraulein Meier suggested to the bus driver. The children watched in horror as people searched for belongings in the rubble of collapsed buildings.

Lost for words, Fraulein Meier struggled to find a way to revive the cheerful spirit of her group of children. "If this is the first bombing in the region, I hope it will be the last!" Her voice sounded gloomy.

Anna leaned over her classmate to get another glance. "Where will these people go when it turns dark?" she asked Fraulein Meier, watching a smudge-faced little boy cling to his mother's apron.

Everyone was surprised that the neighboring city of Mainz had become the enemy's target. The attraction may have been its many factories and the busy harbor. Anna recalled Master Karl speaking about his concern regarding the grain shipped on barges from Xanten down the Rhine.

As the news of the bombing in Mainz spread, curious people traveled from neighboring villages along the Rhine to see the destruction. Most of the people had ignored the importance of preparing air-raid shelters. Blackouts for the entire German population at once became mandatory. Streetlights no longer illuminated parks and neighborhoods, leaving cities in a gloomy state.

Guenter came home from his regular Hitler Youth meeting with his face looking like plaster. The early evening gloom did not help matters. Anna followed him into his room. He drew the door shut and furiously threw himself on his neatly arranged bunk bed, his hands clasped behind his head.

Anna shook from fear. She had not seen her brother in such a somber mood. "I am leaving in two weeks," his voice quivered. "My entire group volunteered to train to be soldiers. What was I to do? They would have laughed at me if I had not joined in with them. Mutti will be getting a note today!" He turned his eyes away from the clouds that moved across the sky, visible through the skylight, and turned to Anna.

"What about me!" Anna cried. "Everybody is leaving me."

"You and Mutti still have the priests at church," Guenter assured her. She quietly began to sob.

Their mother's footsteps startled both. "May I come in?" she whispered. Her cheeks turned pale as she looked at Anna and Guenter in disbelief. Fighting to hold back tears, she took them into her arms. "Perhaps it's all a mistake," she questioned. Then she stood up, arched her back affected with arthritis, and sighed. In her hand, she held the note from the Hitler Youth leader. "What can we do?" she asked. "We must be strong, your father wants all of us to be strong! Besides, what can we do?" she repeated. But Anna knew her mother burned with anger. Guenter had no business joining the Hitler Youth group, she confided in Anna. "But they just did not listen!"

Anna felt elated about her mother's comment with reference to their father, but again was afraid to ask questions.

In a calm and measured tone, Guenter assured Anna and their mother, "It's only six weeks. By that time it will be Christmas, and we will all be together." Visibly disturbed and at a loss for words, he left to run their grandmother's errands.

"Will you go with me to church to light a candle?" her mother asked Anna.

"Of course I will!" she answered, somewhat disappointed at having to cancel her visit to the stables. Anna felt helpless to comfort her mother. The familiar and soothing smell of incense hung in the air as the two walked into the old Catholic Church. She watched the priest, dressed in his long black robe, walk around the altar as her mother knelt before the vigil lights. With her rosary in hand and her head covered with her lace kerchief, she cupped her face in both hands.

Anna sat silent. For as long as she could remember, she had been fascinated by the slender statues of the beautifully calm saints that surrounded the sanctuary, and the stained-glass windows that gave a sense of mystery and heavenly illumination. Although the day was dark and dreary, the old church offered comfort for the fear-stricken young girl and her mother. She knew there was no one left to look after the family as she too prayed and searched for answers.

Her mother's sobbing finally stopped. Utter silence filled the church. *If only the bells from the bell tower would disrupt this silence*, Anna thought. She knew her mother looked forward to the musical sounds of the bells ringing down the week on Saturday evenings. Perhaps this would cheer her up.

Crossing herself, her mother gently rose and walked toward Anna. Her face revealed renewed hope as she lifted the kerchief from her face. "Come on, Anna, we will look for Guenter," she suggested.

"Why does everything keep on changing?" Anna asked her mother as they walked down the hill to their home. As usual, her mother just shook her head.

Guenter had two weeks before reporting to Mannheim. Anna's mother desperately searched for consolation. She resented the fact that certain men remained in their jobs—men like Herr Dietz, who continued to single out Anna, making her studies difficult. Although Anna was on her own with her homework, Guenter came to the rescue whenever necessary. To continue in the training program offered with the Opera House, Anna needed passing grades. The tutor provided by Herr Kummel through the system, a young member of the Hitler Youth, seemed more interested in enhancing Anna's interest in Hitler's goal. "This is the requirement set by the new regime," he constantly reminded Anna. Now with Guenter leaving, Anna wondered how she would be able to make it.

Two weeks passed quickly. Anna's mother spent much of her time mending Guenter's socks and making sure his clothes were in good order. Anna helped their grandmother bake his favorite cookies and carefully packed them into a shoebox.

Guenter spent much time in Anna's presence. He refused to leave her and, for the first time, sat in during rehearsals. After performances, he faithfully waited for her outside the stage door. Together, they rode their bicycles over his favorite trails and stopped for long talks along the scenic Taunus. Occasionally, Guenter helped Anna with her chores at the stables. He enjoyed Master Karl's sense of humor and asked him to watch over Anna during his absence. "Why can't it always be like this?" Anna cried in Guenter's arms during one of their stops along the trails.

The day of Guenter's dreaded departure, a Saturday afternoon, arrived. An army band's effort to serenade the boys to ease tension failed miserably. Dressed in their Hitler Youth uniforms and loaded down with gear, several hundred boys met in the schoolyard. With tears streaming down his face, Guenter had a difficult time responding to his leader's command to climb into the truck. "I'll be back in six weeks, Anna!" his voice quivered. "I'll bring you something!" He shouted again, "I'll write to you," as the caravan of covered trucks pulled out of the schoolyard.

Anna watched her mother's fragile body shake. Their grandmother fought back tears—her eyes focused on the trucks driving away. She found it difficult to watch Guenter cry. It was a heart-wrenching experience for Anna and her mother. Both found Guenter's departure difficult to deal with. Anna's father, Eric, Sister Renate, and now Guenter.

Anna's mother pulled herself together. She reached for Anna's hand and gently pulled Anna's arm around her own. She paid no attention to the grandmother who stood alone, just staring into space. "I feel bad for grandmother," Anna whispered. She recalled her mother's anger toward her.

Walking at a slow pace, Anna's mother tilted her head, looked into Anna's eyes, and spoke calmly, "We must remember to rise above our circumstances. Please remember this, Anna. Sister Renate and I talked about this many times. She was capable of handling tough situations. I am not sure I can do the same. But I will try, and I will thank you for your help. We should not grumble about things we do not have, but we must remember and thank God for the things we do have."

Anna listened intently to her mother and detected strength in her composed and pleading voice. She felt reassured. After weeks of searching for the crippled classmate who always sat in the shade of nearby chestnut trees and watched the other children play, Anna felt discouraged. Herr Dietz would know the answer to the girl's whereabouts, but she could not ask questions.

Chapter 7

1940 ... Suffering of Jewish neighbors escalates ... Hitler attends performance at the Opera House.

It was no secret that the SS [Schutzstaffel] became leaders of the Nazi Party's political movement. Soon after, the Waffen-SS organized a fanatical, highly politicized force, determined to achieve the Nazi regime's brutal ambition to crush those who stood in its way. Their mission was to create a "new order" by getting rid of all Jewish influence.

Conversations with friends and neighbors revealed little calmness and strength. Fear struck nearly everyone who became aware of the war. Hitler was not stingy about boasting. "Our troops have taken over Norway, Denmark, Holland, Luxembourg, and Belgium! We are close to victory!" he bragged over the radio, with his voice at a high pitch and fists continuing to pound against the podium. "In addition, we will soon begin massive air raids over London, England."

In his speeches, he talked of humiliating the French army by overrunning them in only forty days.

"What is the purpose of blackout if we are winning the war so quickly?" asked one neighbor as she stood in line for her weekly meat ration.

Not paying attention to the woman who displayed the Nazi insignia around her sleeve, an older gentleman with a distinct Bavarian slang replied, giving a laugh deep from within his beer belly, "The man is mad!"

Anna's mother stood and watched in horror as two men dressed in civilian clothes walked him away before he made it to the front of the line. No one saw his familiar face again.

Gradual and involuntary changes in lifestyle could not keep Anna's mother from smiling. She cheerfully followed her daily routines while keeping a close watch over her daughter. The biggest challenge she faced daily was not only the constant shortage of essentials, but the nagging reality that people in her immediate surroundings experienced little change in their lifestyle.

Across the courtyard of their apartment house, she watched as one of her neighbors frolicked with his children. His daughter Inge frequently left Anna in tears. "My father thinks he knows why you don't have a father, Anna. My father is a high-ranking officer, he just returned from France and brought us chocolates and, for me, my fuzzy little angora sweater." She ran her fingers across her chest. "Do you like it?" she bragged.

Anna's mother remembered once again one of the Nazi Party's favorite slogans, "Get right with Hitler, and your needs will be given you!"

"Sabina's family seems to have no access to such luxuries either," she calmly reminded Anna.

Positive developments continued to surround Anna, especially in her school. She had promised Guenter to do her best during his absence. Until Fraulein Meier came along, she was doubtful about keeping this promise. She realized she had stumbled through to this point and did not know that her schoolwork could actually become a gratifying experience.

Fraulein Meier planned regular weekly field trips through some of the quaint Middle Ages towns along the slopes of the Rhine. Her love of history and fascination for the castles dating from the thirteenth century soon spread among all of her students. Anna's new teacher became her friend. Fraulein Meier was familiar with the operetta *Saison in Salzburg*. When she learned about Anna's part in the operetta, she immediately bought a ticket for the performance. After school, Fraulein Meier and Anna danced the Bavarian polka, mixed with a touch of the mazurka, through the corridors outside her classroom.

So intrigued was Anna with her activities that she hardly noticed the dangers around her. She focused on school, daily visits to the Riding Academy, spending time with Sabina, ballet lessons, rehearsals, and performances. On Saturday afternoon, she found time to help in the neighbors' busy bakery. Because of rations, long lines reached nearly a block away. She was quick in packaging the breads while Herr Ramspott, the owner of the bakery, worked the cash drawer. He treated Anna as his own, and Anna enjoyed his endless sense of humor. Each time, the baker compensated Anna with a loaf of fresh-baked bread and some pastries. During the week, he made certain Anna's mother did not have to stand in line. This eliminated the problems of pain caused by her severe arthritic condition.

Because of Guenter's absence, their grandmother became more demanding of Anna's time. Carrying the heavy basket of pretzels several city blocks each week proved difficult. She found it even more difficult to digest political conversations with her grandmother during her midday and only meal.

"Instead of spending so much time on your present activities, you may want to join the BDM [*Bund Deutscher Mädel*]," her grandmother suggested in an angry tone. "Today's proper German girl is expected to serve the führer. Furthermore, I hope to see you and your mother involved in our Sunday morning rallies!" she continued.

"But we go to church on Sunday mornings," Anna protested.

"Then start spending time with people who can do you some good! Those priests and nuns do not care a thing about you!"

Anna was shocked at her grandmother's remarks. "The nuns are no longer there! We do not go to church to see the priests, although they are very important. Mutti takes me to church because it is God's house and it is the right thing to do!" Anna cried out.

"You don't want to go into hiding like another member of the family by refusing to join our führer's cause, do you?" Anna's grandmother insisted.

Anna watched a pinch of salt slip through her grandmother's fingers and into a pot of boiling potatoes and sauerkraut. "Are you referring to my father? If so, please tell me what you mean," Anna insisted.

Her grandmother nervously wiped her hands on her apron. "There is nothing to tell!" Her voice revealed impatience as she slammed the lid onto the iron stew pot. Anna placed the peelings from the potatoes and cabbage leaves onto a cutting board and proposed, "I'll go out and feed the rabbits." Her grandmother impatiently waved her on.

Undisturbed by Anna's stroking of their soft fur, the rabbits chewed away on the scraps of vegetables. She was struck by the peaceful temperament of the rabbit with her litter of young crouching in the corner of the cage. Anna reflected on her grandmother's disturbing statement. *Should I tell Mutti about this?* she pondered. *Guenter's time in training is halfway over. I'll talk to him when he gets home.* Excited about seeing him soon, she dashed into her grandmother's living room, picked up her book satchel, and kissed her grandmother on the cheek. "Thank you, I'll see you tomorrow!" From the stern look from beneath bifocals, she knew her grandmother was not pleased to see her leave.

So many thoughts went through her head that she paid little attention to a caravan of vans parked under the chestnut trees along Taunus Avenue. Soldiers carrying rifles stood near the entrance of a fashionable apartment house. Nearby, a man dressed in a gray coat and hat leaned against the wall, conversing with one of the soldiers. Between an occasional puff on his pipe, he carefully checked over the avenue. Sudden fear struck Anna. She ran the short distance to find her mother. Exhausted and shaken, she burst into their apartment.

"I am glad you are home!" Anna threw her arms around her mother, who was surprised at her outburst.

"I was going to visit Frau Osterbaum for only a short while!" she said, smiling at Anna, who gasped for breath.

"Please don't go there, Mutti!" said Anna.

Anna's mother slipped into her coat. "You come with me. We'll go to the corner and take a look." She turned briefly to check the fire in the kitchen stove.

Anna walked close to her mother. Both trembled with fear. From a distance, they saw the vans pull away. "Let's go to the Osterbaums' apartment and make sure they are all right," Anna's mother said with concern.

Anna stretched to ring the doorbell. There was silence.

"Try again," her mother said softly. Again, not a sound.

Anna shook the handle of the huge double door and whispered, "It's open." Without saying a word, they entered. Dark shades covered the huge windows. Once light and airy, the marble stairwell that surrounded an open-cage elevator shaft produced a dreary feeling. Quietly they began walking step-by-step until they reached the Osterbaums' apartment. The only sound came from a neighbor's radio across the way.

Anna's mother pressed her forefinger against her mouth and pulled back Anna's hand as she reached to push the bell button. She knocked lightly and gingerly pushed the partially open door. Anna's mother reached for her hand and pulled her through the entrance hall and into the kitchen. Herr Osterbaum, his face cupped into his hands, sat near the kitchen window staring into space.

"Herr Osterbaum," Anna's mother whispered. In a rocking motion, he turned toward her and half rose.

"Please forgive the mess." He looked old for his age. "They have taken the girls, both of them—they are my life, you know."

"Where have they taken them?" Anna's mother asked.

He shrugged his shoulders. "To some kind of camp—that's all they told me."

Lost for words, Anna's mother asked his permission to straighten up the apartment. "Thank you, you are very kind," he responded.

"Look, Mutti, Trudie didn't take her doll." Anna stooped over to pick up the doll lying in the corner of the room and carefully placed it on Trudie's bed.

There was little Anna's mother could say to ease the pain of her friend's husband. They had taken Gertrude and Trudie from him, and that seemed too much for him to bear. She gently touched his hand and said, "My heart goes out to you. I know the pain, but there is hope. We must have faith! I do not know where my husband Ludwig is, it's been nearly seven years." Amazed at her mother's courage, Anna bit her lower lip to keep from crying. "You know where we live, please feel free to visit." Anna's mother motioned her on as she gently closed the door behind them.

The first snow of winter covered the ground and, because of the blackouts, the days seemed remarkably short. For a period of three weeks and without notice, all activities at the Opera House were cancelled. Sabina and Anna spent much of their time at the Riding Academy. While Sabina and her cousins had the privilege of riding the trails each day, Anna busied herself wherever necessary inside the stables. "Pretty soon we will count on you to run this place," Master Karl chuckled as he pushed open the heavy sliding doors that separated the ramp from the stables. Again, Anna recalled her mother's constant reminder: "Let us thank God for the things we do have." Indeed, she was thankful for Master Karl. She looked down the long rows of stalls. *I am thankful for my four-legged friends too*, Anna thought, smiling at Master Karl.

She found her mother waiting for her outside the stables, nose reddened from the cold. Anna knew by looking at her that she was elated about something. "I have some wonderful news for you, Anna! Our cousin Juergen is moving here from the Black Forest. His asthma is keeping him out of the army. He has a job as head chef at one of the hotels. His wife, Inga, and the children will join him as soon as they decide on an apartment."

Finding apartments, as Hitler promised the German women in his speeches, was no longer a problem. This is what Hitler meant when he promised higher standards of living and more living space for his people. But he failed to reveal that this would come at someone's cost. The people in the local municipal offices assigned Juergen and his family an apartment a block from the train station. A neighbor revealed that the apartment had belonged to a Jewish family. "They were given no notice," explained the heavyset woman who could not hide her anger. "They were vacated just like that!" She balled up her fist and snapped her fingers in disgust.

Speechless and distraught, Anna watched the woman slam the door behind her. She thought about the families in her neighborhood who were forced out of their homes in the middle of the night. "Is she angry at us?" Anna asked her mother.

"Oh, no! She is angry at the system. But she must be careful. Someone else may turn her in."

Anna stroked the flower petals in the bouquet she held in her arms. She listened to heavy footsteps as her mother rang the bell. Juergen opened the door and looked down at Anna. "Look at you! It's been a long time. I haven't seen you since you were Claus's size." Anna looked around as the round-faced toddler, sucking his thumb and dragging a worn-out blanket behind him, waddled toward them. Blond curly hair fell neatly into place around his neck. She could not keep from staring at Juergen. He bore a striking resemblance to Eric. Like Eric, his personality was dominated by warmth and humor.

Taking Anna and little Claus by their hands, he showed Anna's mother and grandmother into the light and airy living room. He thanked them for the flowers. "We can still get flowers," Anna's mother admitted, "but bread, cheese, and butter, that's another story."

"This is your aunt, Anna," Juergen said, gently pulled Anna toward the woman as she walked into the room and gave Anna an affectionate embrace.

Holding on to Anna, Inga shook hands with Anna's mother and grandmother. "The baby is still asleep, he is just getting over the measles. And don't fret," she continued, "we still get supplies of bread and cheese from our friends in the Black Forest. We'll share with you!" Anna's mother let out a sigh of relief and so did her grandmother.

Juergen spoke mostly about Eric, Guenther, and Anna's achievements in the opera. He knew their grandmother's stand on politics and wanted to avoid confrontations with her. He longed to see Eric and Guenther, and suggested they all plan to take the train to visit Emma, who had taken the children to live with her mother.

"You are both a ballerina and a little tomboy," he boasted, referring to Anna's surprising activities at the Riding Academy. "Inga and I would like to see you perform in both places," he added. "That is, if your mother and grandmother will watch the children."

Anna's mother smiled with approval, but her grandmother sat aloof with both arms folded. "We must go! The buses only run every hour instead of fifteen minutes nowadays," the grandmother grumbled. Holding a shopping bag of bread, butter, and cheese, Anna waved until they were out of sight. It had been a long time since she had experienced a joyful family gathering, and once again she had a reason to dream.

Juergen stopped by often for brief visits. His three-wheel truck parked in front of their house was indeed a welcome sight. His presence brought laughter. "Inga apologizes for not having enough sugar for the streusel that goes with this cake." He lifted a cake from the small basket Inga had prepared especially for Anna and her mother. "I brought you some of her boysenberry preserves for the topping instead." His deep blue eyes sparkled as he smacked the tip of his forefingers.

"Tomorrow I will take you both for a ride—that is, if you are not too busy." Anna's mother smiled as Juergen offered one of his strong and comforting hugs. "Throw me a kiss," he urged Anna, smiling, as he closed the door behind him.

The following day, Juergen found Anna distraught, her eyes red from sobbing, sitting on the doorstep outside the apartment. "Shh, just what is the reason for this somber mood?" Juergen sat close to her and stroked her long brown hair.

She handed him a small envelope smudged with tears. "Oh no!" Juergen gasped. "I was afraid of this! There seems to be nothing but deception in our system. Hitler is a madman, when is this ever coming to an end?"

Startled at Juergen's loud outburst, Anna, who had grown accustomed to watching out for anyone listening, looked around.

"Mutti, Anna, and grandmother," stated the note in Guenter's handwriting. "Please, please come soon. We are not allowed to come home for Christmas. All of my friends are upset as I am. I have been crying myself to sleep every night since we have been told this. Please come soon, and if you can, bring me some of grandmother's cookies. We may not be here long, and I do not know where they will be taking us!"

The news came as a shock. Anna's mother walked the floor. Her emotions revealed anger, but Anna's grandmother remained surprisingly calm. "Guenter is there for an important cause," the grandmother insisted. "You should be proud of him—instead you sit around whining." Anna's mother ignored her statement.

"It is truly a blessing you dropped by again today," Anna's mother said softly to Juergen. "I am thankful you are here in the city. We must pray that we can all stay alive through these stressful times."

Anna watched her mother out of the corner of her eye. *Why can't we just be a normal family?* she wondered. She felt saddened by the constant bickering between her mother's stand of faith and her grandmother's ego to support Hitler. Granting Guenter's wish to take the train ride to Mannheim would not be an easy task. There were rumors of expected bombing because of the city's heavy steel industry, and there was no place for the family to stay. But Anna desperately wanted to see Guenter.

Fraulein Meier warned Anna about the danger. "They are taking precaution there because of expected heavy bombing," she confirmed. She located Mannheim on the huge map in the classroom. "This is where the Rhine and Neckar rivers come together. You see Ludwigshafen?" She watched for Anna's nod. "Because of the location and the many factories of metal and chemicals, Ludwigshafen is one of our most important river ports.

"On the sunny side, you may look around," Fraulein Meier encouraged Anna. "Your favorite composer, Wolfgang Mozart, and the poet Friedrich von Schiller, about whom you show much interest, spent much time in Mannheim. Herr Schiller's first play took place there, and even his friend Johann von Goethe visited him there. They loved Mannheim and its famous orchestra. During their period of time, the city became Europe's most famous musical center."

Anna struggled to fall asleep that night as she pondered over Fraulein Meier's conversation earlier in the day. *Perhaps I can fall asleep in Guenter's bed,* she thought. She slipped into the robe her mother placed at the foot of her bed, "just in case the sirens go off during the night," her mother warned. Peter already lay purring on Guenter's bed. Anna crawled under the featherbed. Light snow had covered the skylight in Guenter's room, and it seemed unusually cold. She was thankful for Fraulein Meier's interest. No matter what, she recalled, Fraulein Meier always finds good things to point out. "Just make certain to look for the air-raid shelter signs wherever you go," she cautioned. "And," Fraulein Meier added, "I'll help you catch up your assignments."

The next morning, Anna smelled the rare aroma of fresh-brewed coffee coming from the kitchen. On the table, neatly arranged, sat two of her mother's fine china cups and breakfast plates. A customary pink rose seemed to stretch toward a ray of sunlight that managed to peek through the cloudy sky. From the cupboard, the scent of spruce that shaped the small Advent wreath gave warmth and reassurance.

"Your grandmother and I have decided that the two of you will take the train to visit your brother," Anna's mother announced while preparing for church.

Surprised at her mother's suggestion, Anna asked, "Are you not coming?" Her mother stared out of the window. "You know Guenter wants to see you!"

"I know, and I yearn to see him also," her mother answered. "But I must stay here in the event that … " she paused and stopped braiding Anna's hair.

"What do you mean?" Anna pleaded.

Her mother quickly changed the subject. "This is the second week of Advent," she spoke gently. "We must hurry or we will be late for church."

Anna knew she should not continue to pry. Sensing her frustration and concern, her mother squeezed Anna's arm. "Please don't worry about unanswered questions. Just have faith and always remember to fear God. Let us stay on track, and everything will turn out fine."

In a light snowfall, Anna and her grandmother walked through half-frozen slush and whistling wind toward the bus that would take them to the train station. Clutched under their arms were two shoeboxes of cookies the grandmother had baked and a thick woolen hat Anna had knitted for him. Frau Schmidt, Sabina's housekeeper, contributed cocoa and a few hazelnuts when she learned about the family's disappointing news. Sabina and her cousins offered to assist

Master Karl with the horses during Anna's absence. Herr Kummel dropped by to remind her of the upcoming rehearsal for the *Puppenfee*. She took to heart her mother's reminder to be thankful that God provided these wonderful friends.

For as long as she could remember, Anna had longed to take a train to the Black Forest to visit Juergen. She envisioned hiking with Guenter along the heavy stands of fir she had admired in postcards sent by Juergen. Now she recalled the time Guenter stood beside her to say goodbye to Eric. She had not imagined her first train ride would take place in the turmoil that descended on the train station.

Conductors, mostly women, directed groups of soldiers arriving from various points. Others scrambled to get on—some were left standing on the platforms because of lack of space. Two women struggled to uncouple one of the locomotives. Anna felt the urge to call to them, "Be careful, our friend's daughter was killed doing that!" The startled women turned and looked at her. Embarrassed, Anna turned to stare at the surroundings. On one of the tracks, a rusted crane and a rotting boxcar sat deserted. In the distance, a string of cars lined up for repair. She wondered about the destination of the geriatric rails.

"The train to Mannheim has been delayed for approximately two hours," announced the firm voice of a woman over the loudspeaker. Anna's grandmother let out an unhappy sigh. She looked around in hopes of finding a seat in the drafty terminal. It was a miserably cold day, and damp air cut through their bones. Huddled together, they sat and waited.

Finally, several hours later, the train arrived. Anna's body shook at the sound of squeaking brakes as the train stopped in its tracks. With both hands covering her ears, she looked up at the locomotive covered with a huge swastika banner. Displayed above the banner was the depiction of an eagle with its wings spread across the gigantic machine. "Look at that! Don't you love the contrast of our red flag against the background of the black locomotive?" her grandmother prompted Anna. "And isn't it inspiring?" Disappointed in Anna's lack of enthusiasm, she pulled her through the crowd of people and onto the train.

A young soldier offered Anna's grandmother his seat next to the window of a crowded cabin. The familiar smell of leather combined with sweat hung in the air. Hunger pains distracted Anna's thoughts.

"Are you hungry?" she asked her grandmother.

"No!" her grandmother answered.

One of the soldiers, who overheard the conversation, handed Anna bread wrapped in paper. "It's baked this morning, please take it!" the soldier insisted. "I am just too homesick to eat."

Anna glanced at her grandmother, who hesitantly nodded approval.

Another soldier handed Anna a small bottle of apple juice. "It's yesterday's ration, I have more!"

Anna stood up and shook the young soldiers' hands. "Thank you!" she whispered.

Anna's hunger pain decreased. From time to time, the train picked up pace. Still holding on to her two boxes of cookies, she thought about Guenter. *It's only a few hours away*, she told herself. A group of soldiers from another cabin began to sing songs about the fatherland. The tone in their voices reflected sadness. Anna's grandmother began to sing along. Another soldier retrieved his mouth organ from his backpack and accompanied the grandmother.

Suddenly, the dim lights went off and the train came to a halt. Sirens disrupted the soldiers' sing-along. Anna looked out the window. Searchlights shot across the blackened sky. Everything else became pitch dark. She recalled that the blackout was now enforced. The train sat in darkness, and there was complete silence. Anna looked up at her grandmother, whose eyes were closed. *She looks so tired*, Anna thought as she, too, dozed off. She awoke as the train began to move again.

Using their backpacks for pillows, several soldiers had fallen asleep on the floor in the aisle of the cabin. From the different sound of the sirens, Anna knew that the danger had passed, at least for the moment. "Do you suppose we will ever get there?" she asked.

Anna's grandmother rose to stretch her back. She sat back down. "Put your head into my lap," she suggested to Anna.

Watchfully, Anna placed the shoeboxes overhead before she lay down.

At last, the train pulled into the station. Anna shivered as they stepped onto the platform. The ground beneath their feet had turned into ice. "Be careful, Grandmother," Anna warned while reaching for the old woman's hand. She thought about her mother. Anna knew this trip would have been much too stressful for her, and was thankful she did not come along.

At a complete loss, her grandmother stood, looking in all directions. A shaky voice through the loudspeaker announced, "All buses around the city have been cancelled because of last night's bombing."

From the directions Guenter had given on the postcard, the camp was located six city blocks from the train station. "We have no choice," her grandmother's voice quivered. "We have to walk."

They began to walk the narrow curving streets of Mannheim until they reached the wide boulevard that connected to the camp. "I will just pretend that this is Fraulein Meier's field trip," Anna thought. She reminisced about her favorite poet, Herr Goethe, and reflected on the medieval architecture Fraulein Meier had described.

Anna's heart leaped from excitement. After nearly twenty-four hours and with little sleep and nourishment, she and her grandmother finally reached the camp. A young boy, dressed in his Hitler Youth uniform, stood close to a fire outside the gatehouse. He checked a long list of names before pointing to a two-story building a block away. He shrugged his shoulders. "I believe you will find your brother there, that is, if he hasn't left yet."

Anna looked at the boy in disbelief. Her heart sank. "Maybe they let the boys go home for Christmas after all," Anna's grandmother assured her.

Anna ran ahead of her. "Have you seen my brother, his name is Guenter," she said, pulling at the arm of a soldier who walked out of the building. He looked like a grandfather.

"No, but I will find out for you!" He led her into a drafty, cluttered office and picked up the telephone. After a brief conversation, the soldier slowly put the phone on the receiver. "I am truly sorry, your brother's troop left this morning, actually, only an hour ago."

"Where to?" she cried out.

"I am sorry," the old soldier repeated. "I saw the caravan of covered trucks leave. No one seems to know its destination."

"How can this be?" Anna begged the soldier for an explanation.

"Everything is in such a state of confusion," he responded. "The boys spent most of the night in our air-raid shelters. We thought the bombing would never cease, I guess they wanted to get the boys out of here."

With her habitual stern look, Anna's grandmother said, "We didn't see any destruction on our way." The soldier gave her a strange look and asked, "Shouldn't you consider yourselves lucky? Most of the destruction took place east of here. I understand they brought one of our factories to the ground. Some of the workers, most of them women on night shift, are buried beneath the rubble. Nobody seems to know how to get them out of there! It's a mess!"

Anna sat in the cold metal chair and stared out the window. She looked at her grandmother, who sat silent in disbelief. The soldier looked at the shoeboxes Anna still clutched in her arms. "Would you like for me to forward this to your brother?" he asked.

Anna detected kindness in his voice. She nodded, forcing back tears.

"You remind me of my granddaughter. I have not seen her for several months, and I miss her terribly." The soldier obviously was looking for words of comfort. "I'll tell you what, before you go back to catch the train home, let's go to the kitchen and see if there is something left from breakfast."

He led them into the dining hall. "Please, have a seat," the soldier said, smiling.

Anna sat at the end of a long and narrow table and watched a boy her brother's age remove stacks of dirty tin dishes. She wondered if Guenter sat at this table before he left this morning. *He must have been very sad*, she thought to herself.

The soldier placed a tray in front of them. "Look what I found! It is the best I could find, very nourishing on a cold day."

The bowls of oatmeal topped with raw sugar tasted good. Anna's grandmother shared an infrequent smile with the soldier. "Sugar is such a rare item these days, thank you!"

Anna handed the soldier the boxes of cookies and started out the door. "Oh, I almost forgot." She pulled the red woolen hat out of her coat pocket and asked, "Would you see that Guenter gets this hat? He is always cold, you know?" The soldier nodded. She felt a lump deep within her throat.

Her grandmother spoke not a word as they walked to the train station, and Anna did not dare to speak. She watched her grandmother count out change from her small purse at the ticket booth. There was no waiting in line, and no one pushed to get on. Only a handful of passengers boarded. With the exception of the rumbling sounds of the boxcars moving over the crossbeams, Anna sensed an eerie quietness. The train continued at a steady pace through villages and forests. A conductor entered the car and urged Anna to move to the opposite side. He brought to her attention a colony of antelopes. "They must be in search of food. I knew you would enjoy this beautiful picture," he said with a smile as he went on his way. Anna pressed her face against the window and, although hurt and disappointed, she enjoyed the train ride back home.

Anna's mother responded in anger when she learned about the trip to Mannheim. "My son would still be at home and in school if you had not pushed him into joining the Hitler

Youth so early on. Your Nazi friends have taken my parental rights from me." She placed her hands on Anna's shoulders and, looking straight at Anna's grandmother, she said loudly, "I beg you to leave Anna alone!"

Anna's grandmother threw her head back and left without saying a word.

Anna was amazed at how quickly her mother forgot the unfortunate incident. "We have so much to be thankful for. God will take care of your brother, but we must do our part," she reminded Anna.

Anna's mother meant business. She stayed close by Anna's side. Rehearsals at the Opera House resumed. A new program director, who flaunted the Nazi banner around his shirt sleeve, screened all performances. His ostentatiously pompous personality intimidated everyone. There was talk about several key performers having been moved to "more exciting" opportunities.

The basement underneath the Opera House, in which rejects of stage props and uniforms had previously been stored, now served as segregated air-raid shelters—one for officials only. Arrows from all directions throughout the six-story building pointed to the shelters. "The doors into the shelters are as tight as the doors on a submarine," explained Herr Kummel, "just in the event you are without your gas masks." Herr Kummel's wonderful sense of humor had not changed.

Nothing dampened the spirits of those chosen to perform in the highly promoted and popular Christmas musical *Puppenfee.* Every rehearsal proved to be an exhilarating occasion. Despite threats of bombing, the event was a complete sellout. On opening night, as the orchestra finalized its tuning and the curtain rose, the several thousand in attendance included Anna's mother, Juergen, Inga, Sabina and her family, and Emma, who had come from her village on the Rhine. Only Anna's grandmother would not be there because of a neighborhood Nazi rally.

As always, Anna's mother walked Anna the short blocks to the Opera House. "It's strangely quiet," her mother remarked as traffic moved without headlights through the dark streets. "We do not have reserved seats, but I hope to sit with the family."

Anna chuckled as the massive curtain rose. "Who am I," she whispered beneath her breath, "a nutcracker?" This was not a fantasy, this event was real, and she wanted her performance to be flawless. Her body felt tense as she stood high above the stage. With only an occasional wink of her eyebrows, she managed to glance over the audience. The familiar black and brown uniforms stood out from the six-story circular tiers of boxes. Unsuccessful in spotting her family and friends, she saw hundreds of BDM girls dressed in white blouses seated in the orchestra seats. Immediately behind them were equally as many rows of boys dressed in their formal light-brown Hitler Youth uniforms.

Slowly, skilled stage workers lowered the massive props. With graceful and controlled moves, each ballerina stepped out of the giant chatterbox. Applause began to roar as the audience watched each character come alive. Somewhat awkwardly, Anna began her routine. She had not yet mastered the smoothness of the older ballet students. But she knew that her part as the nutcracker soldier suited her. She had a difficult time believing this evening was real; and, like magic, she mastered her routine.

Not since *Meistersinger von Nürnberg* did the orchestra put forth such exhilarating sounds as this performance came to its finale. The curtain fell and the audience began to shout. Surrounded by his usual entourage, the man with the comical mustache, pale-faced, his dark brown hair slicked straight back behind his ears, rose to his feet. Few paid attention. "This is indeed unusual. The people came to escape reality for a couple of hours," Herr Kummel commented to one of the stage engineers. "They are not even paying attention to Hitler."

Then, with an anxiety-ridden expression beneath his thick gray hair, he glanced around to see who might have been listening. Color returned to his face as he took a deep breath and smiled. No one heard except Anna, who waited for the principle dancers to take their final bow. She welcomed Herr Kummel's affectionate pinch on her cheek and watched him walk slowly offstage.

On a daily basis, Anna felt the hostility between her mother and grandmother. With both Eric and Guenter now gone, even holidays seemed difficult to plan. "It's a blessing Juergen and Inga decided to move here," Anna's mother said in her usual soft manner. They walked through the slush of snow to meet the grandmother at a bus stop to ride the bus to Juergen's on Christmas Eve.

If I could only talk with Eric or Guenter, Anna thought as the bus drove through the darkened city. She watched both mother and grandmother sitting quietly and with stern expressions. *Juergen will fix that.* She smiled mischievously. *He will bring fun conversations to the dinner table.*

Her grandmother insisted that everyone listen to Hitler's Christmas radio broadcast from Berchtesgaden. Everyone resisted the idea, but gave in to her demand. Anna's mother, still filled with anger and resentment over Guenter's departure, suggested leaving early so that she could take Anna to Mass. A heated argument began and dampened the simple Christmas dinner unselfishly prepared by Inga. "I will take you home," said Juergen, impatiently reaching for his hat as Anna and her mother embraced Inga and the children.

Only Juergen tried to carry on a conversation during the ride home. Through the rearview window, Anna's mother watched hundreds of people, mostly women and children, walk along the tree-lined avenues to join a torchlight parade. She spoke up, her voice escalated in disgust, "Can't they forget about this at least one night? This is Christmas!"

Irritated by her remarks, Anna's grandmother pleaded with Juergen, "Let me off here, please!"

Anna moved closer to her mother. *I am glad Eric and Guenter did not hear this*, she pondered as she watched her grandmother disappear into the crowd of people who scrambled toward a dimly lighted stage set up especially for the local Nazi leaders.

Chapter 8

Spring 1941 … Work of feared SS Einsatzgruppen begins.

As winter drew to a close, the reality of harder times continued. Anna's mother prayed for a better spring and summer. But the hourly news broadcasts stirred everyone's emotion. "We are going into one country after another," was Hitler's message. It was clear to everyone that he meant business. "Germany belongs to us today, but tomorrow the whole world," he continued to boast.

To most of her mother's women friends, Hitler had become an idol. To some, he even became a mystical and astrological figure. "Why can't they see the risks they are taking?" Anna's mother asked her friend and confidante Helga, who too refused to dance to Hitler's drums. It was extremely difficult to keep her feelings to herself. Contrary to what the church had stressed—namely, quietness of heart, security, and peace—Hitler and his people showed evidence of brutal force along with physical and spiritual suffering.

The women could not understand why the Catholic Church offered no resistance. "Perhaps they cannot, but everything that is going on is contrary to our Catholic upbringing," Anna's mother kept saying. They feared that the toughness Hitler continued to stress for the German youth meant letting go of their belief in God. Anna's mother recognized from the teachings of her church that the enemy Hitler's people referred to on signs and posters, displayed everywhere, was not another country, but Hitler himself. She was not fooled by all the mixed messages. She even saw through the purpose of tea parties given for children by Hitler and his close associates. Hitler's SS swore, "Not to serve the country, not to serve the people, not to serve God, but Adolf Hitler."

"The enemy sees you," read one gigantic poster. "Blackout!" Printed underneath in bright colors was a depiction of a skeleton and an English bomber in the sky. Hitler's people left no stone unturned to continue his campaign.

Since the Catholic Church made no provisions for her daughter's religious training, Anna's mother vowed to take over some of the church's responsibility. She routinely read to her from her prayer book. "Why don't we take grandfather's old Bible out of the trunk and learn from it?" Anna asked her mother as she watched her flip through the pages of her prayer book.

"Because," explained her mother, "our priests are specific in telling us that only those in the priesthood are allowed to read and discuss the Bible."

Occasionally, however, Anna's fascination led her to dig into her grandfather's old trunk for a peek at the huge old Bible. The Medieval pictures and old script were far beyond her comprehension.

Hitler continued to stress health and toughness for German youth. Dressed in Hitler Youth attire, healthy-looking boys and girls appeared on billboards everywhere. Bold letters reached across the top, simply stating, "*Auch Du?*" ("You Also?"). Colorful flyers for the popular VW attracted people's attention. "Serve the führer, save five marks a week, and you will become the owner of a new Volkswagen," read the flyers that reached every mailbox.

Soon, joining the Hitler Youth was no longer voluntary. "Every German youth must be engaged! Unless you wish to be an outsider, and you are willing to risk being ridiculed," Baldur von Schirach, a member of Hitler's cabinet, bluntly announced. Anna's mother knew there was an even greater risk. She knew that those who refused to join stood the chance of being sent to work camps.

"If you refuse to let the children join the *Jungvolk* and *Jungmädel*," the grandmother contented, "you will admit to refusing your belief in the Nazi Party. Both will be sent away to *Jugendheime* [youth homes]."

Anna's mother argued with the grandmother, "Are you so shallow that you cannot see through all of this? Have you not followed Heinrich Himmler's plans regarding our young girls?"

But she continued to live with this fear. She understood that this process involved turning Germany's young boys into Himmler's tough and ruthless SS and young girls into healthy, child-bearing women. Heinrich Himmler had publicly stated that many young men would be killed, and it would not be a bad idea if a married man had a girlfriend who would bear his children.

"What happened to the morals we were taught until Hitler came along?" Anna's mother often argued with their grandmother. "And what will happen to my son if he gets hurt while performing his duties? Will Hitler put him aside as he has done with the so-called 'undesirables'?"

Why had one retarded twelve-year-old boy disappeared from his neighborhood? Where had this child gone? His parents were told that he was taken to a special camp in the Alps to protect him from the anticipated bombing. But why were they not allowed to visit the child? Why were they kept from writing to him?

Anna's mother pondered these issues as she sat on a park bench and stared at the poster above her head. Overwhelmed with concern for Guenter and Anna, she once again vowed to protect Anna. She again encouraged Anna to spend her after-school hours with her friend Sabina and on her activities at the

Opera House, and she encouraged her to concentrate on the increasing concern for the horses at the Riding Academy.

Anna continued to bond with all the horses at the stables. By the sounds of their nostrils, it was obvious they welcomed her presence each time she strained to push open the heavy wooden sliding doors that led into the long and narrow stalls. Since they began to shed heavily in the spring, they loved being groomed. She loved taking them into the ring, one by one; with minimal physical force from her small body, they responded to her every move.

Anna became accustomed to the horses' moods. With hay and oats becoming scarce, feeding took place only twice instead of three times daily. She had no favorites but loved them all, a lesson Master Karl taught Anna early on. Watching her care for one of the Arabians and puffing on his pipe, he chuckled, "Anna, I see you have no favorites, but I can't say this for our critters. You are definitely their favorite." She watched as he walked away, leaving a pleasant scent of tobacco from his pipe. Very timely, the spry Arabian gave out a loud snort and rubbed his nose against Anna's neck.

No job seemed too difficult for her. Her daily chores included cleaning the stalls. This became a challenge. Like all necessities, straw and sawdust were rare items. "Use them sparingly, please," Master Karl reminded Anna. She learned how to care for the horses, cleaning their hooves daily and applying compresses of vinegar on infected areas whenever necessary.

Thanks to Master Karl, Anna advanced to a variety of steps and jumps. He always made time to take her up to the ring for private instructions.

"Would you like to take Gypsy Baron to our blacksmith in Sonnenberg? He is due for new shoes."

Anna turned and looked up at the aristocratic-looking owner, Herr Ackermann, who watched her from the bleachers. His broad shoulders and nearly perfect appearance intimidated her.

"Me?" she asked, fingers pressed against her chest, looking around to see if someone else stood behind her.

"Yes, you, of course," Herr Ackermann smiled. "We will let you take him into the ring first so that both of you can get acquainted."

While she felt privileged to ride Herr Ackermann's personal horse and to receive a special riding lesson from him, Anna was reluctant. *Taking Gypsy Baron for such a long ride through the villages is quite a responsibility,* she thought.

Master Karl watched Anna's expression. He leaned on his pitchfork and smiled. "You have a good teacher, if I must say so," he said, moving his shoulders back and forth, "and you are a capable rider! It will be a great experience for you. You told me you hope to some day ride in a foxhunt."

Anna nodded. In her childish desires, she dreamed someday to become eligible to wear the black velvet hat and fashionable clothes that were traditionally worn during the foxhunts. At the moment, however, this seemed far-fetched.

Herr Ackermann entered the stall and placed the special bridle on Gypsy Baron. There seemed to be a distinct echo in the horse's walk along the cobblestone aisle of the stables. She felt her heart pounding as she lead the beautiful Arabian alongside Herr Ackermann up the ramp and into the ring. She listened intently to his instruction as he paced back and fourth in the center of the ring. Thanks to Master Karl's teaching, she controlled Gypsy Baron with ease, using her small hands, legs, and shifting of weight. Gypsy Baron responded to her ease and comfort. Herr Ackermann patiently displayed the use of the extra bits necessary for the high-spirited horse.

Through the swinging doors outside the arena, Sabina and her cousins watched from the bleachers. The three girls ran toward her afterward, leaving a cloud from the sawdust that covered the ring.

"Aren't we something," Sabina hugged Anna.

"Take your time, Anna, but don't forget to brush him down!" Herr Ackermann interrupted. He tipped his hat to the girls and left the ring.

"You best pinch me, because I think I am dreaming," Anna said, her voice revealing a mixture of excitement and concern. "I didn't do too well!"

"You are dreaming all right, if you believe you didn't do too well. You see his ears?" Sabina's cousin pointed to Gypsy

Baron. "Look at the foam in his mouth. He obviously liked his little rider!"

Anna looked into the horse's bright eyes and affectionately kissed Gypsy Baron on his forehead.

That evening, she had difficulty sleeping and wondered what it would feel like to ride her first solo to the blacksmith the following day. Master Karl escorted Anna and the Arabian down the ramp and watched her leave through the courtyard and into the busy streets. Gypsy Baron's hooves pounding against the asphalt created a melodic rhythm. "This is like music to my ears," Anna chuckled.

Why am I so privileged? she wondered as she rode down the deserted avenue and along the portico in front of the Opera House and the flower garden by which she and her mother sat for hours. She rode along the paths behind Sabina's family villa and again felt as though she was dreaming. She rode through the sweeping meadows and hillsides, and past the characteristic farmhouses that hugged the hills around the city.

Master Karl told her about the narrow cobblestone streets in the blacksmith's village, but she had no idea of the closeness of the houses. She reached into the top of her boots and retrieved Master Karl's sketched directions to the blacksmith's house. She jumped off the stallion and led him up the hill that rose sharply. *It's like being in a fairy tale,* she thought, inhaling the scent of flowers that beautified the windows of the ancient houses.

Anna followed the blaring sounds of the blacksmith's hammer. "It's like being in another world," she announced as she walked into his neatly organized blacksmith shop.

"Looks are deceiving at times," the old gentleman grumbled as he reached for Anna's hand. His hand was rough, but his handshake was gentle. "I have no help. My son was called into service a month ago. Those jerks had no business doing that! My son is much too young. And, young lady, I apologize for being such a grumpy old man." He stroked Anna's hair and smiled. "It will take two people to get this beauty fixed up." He held up Gypsy Baron's legs, carefully scraping around the hooves. "You see these little stones? We must always remove them because they cause bruises and infected conditions."

Anna nodded and enthusiastically replied, "I can help!"

With a slap on Gypsy Baron's rear end, the blacksmith smiled and said, "If you are easy on Anna, perhaps we can get your new shoes put on."

Anna sat on a workbench and watched the blacksmith shape the horseshoes, one by one, in the burning coal. The fire dispersing into the air startled her. Unafraid, she lifted Gypsy Baron's front leg and propped it against her thigh. From time to time, the horse jerked slightly as the blacksmith trimmed each hoof. "Well, we did it!" He smiled at Anna.

"Let's give him some water and hay. I will show you how to use the pump at the house."

Anna took a small pail of water to Gypsy Baron, who responded with a joyful sound through his nostrils.

"Are you hungry? Let's see what Liesel, my daughter, is cooking up for lunch."

"I am always hungry," Anna confessed. She followed the rugged blacksmith across the yard and into his small farmhouse. The aroma coming from the kitchen amazed her.

"I hope you like goulash and noodles," he asked. Anna nodded and told him, "I like everything! I have not smelled anything this good in a long while."

Petite, with blond pigtails wrapped tightly around her remarkably beautiful face, Liesel bounced out of the house to greet her. Anna watched as she leaned over to retrieve a small strudel from the oven. "Go, both of you, and wash your hands," she commanded, swishing her hands through the air.

Gypsy Baron's belly was full, and Anna had enjoyed Liesel's wonderful meal. "I'll help you mount," suggested the blacksmith after the visit.

Liesel came running out to say goodbye. "Here is some strudel for your mother, and also for Herr Ackermann and Master Karl," she said.

Anna reached down and shook her hand. "Thank you!" Gypsy Baron responded to the gentle squeeze of her legs and slowly started down the stone alley. Anna rejoiced in having this very special day with special new people and her special four-legged friend.

Ahead of schedule, Anna took Gypsy Baron on a detour past Sabina's summer home up in the hills leading out of the village. She slowed Gypsy Baron's pace and took a glance at the seemingly tranquil city below. Only the rooftops of hospitals painted white, bearing the Red Cross in the center, reminded her of the chaos that might be luring around the corner.

Sabina's cousin spotted Anna across the manicured garden patches and ran to find Sabina. While the girls listened to Anna's description of her exciting visit to the blacksmith, Gypsy Baron felt at home as he grazed in the shady apricot orchard nearby. *What a day*, the majestic stallion must have thought. Anna watched him with gratifying thoughts. A moderate gallop through the park completed another perfect day away from the humdrum and the threat of the unknown.

Much to Anna's delight, this special day brought yet another surprise. Her mother stood in front of their house waiting patiently for Anna's return. A small package and a postcard tucked away in her apron pocket, she whispered, "From Guenter and Eric. I did not want to open the package, it is addressed to you."

Anna clutched the tiny package against her chest. She noticed Guenter's handwriting. Slowly she opened the simple but neatly wrapped package. "Anna, I bought this tiny doll from a lady at a train station. She spoke no German. Hope you will like it. It reminded me of you in one of the costumes you wore during a performance at the Opera House. I miss you. Must go. Take care of Mutti, please." Tears filled Anna's eyes. She held the doll close as she embraced her mother.

Eric's self-sketched postcard contained in an envelope said it all. Buildings reduced to rubble, in the background and hidden by smoke an image of the old Brandenburg Gate, a distraught-looking chimney sweeper looked on, obviously caught without a job. Anna's mother shook her head. "At least Eric is all right," she uttered. "We will take the bus down to the Rhine and check on Emma and the children this Sunday. But first, we will go to church and light a candle for the boys."

Little by little, Anna became more sensitive and unwilling to accept the negative attitudes of people caused by constant ups-and-downs of everyday life. Her grandmother's harsh persuasion to serve in Hitler's youth group continued to clash with her mother's ideals. Anna, therefore, would not share her silent fears.

Like their friend, Anna was deathly afraid of bombing ever since she had witnessed the devastation with her teacher and schoolmates in nearby Mainz. Although Hitler's *Luftwaffe* occupied the nearby airport, her mother felt confident that the British would not bomb their beautiful city. "Other than our champagne and cognac factories, there are few factories nearby. We have much culture, and most of the city will soon again cater to tourism. Why would anyone want to bomb us?" she maintained. No matter what subjects or concerns surfaced, Anna's mother remained positive. But soon, her mother's positive attitude would again be tested.

With great anticipation, Anna and her mother prepared for church. A reflection of sunlight from Anna's dressing mirror danced across the ceiling as she lay on her bed and reminisced about the exciting events the past week had brought. She jumped up and shouted, "Look, Mutti, our birds have returned!" Consumed by giving out its cheerful trill, a sparrow perched on a limb of the old pear tree, acrobatically fluttering its wings from time to time.

"It is indeed another beautiful day, Anna," her mother agreed as she stroked her hair. But then Anna's mother, sensitive to her surroundings, whispered, "There is something not quite right." A group of soldiers passing on motorcycles drowned out her voice. "Try to walk a bit faster," she urged Anna as the stately Catholic church came into view. She looked for the other pedestrians who normally made their way to the church. "There is something not quite right," she repeated. She looked around for familiar faces and glanced at the huge clock as they passed Anna's schoolhouse.

"Perhaps we are just a little late," Anna suggested.

Stunned in disbelief, Anna's mother stopped in her tracks.

"What's wrong?" Anna asked.

Her mother pointed to a bright yellow warning sign nailed across the huge wooden front door of the church. "*Eintritt verboten!*" read the warning in black letters. Underneath, a lock was attached by heavy chains.

"How can this be?" Anna's mother spoke in anger. Her face turned pale. Her petite body trembled. She reached for Anna's hand and led her down the steps. "Let's not waste this beautiful day," she said, her voice quivering. Anna watched her mother's distraught face turn red. She had never seen her mother this angry. "I know it is a long stretch, but we will just walk through the park and attend Mass at the cathedral." A smile came occasionally over her mother's face as Anna demonstrated her ballet jumps through the winding paths in the park. They walked by the ancient remnants of the Roman wall. "Only a few more blocks, I hope that I am not wearing you out! You have to perform at the Opera House this evening," Anna's mother reminded her.

From a distance, Anna spotted a similar sign on the doors of the cathedral. She recognized a priest walking across the front of the cathedral and called to him. "Maybe he can give an explanation," she suggested.

The priest turned and walked toward them. "It's nice to see you again." Anna felt comforted by his gentle handshake. Deep lines in his face revealed compassion and concern.

Anna's mother fought to get the words out as she questioned the signs on the doors of the cathedral. "We have not been told the reason for this, and we hope this will be very temporary." His eyes welled with tears as he nervously twisted the cord that hung from his waist and across his brown robe. He looked into Anna's eyes and said, "Please help your mother to keep her chin up." She did not understand the depth of his concern as she nodded.

"Let us rest our tired feet for a few moments," her mother said, pulling her to a nearby bench. They watched the priest, his long robe flowing as he walked, close the gate to the rectory. "He is a true apostle," her mother whispered.

Anna had observed each week as her mother counted the days and hours prior to Sunday morning's Mass. She knew it was the source of her comfort and renewed courage. *Where will we go now?* Anna wondered as they began the long walk home.

Until now, Anna had never seen her mother lost for words. Locking the doors to God's house brought out an anger she had not seen in her mother. "They cannot stop us from praying," Anna's mother contended. She swiftly draped their dining-room cupboard with a delicate linen runner. "Our statue of the Blessed Mother and three white candles will serve as our temporary altar," she announced. Anna knew her mother acted upon her words as she knelt daily in front of their new altar, and each Sunday morning she lit the three candles.

As Anna took her walks through the parks and to the Opera House several times a week, she recognized the change of scenery. Fine automobiles, now rarely seen because of the fuel shortage, were replaced on the busy avenues by noisy trucks and military vehicles. Everywhere she looked she saw reminders of her duty to serve the *Reich*, and reminders of her grandmother's persistent pounding to join the Hitler Youth.

Once decorated with colorful pictures of faraway places, the storefront of a travel agency displayed propaganda. The brightly lit windows of elegant hotels were replaced by unusual darkness, an eerie atmosphere caused by the blackouts. Soldiers leaning on rifles pointing toward the sky replaced the well-dressed and courteous doormen. Loud folk music indicating celebrations of high-powered leadership replaced classical music from within beer gardens and restaurants.

The new owner of the fashionable hair-styling salon displayed a great sense of humor by creating an unchanged picture of his window displays. "Those are all empty bottles, and there is nothing inside the pretty soap boxes. My wife takes great patience in keeping the dust off so it all looks real," he shared with a potential customer.

For Anna, spring could not come soon enough. She missed the fun winter days she and Guenter shared on the ski slopes or just sledding down the steep hills near their home. Her mother's drawn face revealed worries. Anna understood that her mother and grandmother faced an increasing fuel shortage. This seemed more devastating to her mother than the shortage of food.

To find relief from their frigid apartments, her mother and grandmother made daily trips to the forest. Pulling a small wooden wagon, they gathered branches for their wood-burning stoves. The huge generators at school offered very little heat. Everyone wore heavy clothes and at times even slept in them. All government buildings, including schools, displayed posters with stern messages that read, "*Coalen Klau!*" ("Conserve Coal!"). The comical drawing of a bear portrayed as a one-eyed bandit on posters amused young and old, but this was not a laughing matter. Performances at the Opera House became less frequent because of the fuel shortage.

People ran into movie theaters to catch the propaganda. Everyone seemed to concentrate on the war, especially the fierce fighting on the Russian front. They talked about Hitler's success and the stage of war being at its highest power. With the exception of threats of bombing, families of high-ranking officers in Hitler's Wehrmacht continued to prosper. They moved into apartments in upscale neighborhoods once occupied by Jewish businesspeople. Local social services offered some assistance to those who were not so fortunate.

Anna's grandmother insisted that her mother apply for assistance. "I will not sign my name to documents pertaining questions I cannot answer about my husband," Anna's mother maintained during a heated discussion between the two women. "I will just find more work," she proudly added. Their already tight household budget suffered because Anna was not paid her small compensations for her performances at the Opera House as often, but she was thrilled to continue doing chores for her friends at the bakery. Except for items like tea and coffee, Sabina's family did not yet lack the everyday essentials. The supplies from the hotel and the hotel garden kept them well-supplied for a while. Once a week, Sabina took a basket of vegetables and fruit to Anna's mother and grandmother.

Juergen faithfully continued his regular visits to check on Anna and her mother. Like most, he had no connections for acquiring fuel. Using his self-taught engineering skills, he rigged up a burning charcoal stove as a fuel converter on the back of his three-wheel truck. Anna was quite amused and happy that she could hear him two city blocks away. Some of the neighbors did not find it amusing. "Turn off that piece of junk!" yelled an old man who lived nearby. Reluctantly, after probing Juergen about its safety, her mother gave Anna permission to ride with him down to the Rhine to visit with Emma and the children. Anna and Juergen waved to onlookers who stood amazed at the curious contraption, some smiling, others frowning.

Visiting Emma and the children in their grandmother's small stone and stucco farmhouse also took temporary pressure of being away from Anna's grandmother. Thanks to Emma's mother, who projected fun and laughter, the tiny house tucked into the hillside in the village overlooking the Rhine River was always filled with warmth. On a shelf lined with colorful fruit and vegetables, Emma kept an earthen cookie jar full of pfeffernusse. While the adults discussed serious issues of the jumbled-up living circumstances and the absence of Eric and Guenter, Anna played with the children in the vineyard on the hillside.

An escape to the mountain retreat.

Anna at age ten dressed in her mandatory Hitler Youth uniform.

Chapter 9

1942 … Danger lies in wait.

For many, living with fear, uncertainty, and hunger became a way of life. No one complained about long lines so long as there was something available at the end of the line. Spring, summer, and fall gave some hope that conditions might improve by the following winter. Nerve-wracking became the constant droning of bombers taking off every three hours from the nearby airport occupied by the *Luftwaffe*. Occasionally, Anna's mother cried out in her sleep, "Can't you people stop this?"

Hitler's people began to launch a new campaign to recruit and send away young German girls. Anna's grandmother insisted Anna should sign up. "Uncle Hermann"—she referred to Hermann Goering—"promises a healthy and exciting place for all our children. Not only that," she continued, "they will be safe and away from bombing. Just last week, a thousand British bombers unleashed their bombs and devastated our beautiful city of Cologne."

But Anna's mother challenged her, saying, "Is there any difference when we bomb Britain's cathedral cities? It seems our planes started it!" She continued, "I will not have Anna sent away. Not only that, your favorite radio station out of Hamburg bragged about executing captured enemy commandos!" She threw her hands into the air and continued to oppose the grandmother. "Besides, I do not believe the lies that girls ages twelve and older will only be engaged in sports. Working in fields and getting them out of their parents' control is the real reason behind this!" As evident with Guenter, she knew that Hitler Youth stood for "German Work Youth."

To save her from her grandmother's demands, Anna's mother arranged for Anna to visit a children's health spa in the Black Forest. "Your grandmother insists you sign up for an upcoming Hitler Youth summer camp. We must avoid confrontation with her and especially her circle of Nazi Party friends. Besides, the mountain air will be good for you, and I know you will enjoy visiting there. I will find the money to pay for it," she confided in Anna. "And I will arrange the time to coincide with your school vacation and spring closing of the Opera House. Juergen knows the innkeeper there. They will make the arrangements. You will be safe and have fun."

Anna did not want to go, but she did not complain. She did not want to be away from the horses for such a long time. Most of all, she did not want to leave her mother alone. She sat, alone and anxious, as the train made its way toward the Black Forest, along vineyards and then through thick forest. She looked across the mountain range and felt lonely and guilty for being unable to share these moments with her mother. Except for the winsome sound of the train, everything was quite.

Enthralled by the scenery, Anna slipped the huge nametag her mother had prepared around her neck as the train came to a halt in the tiny village deep within the forest. A red-faced and round-bellied woman walked toward her. "*Gruss Gott*, I am Helga, the innkeeper here. Welcome to Pension Steigermeister. The children are anxious to meet you." After a hearty handshake and a quick bow, she took Anna's bag and placed it on a small wooden wagon. "Our truck sits idle these days. We have no fuel to run it," she apologized. "We'll take the shortcut up through the mountain path. The walk is short and enjoyable." Anna smiled and nodded. She was relieved to meet the bubbling stranger and joyfully helped pull the wagon behind them.

Anna felt at home at the inn. As she gazed at the reflection of the rising sun across the mountain range, she imagined her mother on the other side. She felt a lump in her throat and became desperately homesick. As the days passed, her feeling of homesickness subsided, and the melodious sounds of the cowbells on the hillside behind the inn lifted her spirits.

Each morning, the girls went hiking through the forest. They sang as they walked along meadows and studied rainbow-colored wildflowers. Red bushy-tailed squirrels displayed their acrobatic skills along the route. From time to time, groups of deer pranced along the paths with them. Anna stopped for a brief moment and listened to the girls' melodies ring across the valley. "Just like stories in my books," she shared with a frail-looking girl quite small for her age. She yearned for the horses at the Riding Academy. "They would love galloping through these beautiful trails," she reminisced, shading her eyes from the bright sun shimmering through the thick stands of fir on the upper slopes.

Fraulein Helga apologized for the simple meals. "At least we still have plenty of milk and cheese, thanks to our own critters," she giggled, pointing to the goats out in the pasture. Empty plates and bowls after meals proved that none of the girls objected to the food. Anna welcomed not having to listen to her grandmother's demands at mealtime. This was a welcome change. She looked forward to postcards from her mother—and, although she cherished every moment of being in this fairytale atmosphere, she counted the days until she would return to her home.

On the day of her departure, several girls joined Anna as she prepared for her trip back home. "The train will leave quite early," Fraulein Helga announced. "You must reach your destination before dark, because the enemy begins its bombing campaign after nightfall."

Anna looked back to the dormitory that had served as her safe haven during her three-week visit. "I'll miss you," she cried as she embraced her frail little friend. "When will you go home?" Anna asked.

"I have no home. My parents were lost during last month's bombing," the tiny girl said, shrugging her shoulders. "Will you come back?" she asked Anna.

Bewildered and confused at the girl's reaction, Anna whispered, "I don't know, but I will ask my mother."

The train stopped briefly as Anna got on. Recalling Fraulein Helga's comments earlier, she nervously watched the sun set as the blaring sound of the locomotive made known its presence. She reminisced about the past three weeks and the little friend she left behind. The serenity she had grown accustomed to for the past four weeks dramatically changed as the train neared the city.

From a distance, Anna watched her mother pace back and forth as the train slowly pulled into the station. *She looks very sad*, Anna thought, becoming disturbed as she handed her mother the bookmark she fashioned with the help of Fraulein Helga. Arm in arm they walked through the noisy and crowded train station.

"We'll wait for the last bus," Anna's mother shouted over the train's whistle that drowned out her voice. She pointed to a broken-down bench. "We'll sit and you can tell me all about your vacation."

Anna sensed that there was something wrong. "Please tell me what is troubling you," she finally asked her mother.

"I have been keeping up with the news," her mother said softly. "Guenter has been shipped to Russia. No one seems to know where. Rumor has it that he is on his way to Leningrad."

"That is an awfully cold place during winters," Anna angrily contested. "We just learned about that city in our geography class."

Anna's mother squeezed her hand. "That is not all," she went on to say. "The man in the black leather trench coat is back asking questions about your father." A tear dropped across her mother's face.

"What do you say to him?" Anna asked nervously.

"The man is very curt and intimidating, but I cannot tell him that which I do not know. I just hope that he will not frighten you!" Her voice rose as she stared at the reflection of lights of the approaching bus.

Realizing her mother was lost in her thoughts, Anna pleaded, "We best get on the bus!"

Slowly, Anna began to understand that the stalking of the peculiar-acting stranger had to be linked to her father's unknown whereabouts. She noticed the man's presence mostly after dark, and she became desperately afraid to walk the short distance to her grandmother's home. On several occasions, they both spotted him standing near the stage door of the Opera House. Darkness caused by the blackout made his presence even more spooky. Anna understood her mother's concern, but neither spoke about it.

Anna's mother was not the only one who kept up with the news. Her grandmother continued to boast, "I am proud to be German and more than anything, I am proud of Herr Hitler. He is putting Germany back as a great nation. We must leave everything to him and trust him. Soon, our soldiers will land in England, just wait and see. He is doing a good job!"

To avoid angry discussions, Anna's mother just walked away. Her concern was not about Hitler—her concern was her family.

The tide was beginning to turn. Troublesome times on the Russian front began as winter arrived earlier than usual. Everyone became aware of the problems there. It began with several Russian army groups attacking and surrounding more than two dozen German divisions. While the statistics did not make sense to Anna and her mother, they knew that Guenter must be somewhere in the vicinity. Front pages of newspapers spoke about German soldiers running out of steam. Frostbite resulting from bitter cold temperatures made their lives almost unbearable. Magazines, in addition to the newspapers, showed pathetic pictures of German soldiers whose feet were wrapped in rags, their bodies covered with shawls.

Anna saw that her mother spent much of her time on her knees. "We must have faith and accept conditions as they are. God will see us through this," she continued to assure Anna. "Unfortunately, we have no choice in these matters. What can we do?" She shrugged her shoulders. Anna felt comforted by the strength her mother continued to portray.

But enlightening moments continued to overshadow Anna's daily battles. Additional new teachers were assigned to her classes, so that she only saw Herr Dietz during two weekly classes. She enjoyed her new school projects as she watched her grades once again begin to climb.

Because of the fuel shortage and the threat of bombing, rehearsals and new productions at the Opera House nearly came to a halt. This did not stop the talented groups of performers, young and old, from organizing fun rehearsals of their own. "We must keep up our skills for better times ahead" became Herr Kummel's slogan. From morning until evening, wrapped in coats and gloves, members of the orchestra filled the air with their favorite productions.

Frustrated with his cold fingers slipping off the instrument, an impatient young trumpet player decided to cut off the fingers of his gloves. Others followed suit, as he watched amused and elated. Everyone looked forward to daily gatherings in the stage café. No one questioned Herr Kummel's source, but gratefully accepted hot cocoa personally prepared by him. Fresh peppermint tea donated by Anna's friend Sabina was always plentiful.

Anna's friendship with Sabina continued to flourish. Aware of Anna's difficult circumstances at home, her family invited Anna several times a week for a meal. Since occupation of the hotel had changed to Hitler's elite military personnel, Sabina's mother discouraged the girls from visiting there. "You are growing up to be attractive young ladies now, and you should not be seen around these strangers without my personal supervision," she firmly but lovingly commanded.

"My mother will agree with you," Anna proudly added. "She is so afraid of my getting near boys and men."

Sabina's mother said with satisfaction, "Your mother is a wise lady. I like her," she added with a smile.

Demands to join the Hitler Youth began to accelerate. One by one, every young girl over the age of ten connected with the Opera House joined, and so did Anna. The rules, written by one of Hitler's top guns, Baldur von Schirach, were firm. "If you are for our führer, Adolf Hitler, you will sign the enclosed application. If you are not willing to sign to be a member of Germany's *Jungmädels* or at age fourteen the *Bund Deutscher Mädel*, you must state your reason on the enclosed blank."

"Make the best of the situation," Juergen advised Anna in relation to being part of the girls' group of Hitler Youth. "The youth organization will teach you two things: to take care of your body and to be loyal to National Socialism. It will not hurt you to take care of your body. Whatever you feel in your heart is your choice."

Reluctantly, her mother agreed while watching closely. In the beginning, Anna took part in every sports event. Although she did not excel in gymnastics as others in her group, she attempted to keep up. With her background in acrobatics, she developed skills in diving from three-meter springboards, and soon became one of the best in her age group. Her mother rarely missed a competition. Most took place on Sunday afternoons. Anna's mother nervously watched and admitted that she feared poolside collisions.

Anna's mother was surprised that, so far, no special demands were made on her in her Hitler Youth group. This changed shortly after Anna's twelfth birthday. Anna's first assignment came from her BDM leader. A boyish-looking girl only two years older than she gave the order. "Anna, you are to visit a high-ranking officer who is being treated for depression at the sanatorium," she ordered in a stern voice. Afraid of reprisal, Anna accepted the assignment.

In drenching rain, she climbed the stairs to the sanatorium that rose high above the city's affluent residential area. She stopped briefly halfway to catch her breath. At the top of the hill, she stopped once more to admire the magnificently manicured gardens. Thick ivy wrapped the stone walls of three huge buildings. She stretched to read directions carved into an old wooden sign.

Her hands trembled as she rang the doorbell at the main entrance. A stern-looking nurse answered the buzz. "I am here to visit Colonel Schneider," Anna announced. The nurse looked her over and frowned. "You are too young to be out on your own!" She led her across a courtyard and through a long and dreary corridor. Anna was amused at the nurse's fluent tongue, as she did not stop talking. The colonel, tall and handsome, rose from his chair and met Anna at an open door leading to his suite. She experienced an odd reluctance to enter the high-ceiling room. She paused and, with a swift "*heil* Hitler," stepped forward. With a quick curtsey, she handed him a small bouquet of cut flowers. Sudden fear came over her.

She sat opposite him and began to speak. "My youth leader suggested I visit you because you miss your family."

With his head hung low, the colonel nodded. "Yes, my family lives in Hamburg."

Anna felt bewildered, for she knew her mother would be trembling with fear had she known about this assignment. She stared at the pewter swastika cross that graced his collar and the spread eagle above his coat pocket. A revolver lay neatly in its holster on a side table near the entrance. He motioned for Anna to sit on his lap, but she refused.

Every word her mother had spoken to her about the importance of growing up, staying away from strange boys and men, came crashing into her head. For the first time she realized all her mother meant. "Do not let anyone come near you, and never let anyone take advantage of you," her mother insisted repeatedly. "This would be ugly and dirty!

Our *Herrgott* [Heavenly Father] expects young girls to be clean and pure!"

At first, Anna sat motionless. She felt sweat in the palms of her hands. "I just learned a lesson from the talkative nurse outside," Anna reminisced. She felt a compulsion to talk nonstop and began to tell the colonel about the Riding Academy and her love for the horses. She spoke about her hopes of becoming a lead dancer and her dream to attend the conservatory. Her enthusiasm touched the colonel.

"I must go—we have rehearsals this afternoon!" She reached for his hand and curtsied.

In a noble manner, he bowed and said, "If my family comes to visit me, I shall make certain we will come and watch you perform." He noticed Anna staring at a bowl of apples. "Would you like one?" he asked.

"No thank you," she firmly declined.

"Please do take one, and one for your favorite horse," he insisted. "I know horses love apples!"

Anna returned his smile and watched him carefully select two of the largest, brightest red apples in the bowl. Then he walked her through the garden and watched as she skipped down the steep stairs until she was nearly out of sight.

She did not dare to stop, but took a quick glance at the officer waving high up on the hill. "Mutti is still working, and I am afraid to go home," she gasped for breath. She began to run the five blocks toward the Riding Academy, up the steep ramp and into Rubin's stall. She clung on to the handsome Arabian's neck, and in a whispering tone she cried, "Why must everything be so complicated?" As though he understood, he turned his exquisitely perfect head toward her. "I was so afraid. Thanks to Mutti, I am safe, and we can continue to have fun now. Rubin, do you really understand?" She took a bite out of one of the apples she had stuffed into the hood of her coat and watched as he tenderly scooped the rest between his shiny white teeth. "We'll keep the other one for Mutti, all right?" Still out of breath, she gasped as she kissed the black Arabian on his cheek.

Master Karl had noticed Anna's quick entrance into the stables and went to check on her. She told him about her assignment. He shook his head in anger and disgust. "Nothing makes sense these days, even an old man like me cannot figure out all that is going on," he mumbled. "Just continue to listen to your mother! You are growing up fast, but with your mother's wise guidance, you will learn to take care of yourself." Looking over the stallion, he took his unlit cigar out of his mouth and chuckled. "Since you and Rubin already had this little conversation, why don't you take him out onto the trails? He could use some fresh air and so can you. I must ask you to use good judgment, however, in case of an air raid. So far they have not bothered us during daylight hours."

Anna felt Rubin's nudge and tilted her head back toward his nose. As she led the tall Arabian out of the stables, a faint smile came over her tear-stained face. "This makes everything all right," Anna shouted as they galloped through the equestrian trails along the park that led up to the mountain peak. She spotted a small pasture near the cable-car landing where she and Rubin found a few moments of rest. "Guenter and I loved coming up here with our sleds," she whispered to Rubin, who paid little attention but indulged feeding in the tall grass.

No matter how hard she tried, Anna was unable to disregard the horror of war around her. Although hazy in her memory, she recalled having a fun-filled early childhood surrounded by people who loved her. The beautiful sounds as her grandfather plucked away on his zither, while Eric sang or played his mouth organ, still rang in her ears. The aroma of her grandmother's cooking. Her brother's laughter during her first fall on the ski slopes near her cousin's chalet high in the Bavarian Alps. She recalled the fun and laughter when Eric took her to the zoo. She cherished the hours she and her mother spent in the park feeding the swans and listening to afternoon concerts after attending Mass on Sunday mornings.

She had not forgotten the precious moments with Sister Renate and the children at the orphanage, and the tranquil and comforting times listening to the priests speaking about Mary and her son, Jesus, in their religion classes. She had not forgotten skating with little Ellie on the sidewalks in their neighborhood. But her memory of her father seemed only imaginary. So many of the people she loved were gone. Now the darkened windows because of the blackout added to the restless and depressing surroundings.

The afternoon sun penetrated warmth through the skylight in Guenter's room. His cat lay quietly, watching Anna ponder over her homework. She closed her books and sighed, "One more lesson done without a hitch!"

Peter stretched with a yawn as to say, "I am also content."

Anna smiled with satisfaction and said, "Let's go and check our mailbox, maybe we'll hear from Guenter and Eric today. You make me sleepy." She reached over and gently rubbed Peter underneath his furry chin before skipping down the stairs.

"Yes!" she smiled as she retrieved a plain postcard with Guenter's handwriting.

"I do not have much to report and I really don't know where we are," the postcard read. "I can tell you that we are getting virtually no rest or sleep. On the night of my birthday, we came across a deserted Russian farmhouse. We took turns, and I got about five hours of sleep and a cold shower. That was a great birthday present! We found a few fresh eggs in a broken-down henhouse, gathered some wood, and cooked them over an open fire. You can imagine, this was a rare thing and almost too good to be true. I can't wait to be home again. I miss you and love you." Anna beamed with joy as she read Guenter's message over and over. *At least he is all right!* she thought.

She ran into the bakery to share the news with Herr Ramspott. His bearded round face covered with flour, he reached to retrieve a small package from beneath the counter. His white apron barely fit around his round belly. "I saved this shortbread for you and some coffee for your mother. It's not real coffee, ersatz they call it," he grumbled, "but it beats nothing!" Anna ran up to her apartment and placed her new find next to her mother's tiny flower vase and quickly scribbled her usual note: "I'll be at the stables—back soon! Love you!"

Although the bells of the old Catholic church had fallen silent and the heavy doors remained locked, Anna's mother often climbed the hill to the church. In a gazebo nearby she gazed at the church steeple and stained-glass windows illuminated by the reflection of the sun's rays and yearned for the day the doors would once again be opened.

People knew that Hermann Goering's boasting to the people that "no enemy planes would bomb Germany" had failed long ago. His promise that the German people would have sufficient food and grow a strong nation also began to fail miserably. "This is my promise!" he repeatedly announced, "or you may call me Herr Meyer!" His nickname, among those who dared, became "*Der dumme Herr Meyer*" ("The dumb Mr. Meyer").

To this point, the enemy had spared the city from serious bombing. This too changed, as warning sirens began to cry out night after night. Seized with fear, her teddy bear under her arm, Anna followed her mother down flights of stairs and across the courtyard and into their designated air-raid shelter. Other families scrambled in before a dull sound followed the closing of an airtight door that sealed the residents into the shelter.

Anna looked around in the dimly lit and crowded space that once served as a wine cellar. A damp, mildewed smell hung in the air. A petrified, pale-faced old woman, her gas mask cradled in her lap, rocked away in an old rocking chair. Her body trembled. Others simply stared into space. Anna's mother prayed with her rosary clasped tightly in her hands. She pulled apart the fingers of Anna's tightly balled fist. "You will want to hold on to your prayer book," she said, and an elated smile came over Anna's face.

"Thank you," Anna whispered as she affectionately touched the shepherd and his sheep on the book cover.

She covered her ears to avoid the frightening drone of hundreds of bombers overhead. She recalled Juergen assuring her that so long as one could hear the sounds of engines, there was no immediate threat. "But when you hear those piercing and whistling sounds of the enemy's bombs falling, it is time for concern," he warned her.

Once the second sounds of the sirens rang out to let the people know the planes had gone, everyone quickly dispersed to their homes. "At least we were lucky this time," murmured an old man barely able to walk the stairs to his apartment. Unable to get attention, a toddler, amused at all that was going on, reached for Anna's teddy bear, but Anna was not willing to share him during these unsettling moments.

Day by day, Anna's mother continued to show confidence and hope for a better tomorrow. "I know God is watching over us," she cheerfully maintained. "And we must pray that He will watch over our men." She delighted in the most trivial things, and spent hours listening to the finch in concert in the tall linden outside the balcony of her room.

But Anna sensed that a change had taken place in her mother's behavior. She withdrew to her room more often and earlier than usual at bedtime. She was unable to walk with Anna to the Opera House without stopping for a rest. Instead of visiting Anna's friends in their dressing room, she reclined in an easy chair in the gathering space of the stage entrance. Anna shared her concern with Sabina. "I will visit your mother more often," Sabina assured Anna. "Perhaps she just needs me to cheer her up." She brushed her shiny dark hair out of her face and gave Anna her typical affectionate wink.

Regularly, with her mother's permission, Sabina rode her bicycle to their hotel garden to fill her basket with flowers, fruit, vegetables, and whatever she was able to talk the hotel chef out of. Anna's mother looked forward to these visits. Anna soon saw her mother's vitality return, and she was amazed how freely her mother struck up lively conversation with her friend. "I keep seeing those pictures in the magazines of the sad-looking young soldiers on the Russian front." She felt of the flower pedals Sabina arranged as she was speaking.

In her sophisticated voice, yet somewhat lost for words, Sabina responded, "Your son must have learned quite a bit about survival in his youth camps. I am sure he will be all right!" Anna admired her beautiful friend, who showed great pleasure in making things easier for others.

Sabina often shared her learnings from private tutors with Anna. "As soon as I get more fluent, I will teach you English," she promised. "But we must keep it a secret!" Foreign languages were not taught in Anna's school. Interest in history, which Guenter had passed on to Anna, also faded, since the rhetoric of her teachers mostly emphasized the German *Reich.* The educational system proved to be interested only in Bismark's empire.

To make things worse, Herr Dietz's dislike for Anna still surfaced from time to time. When he learned about her nearsightedness, he deliberately seated her at the rear of the classroom. Unable to make out his assignments on the blackboard, her attempts to keep up frustrated her. This played havoc with her most difficult subject, math. She was desperately afraid of his humiliation if she failed her grade. But Anna continued to learn from her mother to do the best she could and to grasp the best life had to offer.

By the end of the fall of 1942, the promises of Hitler's regime to enhance the lives of the German people began to fade. Hitler's people began to grasp for straws. Surprisingly, this resulted in temporary encouragement for all members of the Opera House.

Herr Kummel summoned everyone to an unexpected meeting. From stagehands and shoemakers to the region's most highly respected performers, nearly everyone showed with great anticipation. On the floor of the huge rehearsal hall, Anna and other members of the ballet sat at Herr Kummel's feet. Everyone focused on him as he nervously paced back and forth. His thick, shaggy gray hair seemed almost white, and the lines in his face were deeper. He fumbled nervously for a notepad in his coat pocket as he began to speak.

"We will begin rehearsals for the winter to prepare for the tenth anniversary of the führer's appointment as chancellor of Germany. His people want to show a bit of vivacity during these trying times. During the führer's visit, they requested operettas with music on the light side. Since we have lost some of our best talents," Herr Kummel looked around the room from beneath his thick horn-rimmed glasses, "we will begin auditioning for leading parts in young Johann Strauss's lighthearted *Fledermaus* ["The Bat"] and Engelbert Humperdinck's *Hansel and Gretel.* Because of blackout and bombing, there will only be afternoon and early evening productions." Anna noticed that special sparkle return to his eyes. He raised his arm. "Please get your dancing shoes fitted as soon as possible! Herr Goebbels has made provisions for new materials," he shouted to the enthusiastic band of performers.

With rekindled enthusiasm, the entire group diligently rehearsed for the upcoming festival in honor of Adolf Hitler. Johann Strauss's music rang from corridor to corridor. Because of rumors about an assassination attempt, Hitler showed up unannounced. Uniformed SS, posted at every entrance, made their presence known. In the audience, head covers and coats to keep off the chilled air replaced elegant evening attire. Nothing dampened the spirit of the performers as they watched the audience lift out of their chairs after each production.

Much to everyone's surprise, productions—though carefully scrutinized—continued to flourish. A huge poster outside the canteen read, "Compliments of Hitler's people, free daily lunches will be served in the canteen." Meeting there with other members of the Opera House always proved to be uplifting. After school, Anna hurried to make it there before closing. While she remained devoted to her grandmother, she grew weary of her grandmother's tactics of motivating her into activities her mother discouraged. She found the luncheons at the canteen more beneficial. At least no one there constantly preached about Hitler's wonderful and genius intentions about Germany.

Anna's mother kept her promise to share her faith with her. "Just maybe someone will unlock our church," she kept hoping and praying. But it was not to be. At least she was able to divert attention to other activities around her, thus managing to stay clear of depression. She knew Anna thrived on the emotions of her involvement in the Opera House, and that she worked hard on the fluency in ballet. She felt thankful and secure knowing this.

Anna's Hitler Youth leader did not forget her. She ordered Anna to call on wounded soldiers in crowded makeshift hospitals. To Anna's delight, Sabina and her cousins volunteered to go along and often contributed flowers from the hotel garden. They sang with the wounded soldiers and shared stories about the horses and events at the Opera House. Anna did not object to these assignments. Most soldiers, like her brother, were still in their teens and victims of being drawn into Hitler's *Volksturm.*

Chapter 10

1943 … Reality of war hits close to home.

Night after night, Anna and her mother listened as the ear-splitting screams of air-raid sirens broke the silence. They dreaded the cramped, dark dampness of the air-raid shelter. Huddled together, they sat and listened as waves of Allied planes passed over, ready to unload their cargo. "Our faith will help us through these troubled nights," Anna's mother whispered. "You must not be afraid. God is watching us, but we must keep on praying." Nevertheless, Anna was afraid.

Spring, summer, and fall passed quickly. Winter usually began with torrential rain. Unlike the surrounding mountain region, and because of the hot springs that ran underneath the city, mud froze into ice that followed the snow of winter. This continued to be a time to fear since fuel, food, and clothing continued to be in short supply.

Guenter's infrequent postcards expressed frantic thoughts. "We are not allowed to go into details about our duties," he mentioned each time. "It is cold, miserable, and I am afraid! I want to come home!" In anguish, Anna's mother read his postcards repeatedly. She cupped her hands and hid her face in her delicate handkerchief. Anna stroked her mother's neatly combed hair. She wanted desperately to comfort her mother, but it was of little use. The distraught woman sobbed as she swallowed the tears that ran down her face. "I just miss our boys. It is not knowing their whereabouts that frightens me."

Anna sat beside her mother, helplessly searching for words. She too began to sob. "Why can't we feel free to discuss my father's whereabouts?" she dared to ask.

Anna's mother leaned back and gazed at his picture on her dressing table and turned to look at Anna as she tried to collect her thoughts and said, "If I knew, I couldn't tell you, because it is too risky to discuss. Your father's wish is your safety. He wants you to be protected. Please, I beg you, do not bring your father up again!"

Wishing to please her mother, Anna hung her head and walked away. Bewildered, she vowed not to bring up questions about her father again. She felt a sudden urge to visit Sabina. With the door handle in both hands, she looked over her shoulders and asked her mother, "May I please visit Sabina for a while?"

Her mother gave a half smile and nodded, "Yes, of course!"

Unable to sort out her mother's plea, Anna wandered out into the streets of their neighborhood. A bell announcing the hour clanged somewhere in the dreary distance. A group of soldiers piled out of one of the beer gardens. "Mutti is unable to purchase milk, yet the soldiers can get all the beer they want," she mumbled. "They are so lucky to be here where it is safe." Her heart ached as she began to dwell on the past. She walked by Sabina's grandfather's hotel and wondered how he must be feeling about the changes in his family hotel, built by his great grandfather nearly a century ago. Rainbows of flowers still surrounded the terrace, but the sounds of music from within had changed dramatically. Instead of the once noble guests, Hitler's uniformed personnel enjoyed the luxurious ambience of the hotel and its surrounding gardens.

The half-hour walk to Sabina's villa gave Anna time to think about the concerns that cluttered her young mind. Through bits and pieces overheard, she suspected that her father's mysterious disappearance was because he risked his life to help others. She wondered if he would ever return.

Sabina's family was indeed her place of refuge, and spending time with them was her greatest pleasure. She secretly wished she could live with them. "You may spend the night any time you like," Sabina's mother cheerfully acknowledged often, but Anna felt apprehensive about leaving her mother alone.

Finally, the end of March arrived and so did warmer days. Anna's mother closed her eyes and took a deep breath as she opened her window. "Our family is split apart and access to our beloved Catholic church has been denied. These are two serious issues, and I find them hard to cope with. But they cannot refuse worshipping out in God's nature." Anna watched her mother soak her smooth and pale face in the morning sun.

"Who are 'they'?" Anna asked.

Her mother responded impatiently, "I am referring to the ignorant people who have lost their sense of values." She quickly walked to her desk to reach for a notepad and began to jot down ideas for short-distance excursions. "Easter is an important time to spend with God as He brings forth new life. The trees are budding, and the birds are singing! Don't you see? This is God's greeting card! We do not need to look far to see His signs." She smiled as she reached out to close the window. Once again, Anna's mother showed her determination and familiar devotion to her faith.

They walked through nearby meadows on Sunday mornings. Anna heartily agreed with her mother's earlier comments. "You are right, Mutti," she said, her eyes scanned the rolling meadows in front of her. "There must be millions of *Maiglockchen*!"

Anna attended her weekly, mandatory Hitler Youth meetings, but she remained unaffected by the propaganda. Her mother had no problem addressing her many questions.

With all the attention surrounding her, Anna felt happy and content. She knew from her mother's faith and confidence that, eventually, everything would be all right.

Clouds covered the sun, and twilight turned gray with loneliness. Anna wished that her own loneliness would come to an end. *Somewhere behind the mountain ridge must be my father, brother, and Eric*, she thought. A dandelion stuck between her teeth, she gazed at the rushing brook at her feet. She took a deep breath, filling her lungs with the crisp spring air. Rubin and the two mares grazed peacefully just a few feet away. Intrigued by the horses' delicate moving of lips to savor the young blades of grass, she cupped her hands behind her head and closed her eyes.

She recalled how, several weeks earlier, Master Karl had told a group of riders after a jumping exhibition, "I am increasingly concerned over the horses." His eyebrows rose. "If diarrhea sets in because of their unbalanced diet, we are in trouble! I need your help, please! I must entrust some of you to take a group of horses, three to five at a time, if possible, out into the countryside to graze. I need your commitment, for it will save their lives. Anna, you have bonded well with Rubin. Perhaps you can take some of the old mares along at the same time?" While reminiscing about all that occurred around her, she fell into a deep sleep.

She felt Rubin's gentle nudge. She jumped to her feet and began to lead the three horses over a ravine and toward the trail that led back to the city. Rubin stubbornly resisted and pulled back. From his response, she knew they were not quite satisfied. Feeling sorry for them, she sat back on the ground so that they could continue to graze a while longer.

With the confidence of a noble rider, Anna approached her neighborhood as darkness set in. Attracted by the metallic noise of hooves against the cobblestone, her mother waved from her window. Suddenly, a motorcycle swirled around a street corner, barely missing the rider and horses. "Get those horses off the street!" yelled a soldier reclined in the sidecar. Anna remained calm and gently maneuvered Rubin's restraint. With a reassuring smile, she looked up at her panic-stricken mother.

Master Karl nervously waited for their return. "I am truly sorry for being late, it was Rubin's fault," Anna confessed with a grin.

"We do not want you to get caught in an air raid. As you know, they are beginning earlier these days." Master Karl scratched his head as he reasoned firmly. "There is no telling when and what the enemy will do next!"

Master Karl's prediction came true the following night. This time, the air-raid warning sirens blasted longer through the night. Clad still in their nightclothes, Anna and her mother rushed through the courtyard. Ear-piercing whistles, followed by explosions, lit the night sky. In a matter of seconds, the sky turned into a bright orange-red. Anna's mother pulled her along the exit stairs. When they were barely inside the shelter, the second crash of bombs shook the earth and everything above it.

There was no let-up for hours. The only light in the shelter began to flicker and finally went out. With only the light of a small candle, they sat and listened as Allied bombs pounded upon their neighborhood.

Then, there was silence. Warning sirens gave a signal that danger had passed. The light began to flicker. Terrified and shaken, everyone climbed the stairs and ventured out into the streets to have a look. Fire raged through what was left of several five- and six-story apartment buildings. Dust and smoke made it difficult to breathe. "The enemy's bombs made shambles of our beautiful neighborhood," cried an elderly neighbor.

The air cleared and the dust settled slightly as Anna got ready for school the following morning. "Please go and check on your grandmother, and also take a look to see if our church is still standing," her mother pleaded. She began to walk the hill with flames still leaping into the sky a block away. No one came to put out the fires. There was little use, since rubble buried the fire hydrants. In some areas, even the water mains were destroyed.

Anna pressed her book satchel against her chest. She stood mesmerized by the thumping sounds coming from underneath the rubble of an apartment building in which one of her schoolmates lived. She could not bear to look into the perplexed faces of homeless women and children climbing over debris. The thought of people buried in their air-raid shelters frightened her.

Her feet felt like lead as she continued her walk to school. A sigh of relief came over her as she passed her grandmother's deserted street. She stopped to look down. Nothing had been touched. She was glad and, with all her heart, wished her mother and grandmother would stop bickering. *Survival is much more important than one's opinion about politics*, she thought.

Since only a few students turned out, no one bothered to open the schoolhouse. "Who can concentrate at a time like this?" remarked Herr Dietz in a rare mellow tone. Anna wasted no time heading for the stables. She found Master Karl stretched out on a bundle of straw, his head propped on a saddle. He looked drawn and tired. "Did I wake you?" Anna apologetically asked.

"No, I am thankful you came! Our stable boy, August, did not show this morning," he said, looking at his watch. "He is three hours late. I hear his home was among a number of homes leveled to the ground near the Bahnhof. I had no choice but to stay with our critters through last night's hell!" He pointed to the Palladian windows high above the stalls. "I don't know what frightened our horses more, the thundering sounds that shook the walls or the searchlights in the sky. The bombs fell amazingly close!"

"Were you afraid, Master Karl?" Anna asked shyly.

"No, I was too busy calming the critters."

"But your family must have been quite concerned about your not going to the air-raid shelter," Anna probed.

"I have no family!" Master Karl pulled his handkerchief from his pocket. "It's just me and the gang here!" He removed his bifocals and turned so that Anna could not see the tears flowing from his tired eyes.

Anna reached for his arm. "You can be my family," she spoke in a whisper.

"That's great," Master Karl responded. "It will mean a lot to me." He held her close.

"I'll tell Mutti; she will be pleased!"

Anna pulled the rickety wagon Master Karl had rigged up for her to distribute the horses' rations through the aisles between the stalls. This day she wanted to be more lenient with their rations, but she did not dare for fear the food would not last through the week. Overcome by a sudden urge to check on her mother, she quickly adjusted a bandage on the infected leg of Maidlie, one of the old mares, and then ran down the ramps and the two short blocks toward her home.

Out of breath, she found the door leading into their apartment half open. She called out for her mother. Then, panic-stricken, she ran toward her mother's pale and lifeless figure lying on the floor in the corner of her darkened room. From the neighbor's apartment, loud propaganda music drowned her desperate call for help.

Her mother struggled to raise her head. "Oh, Anna, I am so sorry; I must have fainted." Anna took a sheet of paper from her mother's clenched fist. "What is this?" She waved the paper in front of her mother.

"You must not know," her mother snapped.

"Please do not keep another secret from me," Anna yelled as she ran out onto the balcony to read the note.

It read, "We are sorry to inform you, Frau Bechtold, your son is missing in action and presumed dead."

Shaking her head in disbelief, Anna knelt by her mother and pressed the letter against her chest. "I don't believe this, there must be a mistake! I will not believe this!" she cried out in anguish. Anna had often seen her mother's sad expressions, but not like this. She wiped her eyes. "I do not believe this!" she repeated, knowing that this would become her mother's toughest battle.

"They say he is gone." Her mother's voice was so low, Anna could barely understand the words. "But I know your brother is alive! Please, you must go and tell your grandmother. I am not able to speak with her until we learn of better news."

Fearing for her mother's health, Anna knew better than to contest her mother's request. "I will go tomorrow," she replied.

The blustering sound of sirens shook Anna out of a deep sleep again the following night. From a distance, the rumbling of artillery gunfire warned Allied planes of its presence.

Nearby, slamming doors and hurried footsteps reminded her of the urgency of fleeing to their air-raid shelter.

She jumped to her feet, wondering why her mother had not called for her. As she pushed aside the curtain that divided their bedrooms, she was shocked to see her mother still asleep. "Please, Mutti, come on," she frantically begged. But her mother did not respond. Anna quickly rushed to find a wet towel and placed it on her mother's head. "Wake up!" Anna begged repeatedly while cautiously shaking her mother's tiny, limp figure. Her mother reacted only with a groan.

Anna sat on the floor and held her mother's hand. Just as Master Karl had described, searchlights lit the skies outside her mother's window. Anna's body trembled—she felt cold chills come over her. But this was no time to be afraid. There was nothing she could do. She glanced at the alarm clock in her mother's dimly lit room, and with the sound of exploding bombs in her ears dozed of.

Nearly an hour passed. Finally, her mother turned and, in a weak tone, asked, "Why are you up, Anna?" She removed the wet towel from her forehead.

"Everyone is in the shelter except the two of us!" cried Anna. Then, the second but welcome sound blasted through the night. With a sigh of relief, they listened to shutting of doors indicating that their neighbors were returning from the shelter.

So much had happened during forty-eight hours. Anna's head was once again spinning.

Her mother's fainting spells upset her. Grateful that nothing serious had occurred during the air raid, she fluffed her pillow and stared out the window. It was daybreak. She needed to inform her grandmother of the news from Guenter, but first she would look for Dr. Stadlmeier.

The dust had settled from the horrifying experience of the bombing. As she walked toward Dr. Stadlmeier's house, she mulled over all the events around her. She knew she had a difficult task ahead of her. For the first time in her young life, she knew she must take charge.

"Sometimes," she recalled Eric saying, "we must grit our teeth and fight!" For the moment, this meant that she must put looking after her mother before all else. She felt privileged that her mother's words continued to seed her heart. After all, it was her mother who continued to teach her the meaning of contentment. As she watched her mother praying on bended knee, day after day, she hoped that one day her family would be together again and the troubles that tormented their lives would pass on.

Much to Anna's surprise, she found the elderly doctor and a family friend in the apartment adjoining his office. Dust from partially collapsed ceilings coated the rich oriental carpets. On the doctor's desk, broken glass covered an unorganized array of files. A bewildered expression on his thin face prompted her to offer support. "May I please help you, Dr. Stadlmeier?" she whispered.

He shook his head. "I suppose we are lucky it is not the middle of winter. Every window is shattered." He glanced at the frame of the tall French doors. "There is no one around to fix anything!" His exasperated voice startled Anna. He brushed the flour-like dust from his hands and turned to her. "Anna, to what do I owe the honor of your visit?"

She hung her head. "Mutti is ill, and she refuses to go to the *krankenhaus*!"

Without hesitation, he responded to Anna's desperate plea and followed her to their home.

"There is no need for alarm, at least not at the moment," he told her after a brief examination. "Your mother seems to be going through the change."

Anna looked puzzled and asked, "What does this mean?"

He reached for a small package as he closed his satchel. "Here are some vitamins for both of you. It will be good for you both to take them." He gently touched Anna's shoulder and, with a reassuring wink, tipped his hat and walked out the door saying, "Make certain she gets some rest. Your mother will explain. You know where to reach me, Anna!" His voice echoed from the bottom of the stairwell.

Daily turmoil from the bombing had taken the wind out of everyone's sails. Anna's mother could not fathom that her son, still school-age, could have been killed or have fallen into the hands of the barbarous Russian army. She could not accept the news and was unable to mourn. Anna fearfully watched her mother's change of disposition. Her breathing slowed and her eyes appeared distant.

Through bits and pieces, she again assumed that her father's mysterious disappearance was because he risked his life to help others. She wondered if he would ever return.

onditions in school, too, worsened. Fraulein Meier, Anna's cherished teacher, returned to Bavaria to tend to her ailing parents. Herr Dietz showed no compassion for Anna and her mother following the news about Guenter. Instead, he again sought to punish Anna for trivial things.

However, her nearly unbearable situation at school took an unexpected break after bombs leveled a large portion of the schoolhouse. A new assignment moved her to another school and new teachers. Although the distance there was much greater, Anna rejoiced and hoped for a new start. From here on, she realized she would not need to tremble at the ring of the bell,

It was midday. Anna was glad a dreadful week was ending. Lack of sleep had taken a toll on her energy. She struggled to keep from falling asleep during her last class of the day. Because of nagging hunger pains, she found it difficult to concentrate in her enjoyable new school environment. She looked forward to lunch with her grandmother, but dreaded telling her the news about Guenter.

She quickly sat down in her favorite chair in her grandmother's sunny kitchen. In the garden outside the window, her grandmother's linens fluttered in the gentle spring breeze. For a moment, it seemed as though the events of the week had not occurred.

"We have potatoes, carrots, and cabbage on today's menu," her grandmother chuckled. "I know you both are tired of meatless meals. Just put a potato to the side and pretend it is a pork chop." Anna returned her witty smile. For a moment, her grandmother's old sense of humor seemed more satisfying than the food placed in front of her.

Nervously, Anna twisted her fork and stared at her plate, unable to find the courage to share the news about Guenter. Her grandmother interrupted her thoughts. "Perhaps you will come down to the *Rathaus* with me after we eat? I must collect some discarded coal from the incinerator there, and I could use your help!"

Anna frowned. Her grandmother's request troubled her. "I am afraid that I will get my dress soiled. This is my only school dress." She fondled the edging of the plaid jumper Anna had recently fashioned with material her mother had carefully stored away.

Somewhat agitated, her grandmother answered, "It is much easier for the two of us to pull the old wagon up

Römerberg. I will make certain that nothing happens to your dress!"

The force of the wagon pushed them to walk in a rapid pace down the steep hill.

"Stay here and wait until I signal you to come!" her grandmother ordered. Anna's eyes followed her entering the coal yard. Her grandmother was not alone. Like ants on a mound of dirt, other women ascended upon the coal. Soot covered everything around the compound. Anna noticed how her grandmother methodically examined each find, placing each piece into the wagon like a newly discovered treasure.

"Let us stop for a rest," Anna suggested halfway up the steep incline, next to a field where Guenter once played soccer. She could still sense the tremor of fans cheering for his team. "Come and sit close to me," Anna begged. She reached for her grandmother's battered hands and, with the back of her fingers, gently brushed the smudge that caused streaks on her grandmother's face. Anna felt the familiar lump in her throat. "You must read this note, Grandmother." She fumbled for the note sent to her mother. Tears filled her eyes, and her hands trembled.

The lines in her grandmother's face tightened. "I can't see through these messed-up glasses, please read it to me," her grandmother mumbled while tucking the glasses back into her apron pocket. Anna began to stutter as she slowly began to read.

Afraid of uttering a sound, they sat, each lost in her own thoughts. At first, her grandmother pretended to be unshaken by the news. Moments later, she sprang to her feet and nervously began to pace back and forth. Her hands tightly clasped behind her back, she repeated, "Guenter is serving the *vaterland*, no matter the cost! The führer will make everything *heil*. You will see during our upcoming rally!"

Anna began to pull the wooden wagon, rattling as though it was coming apart, up Römerberg while her grandmother pushed from behind. She placed the wagon into the shed in her grandmother's garden spot. After a quick hug, she left her grandmother standing at the front door. Her grandmother's stern departing glance saddened her, but the brilliant view of the sun, as it began to descend into the mountain range above the city, lifted her spirits.

Anna's mother stood in the corridor outside their apartment, waiting. Unable to conceal the squeaking sound of her door, an elderly woman, small in size, her face as yellow as the moon, stood and boldly listened without saying a word.

"I have been listening for your footsteps for hours, what did your grandmother have to say? Was she upset? Please tell me, it is important that I know. What exactly did she say?" her mother anxiously pressed on in a whisper.

Anna sat on the landing, nervously twisting her hands. She held back, and then hesitantly shared her grandmother's response, quoting her saying, "We must all be true to the *vaterland*!"

Her mother shook her head. "When will she ever see the truth?" Her mother's uncommonly agitated voice surprised Anna. "When will she ever see the truth?" She shook her head and quivered, "*Vaterland*—that's only another word for Hitler!"

"I believe Grandmother means well," Anna interrupted. She stood up to examine the wrinkles of her dress. "Please calm down, Mutti. After all, Grandmother still finds food to prepare our meals every day." She gently kissed her mother. "I have just enough time to check with Master Karl to see if he needs help."

Light rain that had fallen on the rubble of ruins a block away filled the air with a peculiar stench as she walked toward the Riding Academy. Her mother followed her into the street. "I am sorry, Anna, it is not fair to burden you with our disputes."

Anna took her hand and pulled her toward a bench outside the stables. "I'll be back shortly, and we will talk some more." Her soothing voice brought out a faint smile in her mother's face.

During the coming weeks, Anna's grandmother stayed much to herself. Sadness in her eyes illustrated a sorrow she could not hide. She avoided speaking to Anna's mother, so that Anna became their only source of communication.

Because of the frequent bombing sessions, all performances at the Opera House had again been cancelled. Anna missed bringing home the small compensation she earned from her performances. Finding their daily necessities became virtually impossible. "We'll make a little go a long way," Anna's mother cheerfully announced each day. But her voice sank as she reminded Anna, "Not knowing what lies ahead bothers me. But we cannot let this get us down," she insisted.

Anna's grandmother's prediction was wrong. Hitler was unable to heal anything. He was unable to cure the misery of the people. Cruelty of war trickled down even to his followers. Headlines in newspapers spoke of "heavy bombers, B-17s and B-24s, playing havoc with many cities. Fifty thousand people have been killed during air raids in Hamburg alone. American forces have joined the British air force, taking turns with their daytime and nighttime missions."

Sizes of planes meant nothing to Anna and her family. No one knew when the trapdoor of the planes opened. Worst than the rumbling of bombs and the horrible feeling of being shut inside a cellar below a five-story building was the fear of firebombs. No one knew what to expect from one moment to another.

At last, the silence between the two women came to a halt when Anna's grandmother returned from an exasperating trip to visit a cousin on a small farm in the foothills of the Black Forest. Carrying a shopping net filled with brown bags, she skipped up the four flights of stairs. Nearly out of breath, she impatiently rang the doorbell. "I have sent young Fritz, my neighbor's son, to invite Juergen, Inga, and the children over for dinner tomorrow evening," she gasped, pushing herself through the entrance.

Anna was amazed to see a sparkle in her grandmother's eyes. "I managed to bring back a generous supply of food from our cousin's farm. Stretch it as far as you can," she commanded Anna's mother while placing the basket of food in the cupboard.

Anna watched as her mother laboriously climbed the few stairs to her grandmother's apartment. She hoped with all her heart to see her mother smile again. "Maybe this day will be like the old times," she whispered as she helped her mother the last few stairs.

The aroma coming from their grandmother's apartment was unbelievable. She watched the beef brisket bubble in sauerkraut juice as her grandmother opened the lid of the heavy Dutch oven. "I added color to our meal with the carrots and potatoes from your friend Sabina's hotel garden," her grandmother added cheerfully.

Knowing that tensions might run high, Juergen arrived early with Inga and the children. "It took us nearly two hours to get here," he said, taking a puff on his pipe. "The trolleys were overloaded, people were hanging off the sides. So we kept walking until we got here."

They sat at her grandmother's huge dining-room table. Anna stared at the two empty chairs. Her favorite teddy sat in a third empty chair in the corner of the dining room. For as long as she could remember, she had secretly pretended that he was saving her father's seat until his return. It seemed natural to have Juergen sitting at the head of the table.

Inga served a cake while affectionately apologizing for not having the butter for crumbs again. Anna sat quietly and was thankful for an evening that brought memories of better times. Once again, she wondered if her father and better times would ever return.

With her typical authoritative tone, her grandmother plied Juergen with one question after the other. "Are you finding time to attend the local party meetings?" She looked around the table. "Why can't all of you show more enthusiasm and attend the meetings? Are all of you doing all you can to help our führer?"

The cuckoo in the old cuckoo clock broke a brief moment of silence. The grandmother jumped out of her chair and reached for the knob of her radio. "It is time for Dr. Goebbels's speech," she proclaimed.

"Keep up your spirits," Dr. Goebbels's stern voice began his speech over radio waves.

"How timely," whispered Juergen with a hint of sarcasm and a funny smirk on his face.

The lines on Anna's mother's forehead deepened. "I am very tired, we must go," she said, beginning to clear the table.

"We too must cut the evening short." Juergen rose to his feet and took hold of Inga's hand. His affection toward his wife and children touched Anna, who sat and watched. "As you know, it's a tough journey back. But we want the three of you to spend a Sunday with us next month."

Anna's face lit up. "Maybe the trolleys won't be quite as busy on Sunday. I will walk, even if it takes all day," Anna excitedly called out.

"I will make a star on your grandmother's calendar," Juergen said with a smile.

"A star? Over my dead body!" The grandmother jumped out of her chair and protested. "There are better ways to mark our calendar!" Her face flushed with anguish, she drew a swastika on her calendar that was graced with Hitler's picture.

Juergen had a real knack for making everyone laugh. Although it was difficult, this time he made light conversation and squeezed laughs out of everyone except the grandmother. Mostly, however, he said little but smiled mischievously. "Well, we almost made the evening without raising our voices." His final wink, as he closed the door behind them, relieved Anna's frustration. She stood in front of the calendar, the back of her hand pressed against her face. "Nearly five weeks," she whispered. "That's an eternity!"

Her mother looked over her shoulder, gently stroking Anna's long dark hair. "It is the weekend of Juergen's birthday!" She detected a touch of excitement in her mother's voice.

"Well, that makes waiting worthwhile." Anna embraced her mother.

"Not so hard, you are taking my breath away!" her mother laughed.

After grooming one of the mares.

A quiet moment at the Cathedral so characteristic of Anna's mother.

Chapter 11

1944 … Shocking developments.

Anna began each day by making a mark on Guenter's slate writing board. The invitation to visit Juergen's home, she soon discovered, was not the only event she had to look forward to.

Her mother sat quietly in their kitchen. She tilted her head to avoid the bright sunbeams bursting through the skylight. Her pretty face showed concern and stress as she nervously rubbed her fingers against the grain of the old wooden tabletop.

"What is wrong, Mutti?" Anna questioned.

"If we could just get hold of some signs of life from Guenter and Eric, just some signs of life!" her mother repeated. "Just some signs of life!" She arched her back. Sounds of footsteps interrupted her thoughts. Her body shook at the steel sound of the doorbell.

Anna ran to the door. "It's Herr Ramspott!"

With his face covered with flour, his apron tightly tied above his huge belly, Herr Ramspott fought to catch his breath. "You have a visitor, a man with his brewery wagon is looking for you, and he asked me to find you. He is attending his horses in front of the house."

Anna's mother ran down the landing of their steep stairwell. "I give up," she murmured, watching Anna slide down the wooden banister. Anna's mother held her back as they cautiously walked out to look over the mysterious stranger. Anna focused on the two gigantic horses.

"I see she loves horses," exclaimed the chubby and somewhat grubby-looking stranger. "They will get along just fine." His eyes sparkled from beneath his heavily bearded face.

Anna thoroughly examined the chestnut-colored horses. "I believe it is love at first sight!"

The stranger held out his rough-worn hand. "I am Rudolf Singer, your cousin's neighbor from down the Rhine Valley. Emma thought you two might welcome a few quiet days away from these air raids and wondered if you would like to catch a ride with me to her mother's farmhouse. I am making several trips to deliver these barrels to one of the makeshift hospitals not far from here. It will be a pleasure to be your servant if you two would like to catch a ride." He bowed as he tipped his frazzled hat.

With her head slightly tilted, Anna listened before asking the stranger, "Do these horses tire easily?" She pointed to their legs. "Their legs are so short, and their hooves are very small."

He shook his head and smiled. "By the way, their names are Lorilie and Goliath. Their ancestors came from Belgium. Heavens no! This pair can travel to the big brewery in Munich and back without running out of steam. That's just a bit exaggerated, of course." His belly bounced as he laughed.

Her mother pressed her thumb against her chin as she circled the wagon. Anna began to beg, both hands clasped. "Just think, Mutti, no air raids for a few days."

Her mother's frown turned into an irresistible grin. "You are right, Anna, the change will be good for us!"

"Your cousin will be delighted," Herr Singer responded with a smile. "We will pick you up early, around seven, okay?"

"Thank you, Herr Singer," her mother nodded.

"Rudolf will do just fine," the chubby stranger acknowledged as he jerked the rein. "*Komm schon!*" His signal perked up the ears of his horses. Anna watched and listened to the echoing of horses' hooves against the cobblestone street. She waved in delight until the wagon made its way around a group of Nazis pouring out of the beer garden across the street. Her mother briskly pulled her into the doorway and locked the massive door.

Anna went to bed early, a shopping bag of necessities beside her. No warning sirens cried out during the night, but the excitement of visiting her relatives on their farm in the Rhine Valley kept her awake. She wondered how she would meet future challenges expected of her. How would she divide her time? School, Hitler Youth meetings, the Opera House, the Riding Academy, her mother and grandmother. This left only rare possibilities to be with Sabina and her family.

Anna's mother smiled with pleasure as the team of horses and wagon appeared in the distance of a deserted avenue. "He certainly is punctual." With Rudolf's help, Anna pulled her mother up on the wagon seat. Her mother apologized with a groan. "It's my arthritic condition that keeps me from moving about the way I used to."

As the old beer wagon made its way through the war-torn city, Anna sat quietly between her mother and yet another newfound friend. She listened to Rudolf's attempt to make small talk about better times.

"I hope your grandmother finds our note," her mother whispered.

"She will probably be very upset about my missing the Hitler Youth meeting," Anna responded. A mixture of delight and fear came through her voice.

"There is your cousin!" Rudolph pointed his pipe toward an open field as Anna's personal fairyland came into view. Responding to the newly harvested hay, the horses gave out a vigorous sound. The wagon still in motion, Anna jumped off and ran to Emma. A burst of tears and a warm hug overpowered Emma's strong odor of perspiration. She apologized, "It's so tough with all the men gone to fight this crazy war. All of this harvest with the help of only a seventy-year-old uncle, myself, and my mother." She wiped her forehead and frowned.

"About all we can do is to keep our animals alive. The children are at the schoolhouse. They will be ecstatic when they see you." With a quick pat on Anna's backside, Emma ordered Anna, "Go in the house." Her tone changed, "Mother has a little surprise for you. She has been waiting for you for hours."

Anna nodded and looked around. The mountains and meadows, the crisp air—this moment seemed too good to be true. She tried hard not to contemplate on the more serious developments that lay ahead, but to take pleasure in watching her mother relax on Emma's family's farm.

Inside the tiny and neat farmhouse, Anna found Emma's mother stirring the fire in the old wooden kitchen stove. An arrangement of wildflowers adorned the tiny kitchen. "I was beginning to get worried, but I am so glad you are here." Emma's mother embraced the two visitors, and then led Anna into a sparsely furnished loft. "I wanted you to have a place of your own when you come for a visit," she whispered.

Anna smiled. "That's not all!" the old woman said, walking across the room toward a miniature bed. "I couldn't find new yarn, but I was able to unravel one of Emma's outgrown sweaters."

Anna's eyes sparkled. "Thank you!" She cuddled the newly knit sweater in her arms. "It is incredibly beautiful, and you knitted it just for me? It's blue like the sky!" she shouted.

Her mother stood and watched. "You are so kind," she said softly.

At night, with the window open in the tiny loft, Anna felt safe and secure. She dreamed about living in this tranquil place, but she also knew this would be out of the question.

Huge posters adorned the columns in front of the Opera House and in nearby parks. "All events are cancelled until further notice," stated the posters in bold black letters. The five-story Opera House looked deserted. In the afternoons, Anna spent brief moments on the roof garden sunbathing with friends. From there, they saw evidence of their neighborhood turning to rubble from falling bombs during the night. It seemed strange that the enemy very carefully avoided bombing historical sites, such as the Opera House and the exquisite hotels nearby.

Soon came the shock. As usual, everyone responded to Herr Kummel's request to meet in the rehearsal hall. "I have some good news and I have some bad news." Herr Kummel anxiously ran his fingers through his thick gray hair. "The good news," his eyes sparkled from beneath his bifocals, "is that Dr. Goebbels has arranged a grant for all members of this beautiful institution." He walked over and lifted Anna's chin with his forefinger. "Dr. Goebbels even remembered our little ones. While the sum is small," he continued, "compensations await you in the accountant's office." Smiles on everyone's faces brought a flash of light into the dimly lit rehearsal hall.

But Herr Kummel's handsome, wrinkled face quickly changed to a more somber expression as he began to pace nervously. "The bad news," he said, his voice beginning to falter, "is that the führer has asked that all of you perform certain duties in your free time for the cause of winning this war. Details are sketchy, but we will meet again, at which time you will receive further instructions. All schoolchildren are to report each afternoon immediately after school. I know nothing further at this time. Please refer to our bulletin board regarding time and place of our next meeting."

At that next meeting, the unbearable stench of a mountain of shabby and grimy uniforms greeted everyone in the gigantic art and props studio. An army transport truck's engine idled outside the receiving ramp. Anna paid no attention to two high-ranking SS officers pacing the floor near the entrance. Instead, she focused on the spectacular backdrop of the second-act finale of the *Fledermaus* ready to be displayed on the enormous stage at a moment's notice.

Without introduction, his leather club pointing to the masses of uniforms, one of the officers began to speak in a controlling manner. In utter amazement, Anna looked over and recognized the colonel she had visited in the sanatorium. She listened cautiously.

"The führer has called you to work!" the colonel commanded. "These uniforms will be used as decoys in frontline trenches in Russia. Your job is to paint and disinfect each and every one. Fifty thousand of these uniforms are to be shipped to our soldiers who fight this war for you. They are to camouflage their bodies in the snow. Those who refuse in this important endeavor must be summoned to a hearing with our regional SS group leader. Are there any questions?"

Throwing his right arm in front of him, with a click of his heels and a strong "*heil* Hitler," he dismissed the group in a soldierly manner and then vanished into the dark corridor. No one dared to speak. Only heavy breathing broke the utter stillness of the stench-filled studio.

This did not discourage the region's most talented artists. One of the young musicians broke the strange hush. He looked at the group and took an estimate. "I have a suggestion!" He brushed his thick, curly hair from his forehead. "Let us take a vote for a group leader. I shall be honored to recommend Ernst Schreiner to serve as our leader. May I see a hand to second my suggestion?" One by one, everyone followed with obvious respect.

Ernst Schreiner, the shy young man who created phenomenal stagecraft and who for many years served as overseer of the spectacular task of restoring and developing new stage props, stood up and took a bow. A forced smile drew across his good-looking face. "I will accept under one condition!" His smile turned into laughter. "We must turn this stinking studio into a musical place. Let us begin by opening the doors. With fresh air in our lungs, we will sing and dance as we work." He looked around the group as he threw open the huge doors of the loading ramp. Everyone cheered with approval. "You young acrobats and dancers," he pointed to Anna, "please make a sweep through this five-story building and locate every mannequin in our inventory!"

Conductors, choir members, stage directors, stagehands, ballet master and lead dancers, everyone pitched in to keep this treacherous assignment from tearing their team spirit apart. Music, singing, and laughter soon overshadowed the offensive smell, while trucks continued to unload mounds of uniforms each day. Anna's task was to remove rank and decorative items from the uniforms before others arranged them onto the mannequins to receive a solution of paint and disinfectant. "There must be a story behind each of these men," Anna reminisced, placing each item in a huge felt-lined box.

Because no one complained, Colonel Schneider arranged for bagged lunches to be delivered daily. Secretively, Anna took half of her lunch to her mother. On one occasion, unaware of Colonel Schneider's presence and absorbed by the sound of Vienna waltzes coming through the sound system, Anna pretended she was dancing with the uniformed mannequin the lead dancer was beginning to paint.

"Anna, Anna," he called to her, but she paid no attention and continued her flowing dance around the mannequin.

She looked down at her feet and stopped. She saw her light blue sweater reflected in a pair of shiny black boots and two unusual brass buckles she recognized. "I am sorry," she timidly apologized. "I am truly sorry, Colonel Schneider."

"Well, don't be sorry. At least you remember my name! I will look forward to seeing all of you perform when our lives get back to some kind of normalcy." The colonel smiled. "Oh, and from now on," he made a quick turn, "please feel free to take a bagged lunch to your mother, and you do not need to hide it under your jacket."

He fumbled for an apple in the lining of his leather coat. "Here is an apple for your favorite horse. Rubin, I believe, is his name? You should do something about that! Our führer does not approve of such a name. *Heil* Hitler!" He smiled at the stunned lead dancer and, with a click of his heels, walked away.

"Thank you," Anna said as she clutched the bright red apple in her hand. "Perhaps the colonel is just a person like us."

The lead dancer's eyebrows rose above his hairline. "I know," she whispered. "You are afraid to say."

Time seemed to pass quickly. Chilly nights indicated fall would soon arrive. Anna's mother dreaded the thought of winter. Enemy bombers were becoming increasingly more aggressive. She was desperately concerned over Anna's health. At every turn, disarray showed its ugly head. She fought hard to remain positive. "After all," she reminded Anna each day, "we still have some food. God has blessed us, truly blessed us. Even with little food and sleep, we can make it. There is hope!" Against all odds, Anna's mother remained steadfast in her faith. She continued to take Anna for long hikes into the mountain range. "It is here, in God's nature, that we hear His voice, but we have to be willing to listen," she told Anna.

Anna kept the stench in which she worked and the disgusting labor imposed upon everyone in the Opera House a secret. She shared only the occurrences that pleased her. "I just don't want to worry my mother," she shared with her friend Lori. "She is so frail, and if she knew who gives us the bagged lunch, she wouldn't touch it! My grandmother spends all of her time now searching for food. We have learned how to be frugal."

Unconcerned, Lori did not respond. She lacked nothing. Her father, a high-ranking Nazi official, managed to get food from the Netherlands and cheeses from France. Even the soft and fuzzy angora sweaters she often wore came from France.

Another night of intense bombing kept everyone agitated and confined to the air-raid shelter. This time, an unfamiliar whistle accompanied the falling bombs. Juergen's earlier assumption of falling bombs was correct. Last night's bombs fell convincingly close. Anna climbed the hill toward her schoolhouse. She dreaded this day. A day earlier, Herr Dietz spoke of an exam but gave no specific instructions. Once again, Anna felt unprepared, intimidated, and frightened.

Light rain began to fall. A block away, an old woman dug through the rubble of her apartment house and screamed, "The enemy leveled our home during the night. I don't know where they are!" She pointed to a mountain of crumbled walls. "My daughter, my granddaughters, and my sister!" She cupped her face with her grimy hands. "I have not seen them! Our neighbors, everyone is under these ruins!" She kicked a mound of dirt. Smudges covered her face. Anna rubbed her eyes from the burning smell of ashes and dust. She walked over to comfort the old woman. "Leave me alone," the hysterical old woman screamed. "Just leave me alone!"

"I am sorry, so sorry," Anna whispered and walked away.

Only a small number of students made their way toward the partially collapsed schoolhouse. A huge sign leaned against a barricade that read, "Danger, keep out!" Smoke and dust enveloped the grounds of the old schoolhouse. Anna felt bad about the damage to the schoolhouse, but the anxiety of facing Herr Dietz vanished instantly. "No school today," she sighed as she wasted no time in making her way to the Riding Academy. There she would find temporary security with her beloved horses.

At the entrance to the stables, she found Master Karl staring into space. A group of unfamiliar young mares stood nearby. Deep sores and mud covered their skin. Maggots invaded their ears. "They can barely stand. They are only skeletons!" Anna examined one of the mares, which buried her face into Anna's thick long hair.

Master Karl scratched his shiny, balding head. "Our soldiers, I believe, abandoned these poor critters during the night. We have no choice but to end their miserable existence."

"No, no!" Anna screamed. "Please, please, Master Karl, can I take care of them? Sabina will help. We will take them to pasture and brush them every day."

A smile crossed the lines of Master Karl's bearded face. "It will take much more than that! Their sores need constant cleaning. But all right! I'll show you how to prepare the solution. Anyway, I would not want these critters to miss knowing you amazing young girls. Besides, by the looks of it, the war cannot go on much longer!" he moaned from obvious weariness and exertion.

Conditions at the Riding Academy continued to worsen. Several times each week, Anna met Sabina and her cousin Ushi at the hotel to make use of a trailer to haul scraps from the hotel kitchen to the stables. This required muscle action. SS guards posted outside the service entrance of the hotel hurled sarcastic remarks as the girls pulled the heavy contraption through the park and across the cobblestone street to the Riding Academy.

Because of continuous air raids, all schools in Anna's district remained closed. This gave Anna time to attend to the needs of the horses. Anna had grown accustomed to hunger pains. While out in the meadow, she gathered the dandelion greens her grandmother taught her to select for salads. Sabina remained steadfast in sharing potatoes and other vegetables on a regular basis from her grandfather's hotel garden.

"Only three more days before we visit Juergen," Anna said softly as her mother walked into her bedroom.

"We cannot even enjoy the view out to the garden," her mother protested. She pointed to newly repaired windows charred out during a recent night of bombing. "They can't even repair our windows with glass!" She ran her fingers across the quilted plastic paper improvised for glass. "I am not complaining, Anna. After all, we still have each other."

She fumbled for an envelope from her apron pocket. An alarming expression came over her face. "We have news from Eric. It is quite disturbing." She took a deep breath and handed the soiled letter to Anna.

"Dear family," Eric wrote. "I cannot go into details—please understand. Conditions here at Hitler's headquarters have worsened. I can tell you that Hitler is taking residence here. He is now in charge and promises he will never leave Berlin. There is dissention and firing going on at the top within the command post. Hitler makes no bones about it: since his assassination attempt, he does not trust anyone. This, of course, puts all of us in danger. My apartment no longer exists. One of Churchill's bombs claimed it last night. Everything around me is in ruins. I am sticking my neck out as I write, and I am not sure that I will make it. Know that I love you, and I still have hope of *ein-wieder-sehen*." Eric added a P.S. for Anna: "Please remember our little talks of not too long ago."

Anna's mother placed the letter next to her statue of Mary. "She will pray for him," she sighed. A sparkle of excitement returned to her face. "Juergen's birthday is only three days away. I know you are anxiously waiting for the moment." She held Anna close to her.

Without exception, everyone began to suffer. Fleeing nightly to cold, damp, and musty-smelling air-raid shelters became increasingly more nerve-wracking. Moans of anguish from the old and cries of restless, hungry children filled the air. From time to time, the roaring and shrieking sounds of planes falling to the ground brought Anna's mother to her knees. "Someone is losing a loved one. It is so senseless, so senseless!" she cried aloud.

The magnificent Opera House.

Sunning on the roof garden

Near the sculpture

CHAPTER 12

1944 … Mandatory public burning of all books.

Over the *Deutsche Rundfunk* (radio broadcast), men in Hitler's top command continued to paint portraits of Hitler as if he were God. "Our nation is unshakable!" insisted Dr. Goebbels. His words, however, turned into dust. People began to doubt their propaganda. Leaflets printed by one of the SS publications stated and called for drastic action against any citizen who grumbled against the war or doubted Hitler's final victory.

Soon, however, Hitler's efforts in smoothing his peoples' anxiety failed—but he kept shouting with his high-pierced voice at occasional rallies and over the radio. He insisted that his people fight to their death and refused to stop brainwashing the children. "Our task is great," he yelled over Hamburg radio. "We must train the young to serve the *volksland*!" It became more and more obvious that Germany's military situation was getting desperate.

Determined to give the German people just one more shot in the arm, Dr. Goebbels reached for straws by joining Hitler in his endeavor of calling for total commitment to "Hitler's cause." He ordered old men and children to give "one more fight." This last scrape of manpower became known as the *Volkssturm* (Home Guard). Daily, a local Nazi leader announced on street corners, "Just have patience, we must continue to look at Hitler for strength and hope. Soon, the führer is coming out with a new weapon!"

During the winter months, those rumors continued to surface. Even Anna's grandmother made an effort to relieve Anna's mother's anxiety, reminding her that "the führer is about to come out with a new weapon."

No one understood the meaning of this. Remarks and rumors were not taken lightly by the tired and confused people trying so desperately to hold on to a spark of hope. Curiosity over flying objects crossing dark skies in the night drew them out of air-raid shelters. Anna's mother also got caught up in the frenzy. On one occasion, she and Anna stood mesmerized watching an object that looked like a fierce, soundless, flying creature crossing the atmosphere.

Each day, loudspeakers roared through the streets ordering that all books written by Jewish and foreign authors must be burned. "There will be severe punishment for those who refuse to adhere to this announcement."

Anna's mother exploded in anger. "They will not take everything from us." She refused to take Guenter's collection of books to the street for burning.

Anna knew that Guenter loved his collection of books and kept them orderly on his bookshelves, but she was afraid for her family's personal safety. While her mother was away, and afraid of repercussions from the local Nazi Party members, Anna took the books of foreign history and Jewish authors and placed them on a huge pile behind their house to be burned. A feeling of remorse and guilt came over her as the flames reached for the sky. With her head hung in shame, she walked away as a nearby loudspeaker played one of Hitler's favorite Alpine folk songs: "In the meadow stands a tiny flower, and its name is 'Edelweiss.'"

A clanging sound of the doorbell through the intercom from below startled Anna and her mother during their meager evening meal of bread and butter. Anna left her bread on the wooden breadboard. She skipped down the stairwell and across the courtyard. The massive door gave a loud squeak. A reflection of bright moonlight revealed a smile on a handsome bearded face. "Juergen!" Anna screamed.

"Surprise!" he whispered. "Quiet," he pressed his forefinger against her lips. Anna embraced his tall, slender figure. He flung her around in a spin. "Quiet, quiet," he urged. "Stop squealing!"

"I have missed you so much," she cried, "and we are excited about visiting you on Sunday, just two more days!"

"Where is your mother?" Juergen inquired. He retrieved a small paper bag from his truck and placed it in Anna's arms. "Some goat cheese and butter for both of you from my friend's farm down the Rhine Valley. I can't stay, but take these and give my love to your mother. We will see you in two days!"

Night had fallen. Amused at the sound of his three-wheel truck, Anna watched him drive away into the darkened streets. "Just two more days," she whispered, clutching the brown paper bag and skipping across the courtyard toward their apartment. Her eyes sparkled. "Look, Mutti, some cheese and butter for our bread."

Another night of heavy bombing left Anna's school totally in ruins. Makeshift classes were held in a building that once served as a movie theater. Teachers were dispersed into various locations. To Anna's delight, Herr Dietz was nowhere around.

For the first time, boys and girls attended the same classes. All children welcomed this refreshing change. Alfred, a younger brother of Guenter's friend, noticed Anna's struggle with math. He quickly came to her rescue during study periods. For the first time, she was seated in front so that she could easily follow instructions her new teacher presented. She enjoyed these rare moments in school without fear of reprisals.

"Just one more day, and not a sound all night!" She reached to shut off the huge alarm clock next to her bed. "It is so wonderful not to wake up tired," she whispered to her mother in the next room.

Elated with her new arrangement in school, she skipped around and over the rubbish still blocking the sidewalks. Light rain had fallen during the night, which left a heaviness in the air.

She reminisced about all she had to do during the day and wondered what might happen if she did not report for her duty at the Opera House that afternoon. "That is far too risky," she sighed. "Besides, I am already hungry, and I would not be able to bring Mutti her bagged lunch. I will make it!"

Much to her delight, she passed a test at school, reported to her duties at the Opera House, helped Master Karl with the horses, and even spent time with her friend Sabina at the hotel at the end of the day, where she was able to take a warm shower and wash her hair. She was pleased that her grandmother chose to attend a Nazi rally instead of making the trip to Juergen's. "There won't be anyone there to argue," she stubbornly shared with her mother.

Sirens did not disrupt her sleep during the early hours of the night, but shortly after midnight, without a warming, an earsplitting boom sounded. Moments later, sirens began to shriek through the night. Everyone dispersed into the air-raid shelter and sat silently staring into the dimly lit space. Finally, the second signal announced that danger was over. Anna and her mother joined neighbors and ventured into the street to look for an explanation. Only the brilliant red sky in the east indicated that a huge fire reached for the sky. Anna's mother sobbed uncontrollably. "We escaped whatever happened, but those poor people!" Anna tried to comfort her, but to no avail. From the distance, rumbling continued until early morning hours.

Without sleep and exhausted, Anna and her mother fought their way through the crowd of people who searched for a ride to various parts of the torn-up city. A mixture of fear and excitement at seeing Juergen and his family on this day overwhelmed them both. A young soldier, his head and shoulder wrapped in blood-soaked bandages, helped Anna's mother onto the crowded bus. With both hands raised high above his head, the bus driver, frail and tired, yelled to the crowd, "Please step back!" The soldier quickly grabbed Anna by her arm and pulled her through the revolving door.

Because of massive debris along the route, the usual twenty-minute ride to Juergen's neighborhood took nearly two hours. Along the way, Anna wondered what her brother might think if he saw the desolation of their city.

Bewildered and mystified, the bus driver shrugged his shoulders. "As you can see," he brought the bus to a screeching halt, "we can go no further!" His grubby bearded face seemed pail. Anna anxiously squeezed through the passengers standing in the aisle. "I will wait for you outside!" she turned quickly and called to her mother.

On the torn-up sidewalk, she stood confused and perplexed. Unable to recognize Juergen's neighborhood, she reached for her mother's hand. "Where are we?" Anna cried.

Anna's mother pressed her fist against her chest. "I do not know!" Her voice trembled.

Anna recognized Juergen's three-wheel truck a block away and ran to get a closer look. Her mother, struggling to find strength, ran behind her. Anna wiped the dust from the front window on the driver's side. A large piece of shrapnel had landed on the seat. "I am glad Juergen was not in the truck when this happened," Anna said, her body trembling as she gasped for breath.

They turned and stared at a deep crater across the street. "Juergen, Juergen," Anna screamed. An elderly gentleman walked up from behind, his face covered with soot. He gently touched Anna's shoulder. A Red Cross band wrapped the sleeve of his torn jacket. "There is no one left!" Tears ran down the old man's battered face. "My wife, daughter, and grandchildren are under there also." He pointed to a reflection of a single five-story apartment building leveled to the ground. "That's all that is left from the entire city block!" He cried hysterically.

Anna covered her mouth to avoid swallowing the dust that filled the air. "What does he mean also?" she said, and felt troubled.

With her mother by her side, Anna stood motionless, paying no attention to the stench that surrounded them. "There is no one left, there is no one left!" The old man's voice reverberated in Anna's ears. She sat on a torn-up park bench, pressed the palms of her hands tightly together, and cried, "Juergen and Inga, where are you?"

Her mother reached for her hand and, with apprehension, suggested, "We must find our way back home."

But Anna refused to budge. "I will not leave here until I find Juergen. He promised to be here for us. Don't you remember?" Her face pale and wet with tears, she ran into the mountain of dirt before her. "Juergen, Juergen," she shouted until her vocal cords no longer obliged her.

Anna was unable to recall details from the bleak surroundings of the once upscale neighborhood and artistically landscaped parks Juergen and his family called home. What stood out in her mind, as they finally began their journey back home, was a sign an old woman erected in the rubble that read: "We don't know who the enemy is. We do know that he can crumble our walls, but not our hearts!" She felt troubled to watch a few lone survivors as they walked around in a daze, homeless, hungry, helpless, alone. No one came to their rescue.

Anna reached for her mother's hand and said, "Let us sit for a moment." They sat on a block of cement to unlace their badly worn shoes, offended by the gravel of debris, and watch the fires still raging, their flames reaching for the sky and turning it a deep purple. There were no firefighters to fight the flames, no one to offer condolences, no arms to reach for a hug, no one to explain the events that led to the obliteration of several city blocks and their innocent residents.

Though no one publicly dared to speak about it, rumors surfaced weeks later that one of Hitler's V-1 rockets unintentionally fell onto his own people. Her voice consumed with anger, Anna's mother questioned the grandmother. "Is this the new weapon Hitler's people have been bragging about? Killing our own people? Nearly all we had left in our family?"

Much to Anna's surprise, her grandmother's demeanor suddenly changed. She withdrew from all Nazi meetings and concerted her efforts on helping Anna and her mother survive. She no longer spoke about Hitler, nor did she throw blame on Anna's father for the family's hardship. The grandmother did not speak about Juergen, but showed concern about Guenter and Eric's return, spending much of her time with Anna's mother in peace and harmony. Anna welcomed this change. She no longer worried about her mother moment by moment.

Regardless of weather conditions, she continued daily to take the horses out into the hills and mountain range. There, as she cared for the horses, she was able to meditate and mourn for Juergen and his family without interruption.

Because of increased bombings, Sabina's mother invited Anna to spend nights at the hotel's air-raid shelter. "I don't believe the enemy will bomb our hotel. They will need this magnificent place when this crazy war is over." Anna recalled her prophetic comment. This lightened her mother's burden. "I believe you will be much safer there," Anna's mother assured her.

"My prayers are being answered all around us!" Her mother's thoughts seemed far away as she observed the grandmother flick a pinch of salt into a pot of potatoes and cabbage.

Anna frowned as the old cuckoo clock above the kitchen table made known the hour. "Colonel Schneider called for a meeting with good news, and I cannot be late!" She frantically placed her empty plate onto the cupboard and kissed both women on the cheek before rushing out the door.

With great anticipation, everyone sat and patiently waited to hear the colonel's familiar footsteps. Pale-faced, with deep circles under his eyes and a slight smile, he removed his hat and began to speak: "As of today, you will no longer serve our führer in the capacity you have served him for the past few months—with great courage, I might add. Thanks to you, our soldiers are now sufficiently supplied. To show the führer's gratitude, we will continue to serve bagged lunches for each of you for two additional weeks."

No one dared to speak. Then Herr Kummel broke the silence. "Are we given a new assignment, Colonel Schneider?"

The colonel's customary stern expression changed into a weak smile. "There will be no other assignment. But may I suggest you people take advantage of the day hours while our enemy is quiet up there," he pointed heavenward, "and nurture your talents? Perhaps we will meet again soon during better times!" The familiar and sudden click of the heels of his boots rang with an echo through the hall.

"So what are we waiting for?" One of the stagehands leaped across the room. "Let's get ready for our upcoming *Maifest*!" he shouted. Herr Kummel quickly responded and wasted no time in organizing customary rehearsals.

Within walking distance of the Opera House, an elegant villa, flanked by well-groomed shrubs and lawns, served as one of many makeshift infirmaries for wounded soldiers around the city. A respected Jewish banker had lived there until local Nazi members abruptly, before dawn, deported him to a so-called summer camp.

Each afternoon, a group of wounded soldiers made their way in wheelchairs, on crutches, and by whatever means possible to listen to the music through a torn-down wall near the stage area of the Opera House. Increasing in numbers each week, they hungered for a taste of "normal times."

"Normal times will return real soon," one recently blinded soldier whimpered.

With the grandmother's change of heart—her earlier enthusiasm and commitment for Hitler declining and eventually turning into anger—Anna's mother grew physically and emotionally stronger each day. She would not wander far from her immediate surroundings, hoping and praying for news about Eric and Guenter. Wherever and whenever possible, she searched for words of encouragement.

Anna spent all of her time within four city blocks. Schools were temporarily shut down, and no one knew when and if they would reopen. With mandatory duties at the Opera House brought to an end, she continued to focus on caring for her beloved horses. She felt privileged and honored to spend nights at the hotel's bunker and took full advantage of the short distance through the park to deliver baskets of leftover food from the hotel kitchen Sabina arranged for her and to check on her mother.

In early summer, rumors continued to spread that the enemy had landed on the beaches in France and would soon reach the Rhine. Bridges were reported down all along the Rhine, and for the first time, Hitler's people revealed news of the massive surrender of German soldiers on the banks of the Rhine. "There is no cause for fear, and we are proud to have successfully launched Germany's V-1, our first pilotless plane over Britain, causing unimaginable damage. We are weakening the enemy," Hitler's top guns boasted across the region.

All of this took place in freezing temperatures. With no place to go, neighbors hauled away their few possessions on carts or broken-down sleds, pulling them through the slush of melted snow and ice.

No one was able to comprehend the immensity of the danger, nor anticipate the harshness of the months that lay ahead. Corridors in schools still standing were converted into hospital wards. In some areas of the city, badly injured people lay in the streets. Because of the "Red Cross" on their rooftops, hospitals remained untouched by bombings, but conditions inside the buildings were nothing short of chaotic, with the smell of death everywhere.

From the skies, bombers unleashed strange and unexplainable bombs that ignited fires on contact in all directions, with smoke clouds visible across the city. Lack of sleep and inadequate nourishment took a toll on everyone. Shelves in stores remained empty, the doors shut. In torn-up and cluttered streets, children played games competing to see who could find the largest pieces of shrapnel.

The owner of the Riding Academy, with a standing reputation of being not only the most excellent but also the most compassionate trainer of thoroughbred horses in the region, made an unexpected visit to the stables. Extreme back pain resulting from a fall during a jumping expedition hindered his daily activities among the horses. He could only spend short periods of time exercising his two white Lipizzaner stallions. Though he was once tall and striking in appearance, his shoulders now slumped over his well-dressed stature. His pasty complexion and deep lines revealed profound concern.

He stood in dismay as he glanced over his undernourished horses. "They are just skin and bones," he said, staring intently into the stall of his personal stallion. "I do not know how much longer we can wait before making the decision of whether or not we need to put these fine animals to rest. There is sadness instead of sparkle in their eyes. I find it unbearable to watch them. To save their lives, we need salt blocks, hay, and grain now, before diarrhea sets in." He stared at fewer than a dozen bags of grain. He knew that it would only be matter of time before he would have to make his heart-wrenching decision about the fate of the horses.

Through a reliable but undisclosed source, Master Karl learned that unusual activities in the sky developed approximately fifty kilometers from the city. "You are no longer safe out in the open, and I expect you to take extreme caution," he constantly reminded everyone willing to help with the horses.

With time on their hands, the girls refused to give up. Only days later, after listening to Master Karl's concerned lectures, the girls led several horses through a shortcut to their usual hillside to search for a spot of grass on which they could feed. It became apparent that the horses had become sluggish. The reality of the fate of the horses troubled the girls, leaving them without their usual gusto. Instead of riding, the girls led the horses on even the slightest inclines.

They stopped to catch a deep breath. "Look at this view!" Sabina pointed to the city below. Suddenly, the horses became restless. Somewhat concerned, Anna looked around and handed the reins to Sabina. Just a few feet away, she discovered a small opening into the wooded area. Camouflaged with underbrush, a number of deserted military trucks with no signs of life came into view. She cautiously moved forward to take a closer look. Fear struck Sabina, who motioned Anna to leave as the horses became more fidgety. "Just one moment," Anna waved to Sabina. With great effort, she opened one of the trucks. A loud clang startled the horses. Anna cupped her chin into both hands and turned to Sabina.

"Look what we found!" Her voice echoed across the hillside. The horses pulled toward her and returned her excitement with an exhilarating whinnying, disbursing a sleepy owl perched on his roosting branch. Huge stacks of hay filled the truck from top to bottom.

"Do you think it is all right to feed our critters?" Sabina asked.

"Of course!" Anna agreed.

Losing track of time and standing in the shivering cold did not seem to matter. The sound of the famished horses crunching away on the hay was music to the girls' ears. "Isn't this great?" Sabina broke out in laughter and swung Anna around.

Snow began to fall steadily as Anna and Sabina made their way back to the stables, leading their horses satisfied and with renewed energy. Master Karl stood outside the stables waiting for their return. Trying to stay warm, he nervously paced back and forth, occasionally gazing at the gigantic clock that graced the church steeple nearby. A sigh of relief came over his tired face when he saw them. He raised his arms high above his head as he took note of the shadows of horses approaching the stables.

His puzzled face concerned both girls. "Do you think Master Karl is displeased with us?" Sabina asked.

"What have you done to our critters?" he asked. "They are not the same horses I sent you out with!"

In a steady stream, they shared their findings of an exciting afternoon. Consumed with delight, Master Karl sat and listened. He scratched and shook his bald head with amazement.

"And there is much more for the others!" Sabina balled her fist as a victory gesture.

"That was my next question. Can we take the others to the site? But first, we must get permission!" His voice faltered. "We'll wax our skis. The snow will be lovely tomorrow, and we will ski up to explore." Master Karl embraced the girls with humble gratitude and enthusiasm.

After the blizzard subsided, Sabina and Anna set out to further investigate their newfound source of food for the horses. Because Anna did not have adequate shoes for skies, her mother gave her permission to buckle up her brother's old boots and skis.

"You may break your neck in those!" Sabina said, looking over Anna's concoction of skis. "We'll find you better ones when we get back!"

At the last moment, Alfred, another of Master Karl's students, asked to join the girls on their adventure. "He will be good for protection," Master Karl suggested with his typical quirky grin while looking at the boy's frail stature.

With the cold wind biting their faces, the magical winter scene, with the sun making its way through the snow-covered trees, made the search of the unknown exciting. "The weather is perfect for skiing," Sabina shrieked. Not far from the site of the deserted hay, the children noticed a cloud of smoke. "Shall we go there?" Sabina's eyes squinted from the bright, sun-drenched snow. Alfred gave a nod. Slowly and guardedly, the children approached a small campfire. Crackling sounds from a radio nearby startled them. Unaware of three strangers' approach, a young boy wearing a uniform much too large for his size sat and looked into space. A swastika was wrapped around his left sleeve.

"He is my brother's age," Anna whispered.

Sabina began to talk nonstop. "We must find the people who can give us permission to get the hay in the trucks." Her fingers began to tremble as she pointed in the direction of the abandoned vehicles.

"*Heil* Hitler!" The boy stood and held up his right arm. "There is no one around," he continued in a hushed tone. He pointed to a familiar inn nearby. "Everyone has gone. I was told to stay and guard what is left. There is no food, only a few turnips. That is all. The hay you mentioned does not belong to anyone. It too has been abandoned. Do you have something to eat?"

A soft gleam came over Sabina's face. She loosened the straps of her backpack and reached for a piece of bread and cheese. "This is all we have, but I will do my best to bring you something else if you give us permission to bring some of our horses tomorrow to munch on the hay."

The boy smiled. "Would you like some coffee?" He pointed to a rusty coffeepot on his campfire. "It's real coffee," he assured them.

"No thanks," Anna said, looking at a soiled coffee mug close by.

"I am Klaus, and my home is in Darmstadt." With the grimy gloves that covered his hands, he reached for the children's hands.

"Pleased to make your acquaintance," Sabina chimed in.

"We will bring our horses to meet you early in the morning," they responded in unison as they skied down the hillside.

Excitement over the temporary relief of the discomfort the horses suffered from underfeeding spread quickly among the students who only infrequently partook in Master Karl's attempt to keep the horses alive. "I believe someone must still have means of transportation to help us," he grumbled. "I suppose they just don't want to stick their necks out.

Everyone has problems. At least so far, the bombs have not hit our stables." His face changed from disgust to a humble frown.

Helga, Anna's Hitler Youth leader, sent an unexpected message to all girls in the district nearing their fourteenth birthday. "You are summoned to an important meeting at noon on Saturday at our usual meeting place. No excuses will be accepted! Be prepared to join our *Bund Deutscher Mädel.* We will discuss your assignments for the *pflichtenjahr* [year of obligation]."

"Is this my fourteenth birthday present? Just more chores, more responsibility, and we are not even getting our education?" Anna objected.

But her mother calmly explained, "You have no choice. Things cannot continue this way. Have faith, things will be better soon," she repeated with confidence.

The girls sat and listened closely to the new demands from their leader. The smell of beer and stale cigarette smoke added to the depressing mood of the deserted pub that served as their meeting room. "*Heil* Hitler!" The stern voice of the chubby and boyish-looking Hitler Youth leader demanded attention. "We have orders from Gertrud Scholtz-Klink, our leader, that effective immediately you are to report weekly to domestic service. Our trained guardians will meet you at your designated location to teach you your tasks."

"What is bothering you?" Anna asked her mother, who was unable to conceal the sudden blotches on her smooth-skinned face.

She gave Anna a hard stare. "This is another so-called duty I am most uncomfortable with. I will go with you and find out who these people are and the reason for your volunteer services."

"Don't worry, I am almost fourteen!" Anna contested, somewhat annoyed at her mother's concern.

"That is my point!" Anna's mother returned her irritated response.

"Promise me you will not embarrass me?" Anna begged.

"All right, I will only stand watch nearby, and I will not say a word."

Anna smiled at her mother's restored wittiness.

Anna pressed the bright yellow apron Emma had made for her during their last visit. She twisted her long hair into a French twist and took one look in the mirror. "I am glad you are coming with me part of the way," she confessed to her mother. "And don't worry, I'll pretend I am in a play."

Arm in arm, they walked the short distance through the familiar park leading up the steep hill near the cable car toward Anna's designated address and began to locate the street number. Her mother stopped abruptly. "This is the Kaufmann's address. They were close friends of Ellie's mother," she said in a low voice. "They have been gone for quite some time. I wonder, could they have returned? Or, who knows?" she quipped.

Her mother was correct. The new name, Schuster, appeared over the scratched out name of Kaufmann on the directory. "Mutti, please don't leave me. This is nerve-racking," Anna humbly admitted. She pressed the button.

Through the intercom, a polished Austrian voice began to speak. "This is Colonel Schuster, may I help you?"

Lost for words, Anna stood silent for a moment. She looked for her mother, who had found rest on a stone wall leading to the entrance. *Another colonel*, thought Anna. She moved her lips but did not dare to speak.

"Hallo!" The colonel pressed for a reply.

Anna began to stutter, "My name is Anna and I am here to meet a guardian from our Hitler Youth group who will show me how I can help you as a volunteer."

"I do not know about a guardian, but please come up." The automatic door opened and Anna stepped into the elegant two-story apartment house. Dressed in typical Austrian attire, the attractive young-looking colonel greeted her in a most gentlemanly manner. Paralyzed on one side of his body, he apologized for his clumsy walk with the help of a cane. A black bandage covered his left eye. Thick blonde curls swirled loosely around his handsome face.

He led her through the neatly and beautifully furnished apartment. "Whoever decorated this place obviously had exquisite taste, would you agree?" he asked Anna, who nodded.

"So what may I do to help you?" Anna asked.

Footsteps on the polished wooden floor distracted Anna's thoughts. An attractive elderly woman entered the room. "This is my mother," the colonel told her.

"Just call me Inge. We have our regular maid who came with us from Austria. It would be wonderful if you could come for a short while on Saturday when it is her day off and help us with our breakfast dishes and organize our closets for us," the woman requested in her sophisticated and mild manner.

Colonel Schuster lifted his cane in front of him. "We cannot share our business with you—I am sure you'll understand one day." His forefinger pointed to the eye patch. "There is still a war going on, you know?"

Anna avoided eye contact with the colonel and, in a soft tone, answered, "I understand."

"What a relief." Anna embraced her mother, who once again patiently waited for her. "Mutti, they are very nice people." She sounded exuberant. "Would you believe that Colonel Schuster showed me how to get egg yolks off his fine china plates? You showed me how to do this when I was in kindergarten! But how and where are they getting such rations? The colonel's cupboard is full of wonderful food!"

"Please keep your distance," her mother begged.

Again, arm in arm, they walked through the park. Relieved after the morning's event, they made a surprise visit to the grandmother's home, looking for something to eat. Grandmother was pleased to see them and equally pleased, as always, to share her sparse supply of food.

Anna did not mind her new weekly responsibility, but she found the surroundings puzzling. While in their presence, she chose her words carefully. She glanced over the former owner's home and wondered what became of the family dog when its owners left in a hurry, with the pet's water and food bowls still sitting on the balcony. Would the children's laughter return, and would they hold in their arms the exquisite toys that were left behind? Would the owners tend their neglected rose garden? And would they return to enjoy the amazing view of the mountain range from their terrace?

Her mother only shrugged her shoulders. "No one knows the answers to these questions. We are not on their side. We are on the other side." With her forefinger, she covered her mouth as she spoke in a hush.

As Anna fulfilled her duties to the colonel and his mother, dotingly placing the former owners' belongings into boxes and moving them into a dark attic, she could only hope and pray for the best.

By the end of 1944, determined to get their job done, the enemy battered part of the city day and night, leaving only ruins. Their bombers dominated the skies and continued to release phosphorus bombs, igniting fires on contact that lingered for days, leaving an atmosphere of utmost doom.

After the attacks, helpless women, dirty and ragged, climbed across rubble of bricks and twisted steel looking for their children. One woman could hear her children crying and knocking underneath the rubble ... then only silence. Old men, too, dug in the rubble for survivors. Confused animals roamed, searching for their owners.

It seemed that in the face of these unthinkable conditions around them, nothing could swerve Anna's mother's faith. "So far," her voice sounded exuberant, "our lives have been spared, and we still have a roof over our heads. We must be thankful!" She closed her eyes and pointed upward. "There is hope, and life must go on!"

Chapter 13

Winter 1944 … A spark of hope.

Unlike the showy and grandiose attention Hitler's leaders drew to themselves in the past, they now rarely ventured out of their seclusion. When they did, they bawled orders from within their comfortable official vehicles to disoriented and troubled people walking around in ruins or standing in long lines in hope for small rations of food. It was the Nazi leaders' last attempt to force Germany's already weak and vulnerable people to serve Adolf Hitler. *But where is Adolf Hitler?* people began to question. Via radio *Wehrmacht Bericht*, Anna's mother and grandmother, in renewed harmony and agreement, listened to Dr. Goebbels's piercing voice make one gloomy announcement after another.

Sensitive to her surroundings, Anna remained acutely aware of the possibility that she might be questioned about her father's whereabouts as she attended school in an adjoining neighborhood. She did not object to the long walks over the debris of bombed-out buildings, especially since, during the course of her last visit, Colonel Schuster's mother, Frau Inge, had surprised Anna with a pair of new walking shoes.

"I would be pleased if you would make use of these," Frau Inge said as she handed Anna the colorful shoebox decorated with the popular salamander. She pointed to Anna's ragged shoes. "I do not know how you keep your feet dry," she added in a sympathetic tone.

Anna looked stunned and lost for words. "They are real leather, and they are my size!" She took a deep breath. "Thank you! You are so kind," she said, fighting back tears.

"You are most welcome!" Frau Inge gently reached for Anna's long pigtails and wrapped them gently around her head. "Have you ever considered wrapping those around your face? You would look like a real Austrian," she said proudly. "Herr Hitler likes that look!"

Upon learning about Frau Inge's kindness, Anna's mother seemed moved but cautious, concerned and afraid that the colonel's mother might become too personal and begin to ask probing questions. "Please continue to do a good job for the Schusters in return for their kindness, but please avoid closeness as much as possible while you are in their presence," she again persisted. "And Anna," she explained, "it is not difficult to understand their source of food and clothing. Please remember, Colonel Schuster is an SS superior who is closely connected to the Gestapo, Hitler's secret police. All are instruments of terror. Hitler will look after those who are on his side. People on Hitler's side include those who report our Jewish friends and even those very poor Gypsies who live in hiding. They turn them over to the Gestapo for monetary rewards or extra rations. This is common knowledge.

"Some day I will tell you the rest of the story," her mother continued. The lines in her face tightened. "Right now, the less you know, and they know about us, the better." She paused for a moment. "Have you seen the stranger lately who has been stalking us?" her mother probed.

"No, I have forgotten about him." Anna grinned.

Pressing both thumbs together, her mother returned her grin. "Perhaps the stranger has run into problems of his own."

Anna wondered what "the rest of the story" meant, but quickly changed the subject. "I love school! So long as the building stands and Herr Dietz does not appear, I want to be part it!" she cheerfully shared with her mother, who constantly reminded her to be watchful and to look over her shoulder. Daily, Anna reflected upon her mother's positive directions. With scores of air-raid interruptions, she followed her mother's guidance, and by staying busy worked out her daily routine.

For safety reasons, Sabina's mother repeatedly encouraged Anna's mother to join them in the hotel air-raid shelter, but Anna's mother graciously declined. "I must be at home in the event one of our men may look for me unexpectedly," she responded with a note of thanks.

I wonder if she is including my father, Anna pondered as she anxiously hoped to hear about him.

Because of additional damage to the Opera House, only parts of the building remained accessible. The huge Palladian windows and doors of the rehearsal studio offered sufficient light for make-believe rehearsals as, once again, music filled the air. Astonished at Herr Kummel's resourceful gifts of cheese and bread, the enthusiastic and talented group huddled in a sunny corner of the roof garden and enjoyed enlightening camaraderie. No one questioned his resourcefulness; they all appreciated his attempts at keeping the region's finest performers together. His eyes sparkled as he, with great pride, constantly reminded everyone, "I must look after my children!"

Much to everyone' surprise, the group of wounded soldiers who weeks earlier visited regularly found their way through the rubble of the torn-down stage area to their new make-do stage.

"We heard you!" shouted the young blind soldier.

"Please allow us to be your fan club!" a young amputee, holding on to two of his friends, called out.

Moved by the soldiers' enthusiasm, Herr Kummel stood up to announce, "Let us give our young friends a hand! They deserve a round of applause!" The few hours spent in the darkened Opera House served, to those present, as a marvelous escape from the ugly war around them.

Spring arrived early. A strange quiet fell over the region. The pompous attitudes of Nazi officials became instead defeated and defensive. "You people deserve what lies ahead. You have chosen your fate!" they shouted at street corners.

A young man dressed in brown uniform with black tie and swastika wrapped around his left arm stopped to chat with a group of frightened women. "Herr Hitler will win this war!" he insisted.

"He is right, you know! Better listen to him!" From within his truck graced with a gigantic swastika, a Nazi official attested to the young man's remarks. "He is one of Rudolf Hess's original boys!" Like a child whose mischief won the battle, his face turned into a smirk.

"Who cares," mumbled an old woman passing by. "Herr Hess got out of this mess a long time ago!"

At the Riding Academy, the fight to keep the horses alive intensified. Because of danger from daytime bombing, Master Karl became increasingly concerned about Anna and the handful of students who daily took the horses to feed at the mysteriously discovered source. He instructed the students to allow the horses to feed for only a limited time, thus stretching the supply as long as possible. Anna found it heartrending to pull the horses away before they could satisfy their hunger.

Trees and meadows burst into greenness against a blue springtime sky. "Nothing can change or touch our creator's work," her mother kept reminding Anna. "He is in charge!"

With this contagious mindset, Anna suggested to Master Karl that, with the help of the other students, they take all of the horses out of the stables and into the nearby mountain range.

"Just think, Master Karl," the frail and shy Alfred agreed, "for the horses, it's like going on a vacation."

Master Karl stared into space. His head swiveled in Anna's direction. "Our critters are in much better shape now, thanks to you, their young friends." His voice trembled. "But how are we going to keep them going?" he asked in a cautious and scowling mode. "I am concerned about your safety!" After a moment of silence, he agreed. "But you must promise to take extreme caution."

It seemed as though the enemy had forgotten about them. For a brief time, people dared to sleep in their beds at night. Everyone seemed more relaxed—except for Anna and her friends at the Riding Academy. Nothing could contain their zest for rescuing the horses from starvation.

Day after day, the familiar clanking of hooves against the cobblestone streets as the riders made their way to the mountain range brought residents out of their homes to greet them.

With Alfred and her four-legged friends by her side, Anna squinted through the sun's rays at the city below. The trill of a bird perched in a graceful river birch drew her attention as she heaved an enormous sigh. She cherished the moment and thrived on the vivid memories of Eric and Guenter. Most of all, she marveled over her mother's patience in dealing with all the problems around her.

Rubin drew close to her while feeding on the young and tender leaves of grass. He seemed restless and gave Anna an occasional nudge. Suddenly, whirling sounds of planes disrupted the quietude. Anna gestured to Alfred to take cover under a nearby row of trees. Stricken with fear, they stood and watched as the small planes repeatedly circled and swept across their heads, barely missing the treetops. Then, with a sharp turn, the planes disappeared into the horizon.

"They are Messerschmitt fighters!" Alfred shrieked with excitement. "We studied them in school. But what was all this about?" Alfred asked as he ventured back into the open. He stared at Anna who, with both hands covering her ears, leaned against Rubin.

"Perhaps they were looking us over?" She shrugged her shoulders in disbelief.

Only moments passed. A familiar droning of enemy planes drew close. "There must be hundreds!" Alfred shielded his eyes with both hands as the planes came into plain view. He took hold of Rubin's rein and tied up all the horses. "Let's take cover under the gazebo," he said, frantically pulling

Anna with him to take cover. Gripped by fear, they sat and watched as the planes began to unleash their bombs. "They are destroying our neighborhood," Alfred screamed. Smoke and mountains of dust rose from below. After what seemed an eternity, the planes disappeared, leaving their trail of destruction.

Anna's body trembled; tears filled her eyes. She walked toward Rubin and sunk her face into his thick mane. With her fingers, she nervously groped the white star on his forehead. Rubin turned his head and gazed at Anna. She gently kissed him. He responded with a content snivel through his nostrils.

Alfred climbed on the banister of the gazebo to get a better look at the conditions below, but was unable to recognize locations. Smoke bellowed from the direction of the children's neighborhood. "Let's take the shortcut back," Anna begged. Anxious, their minds consumed with the uncertainly ahead, they gently led the horses down the steep incline that took them through the park that led to their homes.

Alfred brought the horses to a halt. Unsure of debris that blocked the equestrian trail, the horses became agitated and resisted the children's attempts to move them forward. Anna slid off her saddle and ran to take a closer look at Colonel Schuster's street a short distance away. There was no sign of life. Only the crackling of small fires disrupted a ghostlike quietness. "Oh no, I was afraid of this!" Under a pile of bricks, Anna recognized some of the Kaufmann family's paraphernalia, which only days earlier Frau Inge had instructed Anna to store in the Kaufmann's attic. "Could Frau Inge and her son be trapped under the collapsed building?" Somehow, she had become attached to this lady. Sad and confused, she looked back and wondered as they made their way home.

Alfred, half a block ahead, called to Anna, "Our street is untouched!"

Afraid to look, Anna responded with a whimper, "What about mine?"

Alfred whirled his horse around. "Look for yourself, everything looks unharmed, and here comes your mother!"

Anna slung the horses' reins over Alfred's shoulder and ran toward her mother.

"Oh, Anna, I am so grateful you children are fine! The bombs dropped ever so close." She pointed toward the terraced stairs that led to the street above. "There is nothing left up there, nothing at all." Her mother cried as she held Anna close. "Where will our poor neighbors go?" she cried. "And where are they?"

Relieved but tired, Master Karl embraced the children as they cautiously walked into the entrance of the stables. "As you can see," his eyes skimmed over the building, "the building is standing, but all the windows are broken. We are fortunate this time. The windows have been there many decades. They can be replaced. But who will clean up the dangerous debris?" Master Karl shook his head. His tired eyes sat deep in his pale face. He showed desperation.

Alfred looked at Anna. "We'll clean it up tomorrow!" he proudly suggested. Anna nodded with a smile.

The following day, Sabina, who had recovered from a fever and sore throat, joined Anna and Alfred for the seemingly endless task of cleaning up the broken glass that had fallen into the stalls and along the ramp that led into the stables.

A peculiar look came over Alfred's face as he sneaked a look into the bunk room formerly used by stable boys during riding exhibitions. Anna and Sabina moved away bundles of straw that blocked the door, but found the door locked. Alfred bent his knees and interlocked his fingers. "Step up and climb over!" he ordered Sabina. Anna spotted a small wagon and pulled it in front of the window so that she and Alfred could follow.

Baffled and surprised, they looked around the room and stared at each other. "Someone must be living here!" they shrieked in unison. Neatly folded blankets covered three of the bunk beds. In a far corner, a red-and-white-checked cloth draped a huge round table.

Alfred lifted the lid of a tarnished pot resting on a hot plate. He closed his eyes and took a sniff of the contents. "It's real coffee," he grinned. He opened one of the lockers filled with canned goods and handed a package to Sabina. "I can't read this. What does it say?"

"It's shortbread from Belgium. I can't make it all out. It's written in French!" She shrugged her shoulders.

"Where are the owners?" questioned Anna. She spotted an old record player under one of the bunks. "Whoever they are, they like Johann Strauss waltzes!"

She looked at the record still in place, turned the handle, and gingerly put the needle in place. The music sounded scratchy and far away. "It's practice time," Anna laughed. She reached for Sabina's hand and swirled her around. "Loosen up and bend your knees," she instructed. "Up and down, the waltz is like the waves of the Blue Danube, remember?"

"It's time to finish the cleanup," Alfred insisted.

"After we have some snacks," Sabina persisted.

"We have to ask Master Karl first," Alfred maintained. He glanced at the washbasin in the center of the room. "Okay, Master Karl needs to know about this annoying and constant drip."

Master Karl agreed that they should enjoy some chocolates from an opened box. He did not indicate concern about the children's discovery, but simply encouraged them to continue their cleanup efforts. "I'll board up the windows tomorrow," he mumbled as he made his way back to the stables.

He made a slow turn and gestured toward the bunk room. "Forget you found this!" His stern look startled the children, who nodded. None of them mentioned the bunk room again, but in their young minds, they wondered, *Won't this mystery ever stop?*

To everyone's astonishment, things began to quite down. Once again, sirens fell silent. Instead, in the distance, constant rumbling of heavy artillery roared through the nights. Bleak reports via radio and newspapers revealed that the enemy was now concentrated and had extended its fighting to the Ruhr, the tributary of the Rhine in the west. Three-fourths of the region, whose chief industrialists had helped Hitler to power, ended up in ruins. "Just weeks before Hitler's birthday," the somber radio announcement continued, "Hitler's weak and dismal army is about to surrender."

Anna spent much of her free time with her friend Sabina at the hotel. She checked daily on her mother but rarely saw her grandmother. She often wondered if her grandmother still believed in Hitler, who was to give Germany's people greatness and victory.

Because of low attendance, the uplifting make-believe rehearsals at the Opera House were discontinued. Herr Kummel had fallen victim to the most recent bombing session. Overnight, he joined the multitudes of homeless neighbors and moved away to live with relatives. Only a skeleton crew remained visible in the stately building once bustling with energetic individuals. To stay connected, Anna and friends took advantage of warm spring days as they sunbathed on the roof garden. The blue and now quiet sky overshadowed once again the destruction of the city below.

Somehow, neighbors coped with unthinkable situations. They aimlessly moved from place to place, pulling their meager belongings behind them in wagons or make-do carts. Among the ruins, one neighbor lived in a cardboard box.

For Master Karl, during a night of torrential rain, came an unimaginable bolt from the blue. Just as he began to bunk down on a bed of hay, he heard a caravan of trucks enter the courtyard of the stables. He carefully doused his night lantern and looked around for an inconspicuous place to hide. Accelerating engines and the slamming of heavy metal doors jolted the horses out of their quiet state. Master Karl, fearful of the unknown activity, remained silent and out of sight. Finally, the noise of truck engines ceased. Only an occasional rumbling from falling debris in nearby bombed-out buildings disrupted the spine-chilling silence.

The eastern sky revealed a new day as Master Karl lifted the heavy wooden lid of the storage bin in which he was hiding and had dozed off during the night. His face showed pain as he lifted his body, affected with arthritis, out of the bin. He stretched his back and slowly walked up the ramp to the terrace outside the riding ring. His eyes scanned the once manicured yet still picturesque courtyard below. A gratifying smile lightened up and relaxed the muscles in his wrinkled face. He yearned for better times to return.

Better times when groups of riders under his supervision lined up to begin their traditional foxhunts. With horses groomed to perfection, saddles, reins and bridles shining, and riders dressed in their finest formal attire. He affectionately recalled Otto, his favorite foxhound, who always struggled to keep up with the group. *Will normal times return?* he wondered.

Just then, the melodic clanging of hooves brought his attention toward the entrance of the stables. An elderly, worn-out-looking soldier emerged, leading several mares and draft horses into the courtyard. As though he knew his way around, he led them straight to the water trough. The horses responded with continuing whinnying echoed by some of the horses inside the stables.

Uncertain of his next move, Master Karl decided to check out the unannounced stranger. He slipped on his leather apron and, with pitchfork in hand, ventured into the courtyard.

"I am not here to cause trouble," said the old soldier, intimidated by Master Karl's appearance, raising both hands above his head. "I have walked for days with little sleep or food. Our group commander ordered me to deliver these horses to you. We no longer have any use for them."

"I have nearly forty horses we are trying to keep alive, and we have no food to spare." Master Karl's voice reached an agitated pitch.

"Oh." The old man scratched his chin and pointed to the huge trucks. "You do not know about the cargo in these vehicles?"

Master Karl looked perplexed. "No! What cargo?"

The old man pulled back the cover of one of the trucks. Master Karl stared at the battered trucks while the soldier unveiled each one. Neatly stacked from top to bottom were shiny green bales of hay and bags of grain.

Still confused, Master Karl filled his hands with the grain and savored the fresh scent as he shook his head with amazement. He looked at the soldier and asked, "Is this for real?" He let go a loud sneeze. "*Gesundheit*!" the old soldier laughed. "And now you see that there is enough feed to keep them fed until this mess is over!"

Master Karl once again looked startled. "What mess?" he continued to prod the soldier.

"Indeed, these trucks came through a mess. Our people blew up the bridge just moments after we crossed the Rhine and the cargo was safe on this side of the river."

After a casual introduction, the two men shook hands. "It looks like we are both in for the same haul," the soldier grumbled.

"After all," Master Karl agreed, "our main concern must be the welfare of the horses."

"If need be," the soldier continued, "I can stay and help care for them until this mess is over. I have not yet been in touch with my family in Berlin, and I have no idea if they are still alive."

While he and Master Karl became acquainted and looked over the muscular draft horses—paying attention to their manes mangled with mud, maggots infested in their ears, their gear in need of repair—the soldier spoke about all that was going on farther down the Rhine.

Later in the day, Master Karl was pleased to share the events of the past twenty-four hours with Anna and her friends. His eyes welling with tears, Master Karl thanked the children for their passionate concern for the horses. "Thanks to you, so far they have not developed bad habits, because you took them out into the meadows regularly even under dangerous conditions. They have remained amazingly docile throughout these challenges and, most importantly, they are still free from colic."

Sabina walked over and stretched to look in on Ben, her favorite white Arabian. "Were we really that helpful, Master Karl?"

He smiled and pulled his bifocals to the tip of his nose. "Yes, indeed, they will always be grateful to all of you, and so will I!"

For the first time in a long while, life at the stables went along without the daily concerns over feeding the horses—now increased in numbers. "We will stretch our supply as far as we can," Master Karl cautioned.

During the night a few weeks later, and unbeknownst to Master Karl, someone dropped off in the open courtyard another mountain-sized load of oats and ground-up hay. Upon discovery, Master Karl once again scratched his bald head in amazement and asked the stable boy, "Where on earth did this come from?" He sifted the mixture through his fingers and got a whiff of its contents. His eyes sparkled.

He glanced at the dark clouds moving over the stables. "We need to get this out of the spring rain!" he ordered the stable boy. He looked at his watch. "The children will be here at noon. They will love to help us."

Like magic, everyone took part in hauling the lifesaving treasure into the storage bin. "Where did this come from?" questioned Anna.

Master Karl smiled. "I do not know, little one, perhaps one day we will know so that we can thank them. In the meantime, let us hope we can get hold of some salt as well." Anna watched as he walked away. Relaxed, the stress gone from his face, he looked much younger, and even mastered a familiar whistle during his walk around the stable.

Inside the stables, the atmosphere changed dramatically. Instead of their sluggish and motionless stance and obvious mood swings, the horses became jolly and happy, especially during time for grooming and feeding. "Truly a miracle: no colic, no digestive problems at all set in," stated Dr. Steinmeyer, the old vet, during one of his visits. Only drooling developed with several of the older horses. Anna continued daily to apply compresses on sores that refused to heal on Maidlie's leg. Whenever Anna passed by Rubin's stall, he was always ready to go, quickly moving toward the gate in hopes that she would put on his halter.

A tremendous burden had been lifted regarding the horses. "We must savor the moments," Master Karl repeated as he himself took pleasure in walking through the stalls to monitor the condition of the horses and keep an eye on their weight. His own appearance continued to improve and so did that of the owner, Herr Ackermann. Their faces showed hopefulness instead of despair.

Will these mysterious events ever come to light? Anna continued to wonder.

Around the city, signs of spring began to lift nearly everyone's spirits. Trees and flowers burst with color. Much to everyone's gratitude, activities in the sky remained silent. Instead, sounds of heavy artillery became more frequent and closer during daylight hours.

As obvious sounds of ground fighting neared, Germany's battered soldiers appeared on the scene and revealed the facts regarding the war. "American armies are nearing the Rhine. Bridges are down everywhere. We were ordered to blow them up as a last attempt to slow down the enemy," announced one of the soldiers. Small enemy planes dropped leaflets to inform the German people of their progress. The message: a continuation of the surrender of Hitler's army. Radio Hamburg no longer blast the voices of Hitler's top guns. Only classical music by Hitler's favorite composers, particularly Richard Wagner, filled the airwaves.

By now, most of the hard-core Nazi Party members no longer mentioned their führer, Adolf Hitler. They too came to the conclusion that, for more than twenty years, Hitler had demanded their loyalty, but he did not return the same.

It became evident that Hitler's promise of a better Germany had turned into a nightmare.

Anna's grandmother kept busy working in her miniature garden, making use of every inch of ground. Her demeanor improved. Anna noticed that she no longer wore the party badge that identified her as a National Socialist. She rarely spoke of Hitler, but her voice expressed concern when she spoke about those who mysteriously disappeared. "By the Nazi Party," she gave a stare toward Anna's mother as she spoke, "they are seen as supporters of the enemy." This did not alarm Anna's mother, who, with renewed confidence, remained unshaken. Not surprisingly, since nearly everyone noticed the subtle change that was taking place around the city.

Anna spent more time with her mother, who thanked Sabina's mother for sharing their hotel bunker with Anna at night. Only a handful of servants remained. Some food was still available, and the girls took great pleasure in preparing small meals in the gigantic hotel kitchen.

An alarming silence motivated Anna and Sabina to venture out into the park in front of the hotel. A remnant of bedraggled German soldiers surrounded a caravan of battered trucks. "Don't be afraid," one of the soldiers, wrapped in a blanket that served as a coat, called to the girls hiding behind the guardhouse. "We are on our way home. The Americans are behind us!"

Sabina stepped closer and motioned Anna to move along with her. "Will the Americans harm us?" Sabina asked in a quivering tone.

Taking a puff on a cigarette butt, the soldier replied with a reassuring smile, "No, they too are anxious for this ridiculous war to end! Don't you know, they are coming to liberate us! We have already been driven back on the west bank of the Rhine near Aachen," the exhausted soldier continued with ease.

"There is no reason to fear. The Americans will give you chocolate and chewing gum," chuckled another soldier.

"What is chewing gum?" asked Anna.

Several nights later, the German command that had occupied one wing of the hotel vacated quietly and without bringing their intent to anyone's attention. Only the one-man guardhouse at the entrance remained as a reminder of their visit.

The following day, a strange quietness continued to hang over the city. Then, for what seemed time without end, heavy artillery shells bellowed through the night. At dawn, the weird quietness again sat in.

No one knew what the Americans would do. Would they imprison and hurt people? Recalling previous Nazi propaganda, would they rape the helpless young German women? Anna's mother was desperately afraid for her daughter's safety. How would they exploit their new surroundings and the tired and vulnerable people? Would they follow in the footsteps of the ruthless and intimidating Nazi leaders who had suddenly left the area?

From the hotel balcony once used by Hitler to deliver his high-energy speeches, the girls watched as tanks followed by jeeps and trucks entered their street. Unlike the bedraggled and beaten-down German soldiers, the American soldiers looked surprisingly clean-cut, their faces friendly and relaxed. With ammunition belts and weapons still slung across their shoulders, a group of them followed their commander into the hotel lobby. Across the park, American soldiers escorted a group of worn-out German soldiers to a transport truck to be taken away.

Only moments later, Sabina's mother entered the girls' room. Somewhat apprehensive about the unknown, she began warning the girls to be cautious of the new visitors. "Our hotel manager is in charge. His English is fluent, and I chose him to meet with the Americans. Please stay out of sight."

She pulled back the heavy curtain that draped the French doors and pointed to a group of soldiers below. "This is exactly what concerns me," she whispered. "You are turning into lovely young ladies! Although our food supply has dwindled down, we will temporarily re-establish our wonderful room service just for you." She gave a quick smile as she disappeared into the corridor.

Chapter 14

Spring 1945 … Identity of mysterious friends.

Within forty-eight hours, all artifacts and reminders of Hitler were removed from government buildings, hotels, and in all places inside and out. High-ranking American military personnel quietly began to move in to the newly vacated areas of Sabina's grandfather's hotel.

Because of isolated street fighting that continued during night hours, the Allies' first command was to establish a dawn-to-dusk curfew for all residents of the city and its surroundings. "You must adhere to this rule for your own safety," announced an unfamiliar voice with a heavy accent from a loudspeaker inside an American vehicle. "And," the announcer continued, "there is no longer need for a blackout!"

As the blackout lifted, light once again streamed from within buildings that had withstood the horrible nightmare of bombings. When nighttime approached, residents rejoiced at the presence of light shining from within their neighbors' homes. In spite of the dismal surroundings of ruins, sparks of hope burst through as street lanterns gave an exciting new glow to surrounding areas.

In a daze, homeless women with sacks containing meager belongings thrown over their backs and their children clinging to them continued to roam the streets. Bewildered and sad, they stared at flames still burning in the ruins of what they had once called home. Occasionally, groups of newly released and decrepit German soldiers walked along ruins of buildings with nowhere to go. One bewildered soldier stood on a street corner for hours, unable to decipher the location of his home.

Organizing basic provisions for helpless neighbors became a priority in everyone's mind. Several young German soldiers who were given permission to return to their homes became the first volunteers. Two disabled soldiers organized a trading post. "Bring your clean unwanted clothing and trade it with your neighbors," read a huge sign that graced an empty candy-factory warehouse.

Other able-bodied persons of all ages eagerly volunteered to assist wherever needed. A group of people, their unexpected presence a mystery, suddenly appeared on the scene. Someone suggested their leader may have been a member of the American Red Cross whose mission was to gain access into prison camps and to keep an eye on the prisoners' welfare.

A farmer from a nearby village shared his spring harvest of fresh vegetables from his hothouses and opened a soup kitchen in an abandoned restaurant in the old city. The aroma from within drew long lines of lost and hungry neighbors. Anna and Sabina decided to check out the excitement.

Surprised at their discovery, Anna made a quick turn around as they entered the dining hall. "What an amazing sight!" she whispered to Sabina. "There is my grandmother!" Her voice expressed utter admiration as she took a closer look at her grandmother, who was enthusiastically serving her neighbors. "What a change! Things are really getting better!" she shouted as she ran to tell her mother the enlightening news about her grandmother's compassionate yet unassuming activity.

She found her mother kneeling in front of the balcony door looking out onto her favorite linden trees. "Anna, do you see the tiny buds ready to bloom?" She reached for Anna's hand. Her face showed the sickening pain of arthritis as she pulled herself up. "We have made it through terrible times. Just as it is with those tiny buds, we too are now ready to flourish. Our boys will soon be home, and our lives will once again burst with new wonders. Would you help me remove those dark curtains from our windows?" she asked with a deep sigh. "And what a luxury, we will sleep again in our beds and without sirens blaring through the night! I feel such hope. Thank God, we have come through a lot," she smiled as she fluffed Anna's pillows and placed them on the windowsill to sun. One by one, they removed the dark curtains as sunshine once again flooded their cozy apartment.

Only a small remnant of the talented members of the theater company who had avoided deportation caused by either bombing or other political reasons remained to meet daily on the roof garden above the cold and darkened Opera House.

The warmth of the spring sun felt good as they sat and shared their dreams for the future. "Will they rebuild the damaged part of the building right away?" asked one of the dancers as she gracefully took a cartwheel and flip across an outside wall.

"Not that close!" shrieked a shy and quiet violinist as he gasped in horror at the burning city below. He grabbed his throat and shook his head. "That looked dangerously close!"

Soon thereafter, and because of unstable construction throughout the magnificent building, the local government made the decision to close the Opera House doors until reconstruction could take place.

Although their city was now occupied, everyone remained acutely aware of the lingering fighting and destruction in other parts of their homeland, especially their capital city of Berlin. Whatever was left of the city of Cologne had already been taken several weeks earlier. Anticipation rang high among the exhausted population. No one knew what to expect next. High-ranking German officers who had occupied residences formerly owned by Jewish neighbors suddenly vanished and went into hiding. This left many homes vacant and without supervision.

As the American armed forces settled into the area, isolated looting of valuables, such as fine art, precious metals, Bavarian pottery, and fine china took place. Even personal artifacts owned by Hitler's military became sought-after items for souvenirs that American soldiers found valuable. The well-known German Leica cameras were among the hot items. Suddenly, nearly everyone began to trade these items through the black market. For American soldiers, their rationed cigarettes became the most popular articles of trade.

With no choice in the matter, residents in neighborhoods spared by the destruction of bombs on the outskirts of the city were assigned to vacant apartments in various locations throughout the municipality. The purpose: to make their homes available for the military and their dependants who would soon join them. This created havoc and heartache among many German people. In some cases, family members returning from war zones were unable to locate their families for weeks and even months.

For the moment, few complained about the new rules, but considered them a welcome trade-off for the fear and uncertainty Hitler and his people had created. As Hitler's leadership began to deteriorate and he seemed to vanish from the scene, no one dared to ask questions. Many, however, speculated about Hitler's whereabouts. "His fifty-sixth birthday is coming up shortly," Anna's grandmother said. "Did he abandon us?" It was clear that, in part, her loyalty to the führer remained with her.

"But where is the führer?" the curious questioned. "And where is Hermann Goering, *der dumme Herr Meyer*?" An unidentified radio station claimed that Hitler was spending his fifty-sixth birthday in the bunker at the *Reich's* chancellery in Berlin with his dog Blondi and his closest associates, and that he had married his longtime companion, Eva Braun. "There is fighting among his top guns," the announcement continued. "Hitler fired his defense minister, Hermann Goering, and had him arrested." Very fittingly, the music that followed the announcement sounded of doom. By now, many hoped that Hitler's methods of destruction would soon reach their peak, for war had taken a toll on them.

Since the threat of bombing no longer existed, Sabina's family moved back to their luxurious villa. Anna moved back home to be with her mother. The girls stayed in close touch and, at Sabina's mother's invitation, Anna often spent nights with them. "I would like for you girls to stay busy and useful during these changing times," she gently suggested. "Perhaps you may be of help at the stables. I am certain Master Karl will welcome your presence, and so will the horses!"

Posters in every corner of Anna's district announced plans for restoration of her badly damaged school. "Classes are to be temporarily held in the children's orphanage."

Full of excitement, she jumped on Guenter's bike and rode to the orphanage to investigate. Several American soldiers carried out boxes of paper. "It's all yours," one of the soldiers said, motioning Anna into the front door. "There is no one there," he assured her with his heavy accent. As she stood and watched as the friendly soldiers jump into a jeep, she recalled the frightening behavior of Hitler's SS when they took over the building.

Anna respected her new teachers and enjoyed her assignments. Her goal and determination was to work hard to please her mother, as well as Guenter and Eric when they returned. *Perhaps Sister Renate and the children will return soon, since Herr Hitler's dreadful people are no longer around*, she imagined. Her thoughts brought back to mind Herr Dietz's threats and humiliation, but her mother's faith and positive words abruptly ended her concern. Even so, nightmares about Herr Dietz surfaced from time to time. For the moment, spending school hours in the familiar surroundings of the old orphanage and the wonderful memories of Sister Renate calmed her fears.

Following Sabina's mother's suggestion, Anna put her free time to use. She began to help her mother mend Guenter's old socks and clothes, even though she questioned whether they would ever see him again. Although neither understood the language, they listened to the American radio station and took pleasure in hours of uplifting music. "Perhaps we will learn to speak their language?" her mother laughed as Anna sang along to the lyrics of "You Are My Sunshine."

Her mother felt an impulse to check their mailbox. Upon her return, she waved a stained letter in front of Anna. She wiped her face with her apron and, with a smile surfacing through the tears, she insisted in a low whisper, "They are tears of hope, hope that our boys will soon return. I am amazed that pieces of mail still find us through our demolished homeland," she murmured as she gently dug into the envelope.

In his letter, Eric revealed anguish: "Dear family," he wrote. "Bombs are falling day and night here. Everything around us is in ruins. There is nothing left standing. I believe we are in the most dangerous place on earth. People are running for their lives. We are lucky to have found this bunker because some have 'standing room only.' We are hiding in this deserted bunker in a building next to the *Reichstag*. There is no food and, because of fierce house-to-house fighting between our people and the Russians, we are unable to venture out into the streets. Judging by the sounds of artillery, I believe they are closing in on us. I am desperately afraid of being arrested, since my ID card identifies me as a classified employee in Hitler's headquarters."

The letter continued, "No one has a clue as to Hitler's whereabouts. We do know that Eva Braun arrived a few days ago. Since then, all is strangely quiet just before his fifty-sixth birthday. Even his dog Blondi and her puppies have not been seen. They may have slipped out during night hours. It is possible Hitler and his entourage will attempt to escape to Bolivia or Argentina. All is very strange and frightening."

Eric concluded, "You will note, I have no address, but hope to soon make my way through the ruins of this city toward the roads that lead homeward. From there I may be able to catch a ride toward home. It is the only possibility, since both trains and railroad tracks all over the region have been destroyed. *Bis auf ein wiedersehn*, Eric."

Anna took a deep breath. Like her mother, she wanted to believe that Eric and Guenter would soon return. *But what about my father's whereabouts?* she continued to wonder. While things looked uncertain for Anna, she stayed focused and felt gratitude because of her mother, who continued to look ahead to a brighter future.

Sabina and Anna continued to meet at the Riding Academy. Although August, his stable boy, returned, Master Karl counted on the girls and their friend Alfred to assist with exercising and grooming the horses. Being watchful of shrapnel from artillery shells, they rotated the horses and took them for long rides along the trails. In the city, the snow had melted, but icy surfaces were everywhere until heavy spring rains washed the snowy forest into a picture of spring.

Master Karl was concerned that the feed he had so carefully rationed would again run out before new supplies could be brought in. He continued to lack the manpower, vehicles, and gasoline to get more, and he knew of no one who would risk crossing the damaged bridges across the Rhine.

Every other day, the hotel chef saved raw leftover vegetables that the children hauled away to the stables in the broken-down and deserted trailer. A young American soldier watched their activities from nearby. Somewhat distraught in watching their struggle, he offered to hook the trailer to his jeep. Sabina quickly put to use her limited skill in English. As Anna stood and watched, the soldier cranked up his jeep and motioned for the girls to climb aboard.

At first, Anna protested, reminding Sabina of her mother's strict rules concerning strangers of the opposite sex. Amused at Anna's motherly apprehension, Sabina shrugged her shoulders. "Don't be such a bore," she shouted. "No one can harm us in daylight. Besides, it's for the horses!"

A smile crossed the soldier's slightly bearded face as he watched the girls break out in laughter. From then on, he watched and came to their rescue each time they prepared to take the scraps to the horses.

Boldly, yet cautiously, members of the resistance came out of hiding. Their former mission of rescuing the haunted minority groups in danger of deportation was over. Built-up anger and deep resentment motivated the brave members of the resistance to vent their anger toward Hitler's arrogant SS who had delighted in dragging Jewish neighbors out of their homes at gunpoint, to haul them away in trucks like cattle.

The mystery of the bunk room Anna and her friends had discovered earlier was solved one dreary day. Blaring sounds of a shortwave radio from within the bunk room caught their attention as they led the horses down the ramp. They drew closer to take a look. A handsome young man with curly blond hair, neatly dressed in formal riding attire, paced back and forth, stopping to pay close attention to the radio from time to time. He observed the teenagers mounting their horses and walked toward the open door.

Nervously, Sabina ordered, "We must move on!"

The young stranger held his hand up to get their attention. "Hello, I am Ferdinant Leonards, and I would love to join you for a ride sometime!"

With a quick nod, Alfred tipped his hat and led the girls and horses out of the courtyard and into the street.

"Well, well, well," Sabina said as she brushed off small pieces of shrapnel from a wooden bench where they had stopped to rest. "Perhaps we will soon discover the mystery of the bunk room!"

Anna sat silent and observed the transformed landscape of the city below. "There are so many mysteries, so many," she sighed with her usual faraway stare.

The harmonious sound of the horses' hooves beating against the cobblestone streets no longer produced the echo of days past as Anna and her friends made their way back to the stables. Instead, they were drowned out by the vibration of gigantic bulldozers whose task it was to move the mountains of debris of torn-down buildings and to search for bodies buried under the ruins.

Anna motioned for her friends to detour through the once-fashionable street her mother's friends, the Kaufmann family, and later the SS colonel and his mother, Frau Inge, had called home. All the debris had been removed from the property, but a sign nailed to a wooden post in the center revealed that Colonel Schuster, his mother, and their Austrian servant were among those killed during one of the air raids. Sabina and Alfred looked puzzled at Anna's sad reaction. "They were the enemies!" Alfred raised his voice as Sabina nodded.

"I know, I know, but they were people just like us," Anna snapped. "The only difference, we are smart, and they were stupid!" Anna gave a last look at what once displayed elegance and beauty and now lay in ruins.

Sunshine, warmer temperatures, newfound energy, and absence of fear contributed to an encouraging new atmosphere among neighbors who, like Anna's mother, hoped to be reunited with loved ones. The question "Have you heard anything yet?" echoed among them everywhere.

Anna welcomed her mother's revitalized enthusiasm and sense of humor. As neighborhood stores once again opened their doors, she eagerly offered to help wherever needed. Business owners embraced her uplifting personality. She swiftly balanced her time between bakery and butcher shops.

"I must keep busy until the boys return!" she cheerfully confessed. She again spoke about her youth in a nearby village, her father's gift of music, her mother's love of cooking, and her first job in a cigarette factory as a quality-control operator. She described her first meeting with the children's handsome and intellectual father. Then, as quick as a streak of lightning, she would change the conversation.

Once again, Anna looked forward to her daily visits to her grandmother's small but beautiful apartment. From her grandmother's balcony, she enjoyed the picturesque view of the old city, which the enemy had spared, and the mountain range in the background. Boxes of spring flowers graced the windows and filled the air with their delightful fragrance. "I am preparing for the boys' return!" the grandmother proudly called out to Anna as she spotted the girl gingerly walking toward her through her manicured garden. "And for you and my dear daughter Lina, there is a streusel kuchen cooling on the kitchen window sill!"

Anna stepped onto a wooden box resting below the window. She stretched and smiled. "I can smell it!" she cried. Amazed at her grandmother's knack for coming across ingredients to bake with when no one else could, she took the garden rake out of her grandmother's hand and embraced her while hiding tears of joy that flowed down her face.

Several days later, after taking a group of horses out into the meadow, the children reminisced and compared recent and present-day events. "We are so accustomed to looking over our shoulders. Isn't it wonderful that we can finally express our feelings without being afraid?" Sabina shared with Anna as they neared the stables.

A group of people stood outside the entrance. Alfred made an abrupt stop. "What is all the commotion?" he asked one of the bystanders.

"Something must have happened to the horses!" Anna's voice expressed concern.

Master Karl ran to meet them. "There is nothing to be afraid of. A young Belgian located one of the SS members he has been searching for all over the region, and he is holding him captive until the American military arrives. There is no need for concern. He is on our side."

Sabina gave a stare. "So much for not being fearful!" she mumbled sarcastically.

"And by the way," Master Karl took a puff of his cigar, "you will be enlightened to know that this young man Ferdinant, through his intelligence network, delivered the mysterious cargo of food for our horses, thus keeping them alive."

Alfred nodded, "We met him earlier."

"And yes, he is quite a gentleman," Sabina added with a witty smile.

Calmly, Anna and her friends led the horses to their stalls. A ghostly quietness enveloped the surroundings. Out of the corner of her eye, Anna spotted a man, still clad in his formal SS uniform, leaning against an iron post. Two heavy chains hung from his hands and ankles. Only the sounds of the horses' nostrils added to the creepy clanging of chains.

From across the aisle, Sabina waved anxiously to get Alfred's attention. "I need help with my saddle," she called nervously.

Master Karl saw her struggle, walked toward her, and took the saddle from her arms. "Thank you," she said with a sigh of relief. Master Karl stayed by their side and helped them finish their chores.

During the following two days, the proud young Belgian showed off his catch while appropriate channels processed handing the prisoner over to the proper authorities. Master Karl remained undisturbed and so did the owner. The young Belgian, as it turned out, served as a leader of a resistance group. His only objective was to seek revenge by humiliating the Nazi.

As the news passed around, people swarmed to the stables to see the action. Several of Ferdinant's friends, also members of the same group and no longer forced to function in hiding, stood guard outside the stables. The elderly gentleman who previously posed as a pathetic and worn-out German soldier, and who secretly delivered the cargo of feed, was one of the Belgian's comrades. When Master Karl discovered the old man's secret, he laughed uncontrollably, saying, "You were most convincing. Yes, you had me fooled. Thank you, we will not complain, your mission saved our horses!"

Selectively and in small numbers, people interested in getting a firsthand look at an SS Nazi were guided to view the Belgian's catch. As they walked by, Ferdinant ordered the Nazi to stand on all fours like a horse. Inside the stall, an expensive oil portrait of Hitler served as a dartboard. Each viewer was allowed one throw of a dart onto the painting wherever they chose. A loud squeal erupted when the dart landed on the heart or between the eyes.

The Belgian shared with everyone the pain and anger caused by the Nazi. "He chased down my family and fiancée and hauled them off to be slaughtered like cattle. I have waited five years to vent my anger." His voice trembled. "Now I want this animal to feel like an animal!"

Anna's mother stretched her tiny frame to look in their mailbox for news from either of the boys. She paid no attention to a slender figure in the hallway. "Any good news today, Lina?"

"No," her voice sounded depressed. "No news!"

"Well, do you at least remember me?" The slender image stepped closer.

"Eric!" Anna's mother screamed. "Is it really you? I didn't expect you here in the entrance!"

Eric hugged her gently. "Yes, so I see!" he came back with his wonderful sense of humor.

Anna's mother ran out onto the street and shouted, "One of our boys is back!"

After some food and a hot bath, Eric began to share the events of his travel home. "It took nearly two weeks," he told them. "On the back of a farmer's wagon, with another farmer and his truckload of manure, and in between I walked. And I did not have a penny to my name. Now I am anxious to see Emma and the children. The good news," he held Anna close and promised, "is that our apartment is still standing, and when we get back, I expect you over often! That's an order!"

At first, Eric was unable to talk about the atrociousness of working in Hitler's headquarters, which on several occasions nearly cost him his life. Once he gained confidence in knowing that he was not being spied on by the Gestapo members with whom he worked, he began to share his experiences working in Hitler's headquarters. "I never dreamed that I could beg for food," he laughed. But his laughter quickly turned into a somber mood. "I had no choice but to destroy my ID card, for I became a target of the unknown."

He continued to share the chaotic conditions in Hitler's headquarters. "For months, no one knew what to do or whom we could trust. I trusted no one." He spoke about the cruelty of Hitler's plan as he ordered the death of Allied prisoners by locking them into the tunnels leading into Berlin and then flooding the tunnels. Only moments before, as he and two of his colleagues were on their way to seek refuge there from constant bombing, another co-worker warned them. Eric's head hung low as he attempted to describe the event. "We owe Wolfgang our lives," he whispered."

After a warm and joyful reunion with Emma and the children, Eric began to search for a job. "There is no shortage of employment," he cheerfully announced. "I cannot go for job interviews, however, until I hear an official announcement that we have lost the war. There are dangers still lurking around. It will take years to rebuild our homeland and all we have lost, and I know there will be no shortage of work."

Eric smiled. "We must also give our people reason for an annual celebration! I shall organize and re-ignite the *Fasching* Fest. Lina, would you like to serve as our first volunteer?"

Anna's mother shook her head and smiled. "No, thank you! I must concentrate on more important challenges right now." She gave Anna a stare of compassion. "Besides," she insisted, "huge crowds of people—that's not my cup of tea!"

Eric's presence was a welcome relief for Anna's mother, who continued to handle most of her challenges quietly on her own except when it came to watching over Anna. She closely watched her and warned her of the dangers involved in growing up. She kept a close watch for activity around their church and prayed for the doors to reopen. She actually enjoyed spring thunderstorms, saying as she looked upward, "God is reminding us that He indeed is in control!" She faithfully listened to Anna's favorite radio station, AFN

(American Forces Network) Frankfurt, for uplifting news translated in German.

Through the airwaves, uplifting news soon began to make its way into the homes of the German people. During the first week of May, all radio stations announced that Adolf Hitler had committed suicide underneath the chancellery building in Berlin. "He took with him his longtime companion, Eva Braun, whom he married just days before. He, himself, killed his favorite German Shepherd, Blondi, prior to killing himself," a somber voice described.

"I wonder whose side this announcer was on?" Anna's grandmother wondered.

"Maybe he loves dogs," Anna responded to her grandmother's surprising statement.

Most German people rejoiced when, during the following week, AFN Radio announced that Hermann Goering had been captured by the U.S. Seventh Army. Shortly thereafter, American forces occupied the Rhineland. With great anticipation, people paid close attention to the chain of excitement that moved forward.

Eric felt great relief when he learned that the führer had committed suicide, and that most of Hitler's high command had been thrown into prison. As soon as the Allies divided Germany and Berlin, Eric wasted no time in applying for a position as draft engineer with local government. After his credentials were carefully screened, he received notice to report to work the following day. "I have not even had a chance to rest yet," he cheerfully announced. "I will look forward to doing my best to rebuild our magnificent city!" he cheered over and over.

Good news began to overshadow the bad. By the end of spring 1945, people were running into newly reopened movie theaters to learn the fate of former neighbors who were sent away to so-called labor camps. Russian soldiers were among those who liberated two concentration camps. Anna's playmate Ellie miraculously lived through the nightmare of one of them called Buchenwald. Her foster mother shared the news with Anna's mother in a panic-stricken tone. "They used my Ellie for experimental purposes!" she cried. "She was only a child, and now she is being held in a hospital for psychiatric evaluation."

Anna's mother comforted her. "Ellie will be fine. She will be just fine. We will pray for her."

To celebrate Eric's new job, Emma invited everyone for a simple meal. Heavy clouds hung over the city as Anna and her mother climbed the hill toward Eric's apartment. Suddenly, following a strange stillness, nearly every church bell throughout the city broke into a continuing and harmonic concert. Anna's mother fell to her knees. "I have waited six years for this moment!" she cheered. With Emma's help, she pulled herself up and opened their balcony door.

Neighbors streamed into the streets. "It's over!" one neighbor began to shout from the top of her lungs. Anna's mother ran to meet the grandmother some distance away.

"It's official," another neighbor shouted. "This dirty war is over! The new American president has just announced Victory of Europe Day! That includes us!" Elated, Eric beat his fist against his chest.

During school hours, Anna frequently stared out of the window and wondered if and when others she loved would return. One day, in the rectory just a few yards away, she noticed an elderly priest walking across the garden toward the church. Making certain not to draw attention to herself, she stretched her neck to observe the priest. To her delight, the priest removed the heavy lock and chain from the entrance. Her heart raced from excitement.

Just then, the school bell rang to announce recess. She ran to find the doors leading to the sanctuary wide open and headed toward the old priest and curtsied. "Thank you! My mother will be so pleased. Will we be able to attend Mass soon?" she asked.

The priest looked at her and smiled. "Yes, but you must give our new people in local government time for an inspection. We wouldn't want something to fall on this pretty head, would we?" He placed his hand on her head. "And thank you for your enthusiasm—I hope we'll see you and your mother soon." As she followed the priest onto the street, she looked up and observed pigeons perching high above the sanctuary. "Those birds can be quite messy—they will have to patch those holes," the priest said, frowning, as he pointed to a large gap in the roof, barely dodging a huge dropping from the feathered critters above.

One day, Anna overheard a conversation between several teachers regarding the whereabouts of nuns who formerly occupied the orphanage. In the foothills of the nearby mountain range, the nuns supposedly resided in a villa deserted by one of Hitler's top guns. After anxiously pondering over the teachers' conversation, Anna confessed to her teacher about eavesdropping. Her teacher responded with a smile. "Yes, of course I will share with you that Villa Constantine has been converted into a nursing home after Hitler's people hastily vacated this lovely place," the elderly teacher, her glasses resting on the tip of her nose, confirmed. She took a deep breath. "Be cautious! Those poor devils who were not Hitler's supporters are not yet out of danger." A chill came over Anna as the teacher walked away.

Anna wasted no time in sharing with Master Karl her desire to visit the nuns. "May I please take one of the horses for a ride there?" she begged.

Master Karl leaned on his pitchfork and smiled. "Yes, of course!" His wrinkled face revealed approval. "This is the first favor you have requested since I have known you. Maidlie may enjoy a slow-paced ride into our beautiful mountain range. Be gentle with her. Like myself, she is getting old, but she will be a good choice for your mission."

After a gentle gallop along the trails, Anna dismounted and led the old mare to the rear of Villa Constantine. A young gardener came out of his toolshed to check out the two strange visitors. "I am Anna, and I am here to visit the nuns." She reached for the hand of the boy, who was about her age. "May I please tie up my horse?" She pointed to a shaded area covered with weeds. "My horse will help you with the pruning!" The boy nodded and returned her smile with a smirk.

One of the nuns, dressed in familiar garb, a wooden cross hanging from a rope around her waist, came out to meet Anna and to check on the horse. She motioned for the boy to water the horse; he responded with a nod. "Our young man cannot hear or speak." She took Anna by the hand and walked her to the rear entry of the villa. Beds of tulips surrounded the building. Anna took a deep breath to take advantage of the delightful fragrance. "How can we help you?" the nun probed.

Anna answered, "I was told that some of the nuns who ran the orphanage may be here. I am looking for Sister Renate. I was only seven when my mother and I last saw her."

The nun hung her head and cupped her left ear to listen. "Oh yes, she is with us, and I know she will be pleased to receive a visitor. I will take you to her, but you must be very quiet. She is very ill. It's her heart. I will let her know she has two visitors. A two-legged and a four-legged one, I might add!" Anna felt at ease with the nun's charming sense of humor. "And by the way," the nun once again reached for Anna's hand, "I am Sister Elizabeth."

Sister Elizabeth led Anna into the elegant villa and to a darkened room. Flickers from candles on a narrow table that graced one wall of the room gave reflection of a simple wooden cross. She led Anna to a single bed in the center of the room and said, "Please sit." She gently pulled Anna onto a chair and then walked to the window to draw the curtain ever so slightly.

Confused and distraught, Anna looked at the tiny figure in front of her. *This can't be Sister Renate*, she thought. *Sister Renate is a big person.*

Sister Elizabeth gently touched Anna on her shoulder. "I will leave the two of you alone. I'll be nearby should you need me."

Anna sat motionless and watched the nun in her slumber. Peace covered Sister Renate's pale face. Suddenly, the nun's hand moved toward Anna, who responded by cradling it in her own. She looked down as Sister Renate nervously twisted her wrist. Troubled, Anna examined a row of numbers tattooed into her skin.

"Anna, is it really you?" the nun opened her eyes and whispered ever so slightly. "Where is your mother? How is she?" With a faint smile, she closed her eyes and fell back into a deep sleep.

Full of gratitude that her dearest friend, Sister Renate, recognized her and remembered her mother, Anna thanked her new friend Sister Elizabeth for her hospitality. "Please feel free to return whenever you wish," she assured Anna, "and I will look forward to meeting your mother."

Anna questioned several gestures the young gardener made as he placed Maidlie's reins into Anna's hands. Understanding the boy's behavior, Sister Elizabeth smiled and said, "Willie would like for you to know that the horse is well-fed today. He fed her leftover hay that he found in the shed. The hay is not fresh, but I suppose hay is hay. These days, man has to make do, and so does beast!"

"Thank you again!" Anna's voice bellowed across the hillside as she led Maidlie into a gentle gait.

Anna's mother listened intently as she described her visit to Sister Renate. "When all seemed so hopeless, Sister Renate was our encourager." Anna's mother cupped her chin into her fists and closed her eyes. "Hitler and his people crushed the spirits of many, but not those who remained steadfast in their faith. We are blessed, so very blessed," she repeated over and over. Anna began to understand the significance of the number imbedded into the nun's wrist. According to Ellie's mother, the same ugly and torturous procedure was used on Ellie while in the concentration camp.

After several months of rest, Sister Renate's condition began to improve. Anna continued weekly visits to her bedside until she became strong enough for Anna to take her out into the garden, where Anna shared her wonderful experiences as the result of Sister Renate's kind direction. Because of the distance, Anna's mother was unable to visit, but she enjoyed the messages Anna delivered back and forth.

Sister Renate's younger brother, with whom she grew up in an orphanage, soon found her through the International Red Cross. He sent for her, and the two lived together in a modest cottage near Munich. This time, Anna and her mother were not sad to see Sister Renate move away, for they knew she would be in the loving care of her brother. During Anna's many visits, Sister Renate did not speak a word to her about herself or the children who were taken away during one night of terror.

With one of her favorite horses in front of the Kurhaus.

Eric heading the city's recovery project.

Anna's mother and grandmother shortly before blackout lifted.

With Guenter, age twenty, after his return from the Syberian Labor camp.

Eric as grandmarshal of the first Folksfest.

Chapter 15

Summer and Fall 1946 ... Guenther returns home ... Result of Hitler's ambition.

No one could cover the ruins of four-story buildings, nor were they able to remove the veil of secrecy and suppression placed upon some and more severely on others during recent years. Amazing, however, were the lifted spirits among minority groups who had suffered the most and still found the courage to venture out from their hiding places.

An old Gypsy woman, hunched over from a crippling arthritic condition, reclaimed her former vending spot on the street corner where Hitler's brazen Nazi members had spent most of their time intimidating neighbors. Anna's mother, surprised to see the colorful Gypsy lady, welcomed her back.

"Where have you been?" she asked the industrious old woman who was busy counting her inventory.

"Hiding in my neighbor's attic, talking with the rats, and knitting these hats!" She pointed to a variety of multicolored ski hats and laughed.

"I see they are hot items," Anna's mother called to the woman, who paused to count money a young soldier handed her for his purchase. Enthusiastically he gave her the signal to keep the change. "*Danke schoen, danke schoen*," the old woman replied.

On the familiar windswept hill near the cable car that sat untouched during chaotic periods, Sabina and Anna spent enjoyable moments planning new strategies for their future while the horses fed on the spring pasture. "We must learn to speak fluent English," Sabina insisted. With the help of a small German/English dictionary borrowed from her grandfather's library, she put short sentences together and instructed Anna to repeat them until she became fluent. "Now," Sabina commanded, "if you should leave my house and decide to suddenly go home in the middle of the night as you did once before, and you are stopped by the American military police, I want you to remember and say to them simply this: 'I am not a German girl.'" Amused at Anna's dubious expression, Sabina fell backward into the tall grass. Anna followed suit and both laughed aloud, startling the horses.

Sounds of laughter and upbeat conversations bellowed from within the stables as the girls returned. "That's a nice switch!" Sabina shaded her eyes from the bright afternoon sun. They noticed several jeeps parked in the center of the courtyard. With a new cigar still in its wrapper tucked behind his ear, Master Karl appeared to have been drawn into an enlightening conversation with several American soldiers. The girls recognized one of the soldiers in the group. "No wonder Master Karl is having a fun time," Anna whispered. "It's Joe, the soldier who helps us with the trailer and scraps, and he is translating for everyone?" They tied the horses to a post outside the stalls and walked over to Master Karl.

Pleased to see the girls, Master Karl walked toward them. "Here are two of our little lifesavers!" He smiled as he attempted to introduce them to the visitors. Sabina gave Anna a swift jab in the side, followed by her usual naughty wink. Both girls were captivated by the tall and handsome soldier with impeccable manners who took the lead in speaking with Master Karl. His dark brown eyes showed compassion as he probed Master Karl about the horses.

"I am Peter," he said, reaching for Sabina's and Anna's hands. The warmth of his hands ignited a desire in both to want to know him.

"This young man and his company would like to ride our horses," Master Karl told the girls as he motioned everyone to follow him to the riding ring on the upper deck. They sat in the bleachers and watched the stable boy, August, exercise one of the stallions while Master Karl listened closely to Peter's request.

"Our boys are worn out from fighting their way through Europe and this horrible war. We are in desperate need of healthy weekend recreation for them. Taking a ride out into your beautiful countryside would give them a lift."

Master Karl scratched his bald head and gently explained, "As you can see, our horses are underfed. Thanks to our mysterious sources and teamwork, they are still alive. You Americans ride Western saddle. This would worsen their weak condition. We cannot let our poor critters go through this."

Peter stood up and cupped his chin with his hand. "We understand, sir, but perhaps we can help you." He rubbed his hands together as in a washing motion and, smiling, he suggested, "One hand washes the other." Touching the dial of his wristwatch with his forefinger he assured Master Karl that he would return within an hour.

"I hope they will return," Sabina sighed as they followed the soldiers down the ramp.

"We'll see," Master Karl sighed.

Accompanied by one of his superiors, Peter returned shortly thereafter, and after a brief introduction he put his limited knowledge of the German language to use. "It has been brought to my attention how you have fought to keep your horses alive. If we can come to a mutual agreement, we would like to run our transport trucks across the border into France to see if some of our friends who are farmers will share their supplies with your horses. In return, we would like a few lessons from you regarding riding English saddle."

Sabina and Anna, who busied themselves with the horses only a few feet away, watched Master Karl pace the floor nervously. Except for the clearing of horses' nostrils, there was silence. Master Karl opened his eyes, smiled, and cheerfully agreed. "For the sake of the horses, we could not receive a better offer!"

After a round of handshakes, Peter assured Master Karl that they would take charge of the feed for the remainder of his company's stay. Six days later, a convoy of transport trucks filled to the max with hay, oats, and even salt pulled into the courtyard of the Riding Academy. Upstairs in the stables, the horses broke out with sudden exhilaration. Like a miracle, once again, the atmosphere throughout the stable became a place of fun and safety. Each day, Peter and his friends paid brief visits to check on their arrangement and to shower everyone with gifts of coffee, tea, chocolates, dehydrated soup, and K rations.

One day, as Anna arrived at the stables after school, Peter and Joe were leaving. Using partly sign language, they asked if she would like to have lunch. They signaled her to jump on the back of their jeep and drove her to their mess hall. "We are going to have lunch, and we will bring a sandwich out for you." Embarrassed, she sat and waited. Moments later, Joe brought out the largest sandwich she had ever seen. Thick white slices of bread with peanut butter. Because of her unusual hunger, she quickly devoured the sandwich. Only moments later, when Peter came to check on her, he was flabbergasted that she sat empty-handed.

"Where is your sandwich?" he asked. She felt her face turning red and placed her hand on her chest. Hiding their amusement, they quickly returned to the mess hall to obtain another sandwich.

Master Karl took great pleasure in knowing the faithful new friends of the horses. Daily, he dressed in his formal riding attire and led small groups of soldiers through the equestrian trails and into the mountain range. The owner's seventeen-year-old son, who had returned from an undisclosed location, took great pride in assisting Master Karl with the many responsibilities.

Afraid of no longer being needed, Anna asked Master Karl if she should continue to help. He shook his head and pulled her close for a hug. "Now what kind of question is this?" he asked. "Just as it has been for the past several years and pulling through awful, awful times, this is your home away from home. Besides," he gave a big smile, "we are not quite finished teaching you all the skills of a fine horsewoman." Anna hid her tears and proceeded to attend to the horses.

Several months later, Peter told Master Karl that his time had come to return to America. "I will not leave you stranded," he cheerfully announced. "Your horses will be in good hands on an ongoing basis. Some of my comrades have requested a stay. They will follow up on our agreement to support you and the horses." He became aware of Anna's sad expression as she sat on top of the grain box and listened.

Peter lifted his hands and with a gentle swoop lifted Anna off the box. He reached for her hand and walked her down the ramp and to her favorite bench in the courtyard. His warm hand felt comforting. He spoke slowly so that she understood every word. "I will be back in five years. By then you will be all grown up, and perhaps I will marry you? I will take you to Kentucky and show you our horses there. Would you like that?" He smiled. "In the meantime, you are only sixteen. Do not let anyone take advantage of you. Our soldiers like the company of innocent young German ladies. But soon, they will return to America where girlfriends and wives are eagerly awaiting their return. Many young German girls will be left behind with broken hearts. So please, Anna, stay away from the soldiers," he cautioned.

With butterflies invading her tummy, she listened as Peter repeated himself. "Do you *verstehen*? Do you understand?" She spoke not a word, but sat, fighting back tears, and nodded. Peter walked to his jeep and retrieved a large brown bag. "This is for your Mutti, please give her my love." He quickly kissed Anna on the forehead and drove away.

"He is so kind to my mother," she recalled. "I wish she could have met Peter."

Would Guenter ever return? "Nearly eighteen months have passed since Sir Winston Churchill officially announced the end of World War Two. There still is no news about Guenter's whereabouts," Anna's mother said, shaking her head in anguish. Someone earlier in the day had insisted that there was no hope regarding those who had served on the Russian front. Anna's mother constantly agonized over this, but she would not give up hope. Indeed, she would continue to look for his return.

Anna continued to spend much of her time with Sabina's family. One night, she was unable to sleep and decided to take the walk through the park to her home. She felt homesick and concerned for her mother. "I feel that I must go and check on Mutti," she said, gently pulling back the silken sheet that covered Sabina's head.

"Shall I come with you?" Sabina asked with a yawn.

"Thank you, you stay here so that your mother will not worry." Anna quietly closed the servant's entry that led into the park. She took a deep breath and began a fast walk toward her home.

After checking on her mother, she went to bed and fell into a deep and restful sleep. A frantic knock on the door startled both her and her mother. "It's two in the morning," Anna gasped.

Her mother ran to open the door. "It's my son!" she began to shout repeatedly. "It's my son!" Streams of lights disrupted the darkness as neighbors from adjoining apartments came to share her mother's excitement.

Guenter stood motionless. "It's me," he said, his throat sounding scratchy. Anna uttered a long sigh.

Stunned and perplexed, they stared at his pathetic appearance. His face was ashen and unshaven, and with deep circles under his eyes, he stood motionless. A ragged overcoat covered his thin figure. Rags enveloped his worn-out boots, which were several sizes too large. His head was covered in the dark blue ski cap Anna had knitted and mailed to him shortly before he was sent to the front line. "I know it is really you because you are still wearing that hat I knitted you," Anna sobbed. "I can't believe you still have that hat!"

Guenter looked intently at Anna. "Yes, but you have to give it a good soaking."

He slowly walked toward Anna and held her close. Their mother walked toward them. The surprise overwhelmed her as she collapsed into her son's arms. Anna quickly placed a wet cloth on her mother's forehead. "Is this real?" her mother asked as she opened her eyes. "Is it truly you, Guenter?" she questioned again and again while looking intently at her son.

Anna threw her coat over her shoulders and ran to get Eric. "We'll wait until morning to share the good news with your grandmother," he suggested. As Guenter enjoyed a warm bath and streusel cake she baked the day before, Anna's mother immediately disposed of his clothes. He sank into his bed and slept for hours. Their mother gingerly opened the door from time to time to check on him and kept everyone's voices down.

During the coming days, there were many things Anna wanted to talk about with her brother, and many questions she wished answered. Guenter sat in silence and only shared weak smiles. It was obvious he remained traumatized by the labor-camp events and did not wish to disclose his miserable experience of witnessing the endless field of dead in Siberia.

Guenter fought hard to overcome mental and physical problems. He spent many hours in silence and cried out in his sleep at night. Anna encouraged him to talk about his experiences, but to no avail. On rare occasions, he gently explained, "It is far too difficult to talk about and impossible to describe the pain I felt in the Siberian labor camp." Tears ran down his young face. "Please understand, my thoughts will forever be with my comrades who perished there." He expressed only two wishes. "I would like a little plot of earth to plant a garden for us, and I would like to get back to school. I am not certain I will be able to catch up." He covered his tired face with both hands.

"How did you get out, and what means of transportation did you have to get home?" Anna probed.

"A Russian nurse got several of us out, and we just started to walk. We saw death along the roads everywhere." He quietly began to sob. He looked at Anna. "I am so happy to be home!" She sat beside him and held his roughed-up hand until he fell asleep.

During the following weeks, their mother lovingly and patiently nursed Guenter back to health. She left his side only long enough to attend church. The grandmother relentlessly prepared nourishing meals. Determined to nurse him back to health, both women tiptoed around him as he slept endless hours. Anna and Guenter spent much time together. Severe frostbite on both feet prohibited him from taking long walks. For a change of scenery, they patiently waited in long lines at a nearby bus stop to catch a ride to the Rhine. There they sat undisturbed and talked about their early childhood. As though treading on thin ice, Anna occasionally probed Guenter about their father. Guenter's only response was to stare into space or shrug his shoulders.

Sabina, too, contributed much to Guenter's well-being. She made regular visits with baskets of seasonal fruits and vegetables. During one of her visits, she acted nervous and in a haste to leave. Her demeanor seemed to be befuddled. Finally, she turned to Anna and whispered, "My family and I are leaving tomorrow for England to be reunited with my father."

Anna felt a chill come over her. "When will you return?" she asked.

"Most likely in about one year," Sabina added as she reached for Anna's hand. "My grandfather told me I could give you this!" She pressed the German/English dictionary into her hand. "I want you continue to practice English until I come back. Will you promise?"

Anna nodded as tears began to flow across her face. "Yes, I'll promise, but I will miss you terribly." Anna watched until Sabina peddled her bicycle out of sight.

By way of the American Air Force News Network's translation, Anna learned that from approximately ninety thousand German soldiers who fought on the Russian front, only about six thousand returned. Her brother was one of them. Hitler's ambition and its path of destruction left deep and lasting scars.

Despite constant brainwashing by Nazi propaganda, Hitler's expectations of the German youth never developed. Because of the devastation around them and, worst of all, the pain of separation from families, they grew tired and refused to fight until the bitter end. Around the city, as people came out of hiding, mass confusion among the people set in.

Soon statistics revealed that half of Germany's urban housing lay in ruins. Only eight million homes were available for eighteen million households. Many families were grief-stricken and displaced. Men between the ages of sixteen and sixty died fighting the war or were either lost or missing in action, thus leaving as many widows and orphans. Thousands of women and children died in bombings. Children lacked food and were below their normal heights and weights, and still suffered hunger.

For the first time, Germany's people discovered the extent to which the war made its path of destruction. As the concentration camps, referred to by Hitler and his people as labor camps, were opened, the truth began to come out. Lies preached by local Nazi members regarding the safety of neighbors they carried away like cattle without warning came to light.

The end result turned out to be the exact opposite of all Hitler preached. His goal to create Berlin as the capital of the world was never realized. Hitler's dream of building gigantic buildings he himself began to design never came true. Destruction that consumed the lives of millions and transformed the world was the end result.

Hitler's goal at the beginning of his reign to create the "new order" through the Hitler Youth failed. His attempt to develop a brutal, fearless, and cruel German youth backfired. Instead, those who survived returned humble, meek, traumatized, and frightened. Some suffered from shock caused by the aftermath.

Because of serious damage and the chaotic stage of the country, the doors to the Opera House closed. It would take years to restore the damaged wing of the magnificent structure. For Anna, all personal dreams collapsed, and by the time she reached age sixteen, she had somehow managed to complete the primary and secondary education expected of a girl her age. There was no one who would guide her to follow her dream. No one encouraged her to explore classics of either literature or music. Only the outside walls remained of the conservatory she had dreamed of attending one day.

Anna knew her chance of being part of the "first floor" in the Opera House, an aspiration Herr Kummel had planted into her young heart and mind, would not be possible. Her hopes to become a featured dancer and to become an apprentice vanished into thin air.

Hitler left Germany devastated, and his legacy remains a memory of one of the most dreadful cruelties of modern times.

None of this hindered Anna's desire to prepare for a brighter future. Her interest was to build a life around her family. Several of her peers began socializing with American soldiers. Her mother felt strongly against this. The daughter of one of her friends fell in love with an American soldier and became pregnant. The young soldier, however, left for America and was never heard from again, leaving the young girl devastated. Anna's mother continued to remind Anna of the strict moral rules and standards of the Catholic faith. After all Anna and her mother had been through, she vowed to be obedient to her mother's wishes. She recalled the genuine concern of her friend Peter that she avoid socializing with American soldiers until she became of age.

Anna watched her mother as their struggle for survival continued. Her mother's demeanor showed renewed confidence in faith. Nothing could keep Anna's mother from her devotion to God; she never complained, but constantly thought of ways to please those around her. "Isn't it wonderful that we are free to attend church again?" she constantly reminded everyone.

To help ease her mother's struggle, Anna began to look for a job. Her fascination drew her to a small, newly erected building in the shape of a cuckoo clock near Sabina's grandfather's hotel. Flowerpots filled with bright red geraniums surrounded the fairy-tale structure. On the front entrance a small sign read "Help Wanted." As she took a closer look, the owner, a well-dressed gentleman, came out to greet her. The sound of the doorbell created a magical atmosphere.

"This is amazing!" Anna began to compliment the gentleman. "A building shaped like a clock?" Her voice was exhilarated.

He smiled and took a puff of his pipe. "My wife of many years dreamed about this business," his voice began to tremble. "They took her away one night. Those barbarians killed her!"

In a low tone, Anna responded, "I am truly sorry" and began to walk away.

As she turned to take another look, she regained her courage to inquire about the sign in the entrance. "Does the sign in your window include someone young as me?' she shyly asked.

He nodded and smiled. "I thought you would never ask!"

"But I am only sixteen," Anna confessed.

"Tell you what, let's give it a try for six weeks and see," he recommended. After a brief and enlightening conversation, both agreed that she would report to work the following day.

Anna found her new challenge enlightening but boring. Her job was to sell the clocks and to daily dust hundreds of them resting on glass shelves. Except for an occasional foreign customer, there was no one with whom she could converse in the English language. "I am wasting time," she complained to Guenter each day.

"Then do something about it," he proposed. She shared her feelings with the owner, who understood and respected her desires.

Sabina's two cousins with whom Anna remained in close touch responded to an ad run by the American Military Forces Communication Center for telephone operators and encouraged Anna to join them. Intimidated by their advanced knowledge of the English language, Anna resisted. But Sabina's cousins refused to take no for an answer. "We promised Sabina to keep an eye on you. You must at least give it a try!" they insisted. "Besides, we have some wonderful clothes we have outgrown to give you just for the occasion. You cannot go to work there in your riding clothes," they laughed. Anna gave in and joined her friends in their new endeavor.

A woman, neatly dressed in her U.S. Air Force uniform, her glasses resting on the tip of her nose, met the girls in the entrance of an old building that had once served as headquarters of the regional Gestapo. "I am Sergeant Ryan." She reached for their hands and began to conduct the interview.

Afraid to speak, Anna sat and listened closely. "I hope to become fluent in your language," she apologized to the attractive member of the WACs (Women's Army Corps) as the woman began to direct the conversation toward Anna.

"Perhaps we can teach each other?" the woman encouraged Anna with a warm smile.

After thorough screening and several days of training, the girls were invited to immediately report to work as booking operators. They loved their new American employers and their surroundings. During break, they practiced unfamiliar phrases pertaining to their new jobs until they felt completely at ease. There was much to learn, and they became fascinated with connecting heads of state and famous military personnel across Europe. "I can spell his name," Anna shouted as she booked a call for General Eisenhower for the first time.

At the end of the day, Anna shared her new adventure with Guenter, who spent most of his days catching up on the studies he missed. On Friday afternoons, before she went to the stables, she happily stuck her earnings into her mother's apron pocket. "Make sure you are always on time and better yet—early!" her mother suggested. "Then they will know you appreciate working for them!"

Sabina's cousins left several months later to further their education at a nearby university. This worried Anna, since she depended on them when she failed to communicate with someone. Sergeant Ryan sensed that Anna felt lost and offered to transfer her to the teletype section for training that would eventually lead to a promotion. "While you are in training," she cheerfully shared with Anna, "we will increase your pay."

Surprised but confused, Anna asked, "Where will this place be?"

Sergeant Ryan took her to a nearby window and pointed to an adjoining building. "Just two floors down! As soon as you know how to type, we will need you back with us."

Her new instructor, an attractive female soldier much younger than Sergeant Ryan who everyone called Sunshine, introduced Anna to her temporary office, the fascinating equipment, and its many functions. She was pleased that the sounds of the busy equipment drowned out the slow tapping of her typewriter as she struggled to carry out her assignments. During lunch hour and breaks, she practiced typing with the help of an instruction book.

Slowly she caught on and began to feel sure of herself, but she continued to apologize for her lack of speed. "Don't worry," her instructor assured her. "Your enthusiasm far outweighs any doubt about speed."

Shortly thereafter, Sergeant Ryan invited Anna back to her department to assist her with the simple tasks of filing and typing. "Don't hesitate to ask for my help," Sergeant Ryan said as she showed Anna to her new desk outside her office.

For Anna, things could not have been better. She loved working with her new American friends and worked hard to please them. On Sunday afternoons, Sergeant Ryan and several of her fellow workers invited Anna to join them at a tea dance held in the famous landmark of the Kurhaus. In the past, this magnificent building served as one of Hitler's favorite playgrounds and as the casino of Europe's richest residents. The American Red Cross converted the stately building into an enlisted men's club. Each Sunday afternoon, an eighteen-piece military band, dressed in formal garb, filled the air of the huge ballroom with the sounds of Glenn Miller's popular orchestra. Anna had no problem following her fellow workers' lead with the jitterbug and the sound of "In the Mood."

For Anna's family, life seemed to progress. Her mother's prayers were answered. Her face lit up whenever, in a melodious tone, she continued to praise God saying, "Our boys are home." Only her occasional faraway look revealed longing for the children's father. As always, the grandmother cheerfully invested her small pension on new resources to feed the family.

With stacks of books by his side, Guenter spent most of his time in seclusion. Only their mother disturbed him from time to time to serve him freshly baked bread and his favorite beverage, hot chocolate. Eric kept busy with Emma and the children. His new job, as member of a team to restore the city, perfectly matched his talent and imagination in drawing and art. In his spare time, he began designing floats for the *Faschingszug* (parade) for the region's *Fasching* springfest.

Anna's daily walk to work took her by the Opera House. As though awakening from a dream, she reminisced about her friends and the amazing times, both good and dreadful. She wondered about Herr Kummel's whereabouts and especially his well-being. After work, Anna wasted no time in getting to the stables and her beloved horses. She continued to assist Master Karl and the stable boy with their endless chores. At the end of the day, Master Karl included her in teaching a group of advanced riders the skills required in a foxhunt.

One late afternoon, as Master Karl's group returned from the trails, they took note of a young soldier who regularly stood at the entrance of the stables observing the riders. Somewhat startled, Anna fell to the rear of her group as the soldier called her by name. When she took a closer look, she realized that he worked in telecommunications. The clanging of horses' hooves drowned out his voice. Anna casually waved and moved on with her group.

The following day, the soldier waited for her in front of the office building. "*Guten morgen* [good morning]," he attempted to greet her in German. "May I walk you home after work?" he grinned. She nodded and quickly made her way to the office. At the end of the day, as she was leaving, the sergeant, handsome and well-groomed, opened the exit door for her. Anna felt awkward. She thought of her mother's concerns, and recalled the stern warning from her friend Peter not to go out with soldiers. To disrupt the silence, she began to share with him her concern about a list of phrases Sergeant Ryan wanted her to learn. He unhesitatingly offered to help and suggested they meet in his office during lunchtime. A block away from her home, she said goodbye in front of a friend's house. There she waited until the sergeant was out of sight.

During the tutoring sessions, she began to feel more comfortable in the soldier's presence. She watched him closely and became intrigued with the confidence with which he managed the personnel under his supervision. Anna felt safe, and when he offered to continue to work with her, she graciously accepted.

An invitation to drive through the nearby mountain range with the sergeant's best friend and his girlfriend did not come as a surprise. With Guenter present, Anna shared the invitation with her mother, who reluctantly approved of the invitation. Guenter, however, raised his eyebrows. "You have a couple of admirers at the Riding Academy. Why don't you socialize with them?" he said, smiling cheerlessly.

Anna felt elated as they drove through the scenic mountain range. She recalled riding through the familiar trails during hard times. Impressed by the natural beauty, gentle valleys, and broad forest hugging the hillsides, they stopped to capture the moment with their cameras. The sergeant took

Anna by the hand and walked her to the edge of a ravine. He pointed to the landscape below and slowly spoke so she could understand clearly. "This is how my family's farm looks back home in America." He pointed to an old farmhouse nearby. "We even stack our wood behind the house." He waved his hand across the rolling fields of wheat. "Just as far as one can see," he elaborated. "This is the picture of my home!"

Anna sat and absorbed the picture her friend described of his home in America with such minute detail. "What about horses? Do you have horses?" she asked.

"Oh yes, of course," he added. "We use mules right now, but our pastures are ready for horses." He put his arm around Anna's shoulder. "We just have to find the horses," he laughed.

Anna began to reminisce. *Who is this soldier who is helping me to improve my skills at work, who waits for me in front of our office? Whenever I look around, he is there! At the end of day, he is standing at the street corner near my home when I return with Master Karl's group of riders? Even during the day, he waves from his office window to get my attention.*

Filled with mixed emotions, she finally shared the sergeant's friendship with her mother. "My main concern," her mother began to respond candidly and with authority that Anna had not seen before, "is that you cannot allow yourself to become physical with this or any other man, no matter what the circumstances may be. To do so, before the marriage vows, is sin against God. Please, please promise me that you will not weaken?" Anna listened carefully to all her mother had to say.

As the relationship continued to grow, Anna boldly explained her feelings to the sergeant, and that she would stand firm with her mother's guidance. He stubbornly decided to end the friendship, saying that he would visit a girlfriend in Switzerland and think things over.

Upon his return, he asked to meet Anna. "Soon, I will be reassigned to the States. I will be going into officer's training school, and I want to marry you. But first, I would like to meet your family." The sergeant spoke slowly and in a fervent tone.

"What about my mother?" Anna asked in a bewildered tone.

"She will come for visits," he suggested without reservation.

Anna's mother spoke gently to the total stranger who asked to take her daughter far away across the Atlantic. In a pleading tone, she said, "To give you an answer to your proposal, I want what is best for my daughter. I pray for her safety, and her happiness is most important."

Everyone showed concern, but to please Anna, they agreed to make plans for a small church wedding following the mandatory civil ceremony.

Only minutes after the civil ceremony, Anna's husband, angered by her comment about feeling hungry, humiliated her by striking her across the face on the steps of the courthouse and in front of his two best men. "It will never happen again," he apologized. Ashamed, mystified, and afraid, she did not share the incident with anyone.

Anna sought a few moments of solitude as she climbed the stairs to the upper deck of the Alexandria. Had she used sound judgment leaving behind her family and all that was familiar? She wondered about this as she watched the sun slide down into the sea.

The train ride to the harbor in Hamburg was long and worrisome. Remnants from war and bombing brought the train to a halt crossing one of the high-rise bridges. Rough and windy weather conditions made the transfer from Hamburg's train station to the harbor miserable.

The farewell at the train station back home was painful. Everyone was present except Guenter, who was deeply hurt by Anna's decision to leave. It was obvious he did not approve of Anna's choice and expressed concern. Eric shared his feelings. "Who will be there for her?" was the question that nagged both.

Anna, however, was not concerned. Her new husband was sending her ahead to meet his family and would follow in a few weeks. She was unable to forget the vivid picture he had painted of his family's farm and life in America. If she accepted this invitation, perhaps she would no longer live with the constant fear and insecurities that plagued her young life. The strict rules embedded into her heart by her devout

Catholic mother that a young girl practice sexual abstinence before marriage became Anna's main concern. To abide by her wishes, marriage became Anna's obvious choice.

As her thoughts continued to wander, the ship came to a sudden halt. There were no sounds except for the steady roar of the sea, the buzzing of the engine, and the cries of the seagulls following the ship. The voyage across the Atlantic was expected to take ten days. Anna asked a steward passing by, "Why is the ship already stopping?"

"If you will follow me, miss, I will try to explain," responded the steward with his polished English accent.

She followed the young man to the other side of the ship as she looked across the sea. "You see," the steward pointed eastward, "there are quite a few mines still floating around in the English Channel. They are scanning the sea, and I believe they are just now defusing one of the mines located about an hour ago. One of the Norwegian cargo ships was damaged quite heavily just two days ago."

Anna pulled the heavy woolen scarf her mother knitted for her over her head and braced herself against the strong ocean gust. "You can be at ease now, miss," the steward said, acknowledging a signal from one of the divers who, with the help of another, climbed back into one of the small crafts that escorted the ship across the English Channel.

With her fist clenched against her chest, she leaned against the ship's railing. *What is the reason for this knot in my stomach?* she pondered. Doubt about leaving home hung over the waves blown back and forward. The gentle splashing created a lonesome sound. "You are only eighteen years of age, you have your life and the world in front of you," the voice of Herr Ackermann at the Riding Academy echoed in her mind. "We want you to stay—you are part of the Riding Academy! Besides, my son is disappointed about your leaving. You know he has had a crush on you for a long time."

Spotting the graceful moves of a whale in the distance momentarily relieved the tightness in her chest. One thing was certain—because she missed the horses bitterly, she did not want to think about her friends at the Riding Academy during this time.

"Christmas is only nine days away. What will it be like spending Christmas away from home?" She began to sob. She realized that most of all she would miss her mother, Guenter, and Eric. Remembering her mother's reassuring words, "I just want you to be happy and whatever you do, always remember the things we talked about," all at once gave her new courage.

A violent storm erupted during the fourth day at sea. Nearly everyone aboard suffered from seasickness. After three frightening days of nearly forty-foot-high waves, the storm calmed down and life aboard the Alexandria went back to normal. The captain ordered the velvet ropes throughout the corridors of the ship removed. Rain squalls ceased and so did the eerie squeaking of the ship. Once again, passengers appeared and strolled on the promenade, filling their lungs with the fresh salt air as color returned to their pale faces.

For the remainder of the voyage, Anna spent little time in the close quarters of her cabin. There, a porthole offered only a view of the slashing waves of the windswept sea. She spent most of her time lying on a deck chair studying the starry skies. *At least the horrible war is over*, she constantly reminded herself.

From time to time, she walked along the ship's railings with eyes fixed upon a group of seagulls. Guenter loved seagulls and described them to Anna after a vacation with their grandmother to the Bodensee. Now she too had fallen in love with these graceful birds as she watched them incessantly.

Christmas eve, 1948. The blaring sound of the telephone in Anna's cabin startled her as she ran to lift the receiver. "Guess what, I just learned that we are arriving in the New York harbor around midnight. Let's stay up and watch! Would you like to?" The enthusiastic caller was Anna's new friend Erna from Stuttgard.

"Sure, that sounds exciting," Anna answered. "I will meet you in the dining room."

After dinner, Anna hurriedly ran down to her cabin to get her coat. Nearly all the passengers were gathered on the upper deck. Over the ship's intercom, the captain announced,

"Ladies and gentlemen, you will have a clear view of the Statue of Liberty in about fifteen minutes."

Anna watched as the ship maneuvered its way into the harbor. "Have you ever seen such a red sky?" she asked, turning to Erna. "No, and look at the reflection of these ocean-going ships," Erna responded with an excited laugh as she pointed toward the tugboats nestled against the shore.

With her fingers caressing the necklace her mother had fastened around her neck only moments before departure, she stood and absorbed the image in front of her. She felt as though the Statue of Liberty turned to welcome her personally. Remembering that she would indeed hold in high regard the values her mother relentlessly taught her, she vowed to focus and strive for the best life had to offer.

Oblivious of what lay ahead in her new life in America, Anna stood amazed as she continued to gaze at the skyline of New York.

Soon she would learn that the beautiful farm her new husband so meticulously described during their outing in the Taunus Region of Germany did not exist. There was no pasture suitable for horses. Only a lonely mule stood alongside tobacco barns. Her husband would not attend officer training school—instead, he would become a tobacco farmer. A visit from her mother would be out of the question.

During the following years, Anna would learn to cope with the culture shock. The memories of her mother's guidance became her comfort during constant mental abuse. She would learn to endure labor on the tobacco farm in sweltering heat and climatic conditions her body was not accustomed to. She would learn to deal with her husband's unacceptable social behaviors in the company of his unruly friends. Worst of all, she would learn to survive the physical abuse that threatened her life. Because of her mother's lifelong counsel, Anna refused to crumble under her circumstances.

Then one day, a ray of sunshine broke through the dark clouds that had enveloped her life. She met a wonderful German couple who became her closest friends and would ultimately help set her free. This did not come without the sacrifice of leaving her small son behind. To overcome the pain, she focused only on encouraging thoughts.

Her family, although the mystery about her father remained, was doing well. Her mother faithfully wrote long weekly letters. She reported good news from Master Karl about Anna's beloved horses and the activity at the Riding Academy. "Sabina returned from England with her new husband and lives with her grandfather at their luxurious villa. Instead of riding her bicycle, she visits us in her red convertible so small she parks on our sidewalk. She always showers us with beautiful fresh flowers, baskets of fruit, and vegetables from their hotel garden! I must tell you that I am the envy of our neighborhood. And, they all miss you!" she wrote in her uplifting letters.

"I always think of you as I walk by the Opera House, but there is still no activity," Anna's mother continued. Her many letters also contained clippings from newspapers that displayed pictures and editorials of Eric, who became one of the principal organizers in rebuilding their beautiful ancient city. There were pictures of the grandmother, who volunteered in newly organized events founded by the Church. Pressed leaves from chestnut trees accompanied a note saying, "These leaves came from one of the trees in the park you always passed on horseback. I miss you terribly, Nunnielie, and I hope with all of my heart that you are happy," her mother always brought her letters to a close.

While taking care of the frostbite that continued to plague his feet and fighting emotions caused by the horror of his imprisonment in the Siberian labor camp, Guenter studied day and night and soon went to work as a messenger for a government-controlled insurance company. He began to climb the ranks and became department supervisor in the organization's investigative division. There he met Irmgardt, his secretary and the love of his life, a young lady who lost every member of her family during Hitler's war. The two became inseparable and soon married. Two years later, Irmgardt gave birth to a beautiful baby girl they named Gisela.

Afraid of hurting their mother, Guenter did not make mention of their father. On rare occasions, she spoke about his charisma and elegant manners. As Guenter attempted to file for her government pension, she refused to answer questions because she would not lie about their father's identity. Guenter respected his mother's sensitivity and totally supported her as she lived a peaceful life until age eighty-six.

As Anna continued her journey in the *country* she learned to love and cherish, many challenges began to face her. The language barrier and limited formal education became her immediate test. With an unwavering attitude she followed in her brother's footsteps to *"never give up."*

Cautiously Anna began to surround herself with praiseworthy people and valued her close friendship with her German friends. Soon she found love and married the handsome son of a respected merchant from a family with strong Christian roots. This delightful new family welcomed Anna with open arms, and everyone rejoiced with the arrival of their beautiful daughter one year later.

Seven years later, as they were building their lives, a fatal heart attack claimed her husband's young life. In the sanctuary filled to capacity with friends who paid their last respect to her beloved husband and daughter's wonderful father, Anna prayed for strength. Without financial security, her main focus became her daughter, to keep their home, and to pay off the debts that occurred without forewarning. She managed to obtain a second part-time job to reach that goal.

Once again, dark clouds lifted as the sun began to break through. Through Anna's job she met the love of her life.

His tall stature, fun-loving personality, charisma, and love for sports enchanted both mother and daughter. Two years later, her late husband's family assisted Anna with plans of a small wedding ceremony in the chapel of their church.

Seventeen wonderful years followed. Her husband became Anna's strength and this tower of strength became the devoted father of her daughter. With watchful eyes upon their daughter who blossomed into a beautiful young woman they enjoyed life as a family. His success in his work resulted in a promotion and move to a large city five hundred miles away. There, with his support and Anna's love for people, she became a highly respected and successful Realtor. During their marriage they traveled to Europe on numerous occasions which afforded an exciting opportunity to introduce Anna's husband to her family and Sabina and her mother.

But something was missing. He chose to walk away. Why would her husband choose to walk away from his nearly picture-perfect family, beautiful home, and security? Anna felt confused, helpless, and rejected as she began to search for answers.

A friend from church invited her to *Bible Study Fellowship*. Each Monday evening for the following fourteen years, she joined several hundred women as they sat, listened, sang, prayed, and praised God. As her eyes began to open wide, she began to see things she had never seen before, and answers to her many questions came to light. She began to understand more clearly all her mother so desperately tried to teach her children in the *midst of thunder storms* and *through the turmoil of Hitler's terrifying war.*

But this is not the end. The story goes on . . .

Anna's daughter and grandson bring much joy into her life. Both daughter and grandson enjoy a special, loving relationship with her former husband and the bond between them continues to grow with every passing day. She looks forward to occasional visits with her son who enjoys his life in a coastal town nearby. He proudly shares pictures of his two sons, three grandchildren and their families. Anna's passion to study the Bible, her love and hunger to know the Person her mother so reverently referred to as *"Herr Jesus,"* continues to increase.

Anna has discovered the true meaning of happiness, she enjoys her life, her adorable cottage near the seashore, and her many friends. She has been richly blessed with one special *Christian* companion with whom she has shared her faith and the simple things in life for more than twenty years.

As the writer concludes her story, she shares her final thoughts.

The evening is calm and bright. On an island on the eastern shores, she walks along the seashore near her home. She acknowledges a friendly gesture from a lone angler, his dog by his side. With the warm wind in her face, she stops to reminisce. Then her racing thoughts come to a halt as she looks out onto the sea. During the night, heavy rain cleansed the air of thick pollen. She takes a deep breath and gives a contented sigh.

The beach is deserted and the sea bellows, leaving only the sounds of the seagulls and her favorite black birds. A family of pelicans gracefully maneuvers its way through the current of air while the tiny sandpipers swiftly run to and fro. Under the sunset, the ocean is flooding the beaches reaching across the marsh grass.

A couple of fishing boats reflect the brilliant colors of the sunset. To the east, the islanders' much-beloved lighthouse sends its beam of light across the waves.

With a thankful heart, she sits in the sand to absorb the beauty around her, and with deep love and admiration she looks upon her children far away.

A short distance out into the sea, she watches a lone pelican making one last effort to find food for his late afternoon meal. "What a sight!" she rejoices aloud as the pelican circles the air and examines the waters below. At the last split-second, he dives into the water as he folds his awkward wings and slashes the water like a hurled lance with grace and precision.

The ocean is steel-colored in the fading light. "Nothing but your beautiful creation, Lord: birds, sea, sky, and most of all, your awesome presence and peace." Her hand reaches heavenward. "Thank you for the joy I feel in my heart. Thank you for my family and my beautiful children." She stops to look at the puffy clouds moving across the Carolina blue skies before resuming her stroll back to her cottage. "And one more thing, God," she prays. "Thank you for being my best friend and making me responsive to 'a touch of your hand.'"

The Artist.

With his gift of art, young graphic designer, Jason Chrisco designed the book cover to capture the context of the story "On the Other Side."

Drawing from a very young age, Jason pursued art as a career earning a degree in Graphic Design/Advertising. He works as a freelance designer in his spare time, and his goal is to some day own his own design firm. Jason lives in Graham, North Carolina with his wife Laura and daughter Mollie.

CPSIA information can be obtained at www.ICGtesting.com
Printed in the USA
LVOW13s1522110314

376955LV00002B/330/P

ML 4-14